AND THE WIDOW WORE SCARLET

Scandalous Sons - Book 1

ADELE CLEE

This is a work of fiction. All names, characters, places and incidents are products of the author's imagination. All characters are fictitious and any resemblance to real persons, living or dead, is purely coincidental.

No part of this book may be copied or reproduced in any manner without the author's permission.

Books by Adele Clee

To Save a Sinner

A Curse of the Heart

What Every Lord Wants

The Secret To Your Surrender

A Simple Case of Seduction

Anything for Love Series

What You Desire

What You Propose

What You Deserve

What You Promised

Lost Ladies of London

The Mysterious Miss Flint

The Deceptive Lady Darby

The Scandalous Lady Sandford

The Daring Miss Darcy

Avenging Lords

At Last the Rogue Returns

A Wicked Wager

Valentine's Vow

A Gentleman's Curse

Scandalous Sons

And the Widow Wore Scarlet

The Mark of a Rogue

CHAPTER ONE

Covent Garden, London, 1820

Blood seeped from the wound in Damian Wycliff's thigh as he lay slumped in a dank alley off Drury Lane. The blade had pierced his breeches, had sunk deep into his now burning flesh. A crimson pool soaked the beige buckskin. Had he not broken at least two fingers, had he been able to see out of his swollen left eye, he might have untied his cravat and used it as a tourniquet.

Damnation!

A man wanted to die clamped between the soft thighs of his mistress. A man wanted to die alongside his comrades whilst fighting for king and country, not alone and slouched against a wall reeking of vomit and piss.

A curse vile enough to make a vicar faint burst from his lips.

If he discovered his father was to blame for the vicious attack, there'd be hell to pay. The Marquis of Blackbeck would do anything to prove a point, to teach his bastard son a lesson.

But there were other enemies.

Had Lord Cockram sought retribution for Damian winning the

fool's Berkshire estate in a game of whist? Had Damian's lover, Mrs Sidwell, punished him for giving the woman her congé? Once he discovered the identity of the person who'd paid the four men to beat him to a pulp, Damian would have his revenge—assuming he didn't bleed to death on the pavement.

Hoping to capture someone's attention, he whistled loudly. But only a randy buck or a drunken sot wandered into a dark alley in the dead of night. If he could just send word to his coachman, Cutler. The fellow possessed the skill of a seamstress when working with a needle and thread. It wouldn't be the first wound he'd sewn. It wouldn't be the last.

Depleted of energy after the violent brawl—and after the rampant activities with the actress used as bait—he lacked the strength to stand. The crimson pool continued to spread, saturating the material stuck to his thigh.

What a blasted inconvenience!

"For the love of God, can anyone hear me?"

His cry for help echoed in the narrow passageway though no one answered his desperate plea. Had the blackguards not robbed him of everything except for the one item he truly valued, he might have bribed a gullible passerby.

Despite being an unrepentant sinner, he tugged at his shirt, forced his fingers through the gap in the fine lawn and grasped the gold cross hanging around his neck.

"Mother, if you are watching from your heavenly plane, do something to save your errant son." The words lacked conviction, for he did not believe that the power of love could work miracles.

He did not believe in the power of love at all.

As his life drained from his body, he lay back on the damp cobbles and gave himself over to fate. Carriages rolled past on the street beyond. Distant voices filled his head: laughter, taunts and mocking jeers. Some real. Some imagined.

The clip of footsteps reached his ears—a devil's cruel trick to torment him.

But then a woman appeared, dressed in nothing but a white chemise, a red shawl drawn tightly around her shoulders, her ebony hair tied in a single braid. She crouched at his side, frowned and tutted as she scanned the length of his body before her gaze narrowed on the cross gripped between his bloodstained fingers.

Had she come merely to rob him, too?

"Can you walk?" she asked with some impatience. The panic in her voice highlighted a fear for her own safety, not his.

Damian opened his mouth to speak but found it impossible to form a word. A fuzzy sensation sent his world spinning. Nausea made him retch.

"The door to my lodgings is but ten feet away, sir." The woman's head shot left then right. Her breathing came in rapid pants. "Can you make it there, do you think?" Her dainty hand came to rest gently on his cheek. Then she slapped him. Hard. "Sir, can you hear me?"

Damian mumbled in response lest he receive another beating.

The woman grabbed the lapels of his coat and tried to haul him to his feet. Twice, he collapsed back onto the cold stones. Twice, the woman almost came crashing down on top of him. After some perseverance he managed to stand—only to cast up the quart of brandy he'd downed two hours earlier.

"Mother Mary, give me strength," she muttered, staring at her soiled boots.

"Maria," he whispered, draping his arm around his saviour's shoulder. "My mother … her name was M-Maria."

"Then for her sake try to place one foot in front of the other."

"She's dead."

A compassionate sigh left the woman's lips. "And you will be, too, if you do not heed my advice and hurry."

They shuffled along together. Damian gripped the wall with his good hand while the woman at his side clutched his wrist rather than his broken fingers. As soon as they made it beyond the

3

battered blue door, her shoulders sagged and she exhaled deeply before kicking the door shut with her dirty boot.

She dragged him into a small room, sparse but clean, and settled him onto a bed.

"Forgive me," she began in an eloquent voice so opposed to the crude living conditions, "but if I'm to help you, I need to remove your breeches." Her hands came to rest on his thigh. "It is the only way I can tend to the wound."

Damian nodded but lacked the enthusiasm to offer the usual lewd suggestions.

After tugging off his shoes and throwing them to the floor, she took a knife to the garment and used two hands to rip the material from his knee to his groin. Amid the chaos of his mind, he thought to inform her he never wore drawers, but then her fingers swept up his thigh, grazed his ballocks.

"Good Lord!" Perhaps she was referring to his impressive manhood for her tone held a hint of panic. "I need to find something to stem the bleeding."

Perhaps not.

"Argh!" His groan failed to convey the extent of the pain when she pressed the area around the wound. Damn, it ached like the devil.

"Forgive me, sir, I have no choice but to use a needle and thread." She raced across the room, rummaged around in a drawer and returned with a stocking and a small basket. "Do you happen to have a flask of brandy?" When he failed to answer, she said, "No matter."

She fastened the stocking around his thigh so tight his heartbeat pulsed in his leg, but it would stem the flow of blood.

"N-name?" he managed to say. He would know the identity of the angel attempting to save his life.

She drew a stool up to the bed and placed a bowl of water on the floor beside her. "If you survive tonight, you may call me

4

Scarlett." Grabbing the lit candle wedged into the neck of a green bottle, she moved it to the side table and then took a seat.

Scarlett.

The name didn't suit her. She looked too prim, too wholesome to be loose with her affections. But then he recalled the red shawl draped over her shoulders and pondered the possibility that she used an alias to conceal her identity.

"Now hold still," she said in a voice not too dissimilar from that of his first governess—a wicked devil of a woman who found pleasure in torturing small children. "I'm afraid I have nothing to numb the pain. But if you can resist the urge to cry out, I will be most grateful. This may help." She thrust a ball of material into his good hand. "The stocking is clean. I assure you."

Oh, he'd tugged a lady's stocking off with his teeth on numerous occasions but could not recall ever forcing one into his mouth.

As Scarlett threaded the needle, a sense of trepidation took hold. A woman lacked the strength of heart to stab a man's skin. Cutler's hands didn't tremble when he contemplated the first stitch. Cutler didn't frown and bite down on his bottom lip as if faced with a mammoth task.

"My needlework skills are sufficient," she said, more to reassure herself than him. Lord, if she did not get on with it soon, he'd be spewing bile.

By way of a prompt, he scrunched the stocking and pushed it into his mouth. Even while skirting the edges of death, he found the action mildly erotic.

A wipe with wet linen preceded the first jab of the needle.

Damian closed his eyes and tried to breathe evenly through his nose.

Scarlett dug too deeply on the first stitch. He might have cursed had he not been chewing on the lady's hosiery. With the second stitch, the room rocked and swayed. An ominous black cloud swamped his field of vision. With the third stab, the

5

swirling mass smothered him, sucked him down, down into the dark depths of oblivion.

Damian woke to the distant sound of a door slamming, to the pounding of footsteps on the stairs beyond. His forehead burned, and his neck felt damp to the touch. A homemade splint supported his broken fingers. The wound in his thigh throbbed. Daylight broke through a small gap in the curtains covering the tiny window looking out onto Drury Lane. Lacking the strength to sit up, he glanced around the room and found no sign of Scarlett. He tried to call her name, but the word died on his lips as he slipped back into the void.

It was dark when he woke for the second time, the room lit by a single candle that reeked of the acrid smell of tallow. Scarlett sat on the stool next to the bed, wiping his brow with a cold, damp cloth.

When she noticed his eyes fluttering open, she gasped. "Saints preserve us! You're awake. Do you think you might eat some broth? You must take something to bolster your strength." Scarlett shot to her feet. "It will only take a few minutes to heat."

Damian tried to move his parched lips, to beg for a drink, but his tongue was so dry it stuck to the roof of his mouth. He reached out and captured her wrist hoping to convey his intention, but her sudden yelp shocked him.

Scarlett pulled her hand free and rubbed her wrist. It was then that he noticed the purple bruise. The sight stole his breath. Damn it all. Had he done that whilst thrashing about consumed by a fever?

"You are not to blame," she said, for there was no doubt this woman could read his mind. "In my line of work, men think they own me." Bitterness coated every syllable. "Either that or they're determined to act the hero, desperate to drag me from the pit of despair."

Her line of work?

Damian considered her pink lips and rouged cheeks. As a

virile man with a huge appetite, his gaze had lingered more than once on the soft swell of her breasts spilling from her dress tonight. And yet he could not imagine her sprawled naked on a bed in a brothel. Judging by her shabby lodgings, Scarlett was no rich man's mistress. From her elocution and diction, from the graceful way she walked around the room, from the books stacked on the side table, she had not been dragged up on the streets, either.

"I'm an actress." Her smile failed to reach her captivating blue eyes, and a tidal wave of melancholy swept through the room. "Success, I have discovered, depends upon which gentleman acts as your patron. Indeed, it is not the late hours that wear me to the bone but the effort it takes to keep the lecherous hordes at bay."

Anger flared in Damian's chest.

Resentment festered.

The arrogance of the aristocracy sickened him. The Marquis of Blackbeck was one of those men who claimed the right to bed whomever he wished. The Marquis of Blackbeck had seduced the opera singer, Maria Alvarez, with total disregard for the bastard son he was to sire.

"You … you were not always an … actress." Damian forced the words from his lips. "I may be knocking on death's door, b-but I hear good breeding in your voice."

Scarlett kept her back to him as she stirred the pot hanging over the fire. She sniffed numerous times, but he doubted it had anything to do with inhaling the pungent aroma of vegetable broth.

"No," she said, the answer carried on a deep sigh. "I attended the Rushbridge seminary for young ladies in Bath until a tragedy forced me to return to town."

Had he the energy or the inclination to further their acquaintance, he might have probed her for information. As it was, only one question lingered in his still woozy mind.

"Then why would an educated woman, one tired of dealing with troublesome men, rush into an alley to rescue a rogue?" Innocent ladies avoided men like him. Men whose conscience lay buried beneath a hard shell, one impossible to crack.

Cradling a bowl of broth, she returned to sit on the stool. "Because my mother taught me to help those people less fortunate." She scooped a spoonful of the rotten-smelling liquid and forced it into his mouth. "Because I believe we reap what we sow, sir. Is the broth too hot?"

"No." Damian swallowed the bland concoction, grateful to feel something moist against his lips. "So you hope fate will see your kindness repaid?" Was it kindness or utter foolishness to take a stranger into one's home?

"Look around you. Hope is all I have."

An uncomfortable silence descended.

With patience, Scarlett fed him until the spoon scraped the bottom of the bowl. Exhausted from the effort it took just to swallow, he lay back on the lumpy pillow and speculated how long it would be before a man wore her down and destroyed her resolve. She was pretty, demure, would have an appealing figure had she a little more meat on her bones. If she had any hope of escaping the drudgery, there was but one option open—take a wealthy lover, bleed him for every penny and find a quiet place in the country, somewhere to live off her ill-gotten gains.

By the time she returned from washing the pot in the room across the hall, the fire had burnt to naught but glowing embers. For a long time, she stared at the grate in dismay. The deep furrows on her brow undoubtedly stemmed from more than concern over firewood.

"It's late," she said as she turned to face him. She glanced at her feet before steeling herself—raising her chin and straightening her shoulders. Perhaps she wanted him to leave but didn't know how to broach the subject. "I slept on the floor last night, but the temperature has plummeted. I don't have enough wood

8

to keep the fire burning all night. It is imperative we keep warm."

As a man used to the many ploys a lady used to get him into bed, this one was rather novel. "You wish to sleep with me tonight?" A woman brimming with benevolence would not force him to sleep on the floor.

Scarlett gave a half shrug. "Unless you can think of a better option."

Amorous thoughts flooded his head. Indeed, for the first time since being stretched on his back, his cock twitched. Even in his sorry state, he could rise to the occasion. But that was not how one repaid the woman who had breathed life back into his bones, who had dragged him back from the flaming gates of hell.

"Though I warn you, sir," she continued, reading his thoughts once again, "dare lay a hand on me, and I shall claw at your wound like a wildcat. After I have punched you in your swollen eye and squeezed your broken fingers until the bones shatter."

Damian arched a brow in admiration, impressed by the vehemence in her voice. "Have no fear. My mother taught me to show my host the utmost respect."

And he would never bed a woman who wasn't tugging at his breeches, eager for the first hard thrust.

Scarlett narrowed her gaze. "Judging by your ebony hair and olive skin, I assume your mother was of Mediterranean descent."

"My mother was Spanish. She died some time ago." He didn't want to dwell on sad memories and so patted the faded blanket covering the bed. "As you said, it's late, and talking has taken what little energy I possess."

She nodded and edged closer to the bed though she did not remove her dress. "You need rest. The fever has broken, and I imagine you'll be fit to leave in a few days. Of course, you're free to leave whenever you choose. When the time is right, might I deliver a message for you?"

For some reason, he felt an odd form of peace whilst in her

care. As soon as Damian's friends learnt of the attack in the alley, they would be just as eager as he to find the culprit. To exact revenge.

"How long have I been here?"

"Three days."

Three days!

Good Lord! Undoubtedly, his friends were pacing the streets wondering what the hell had happened to him. "Then I'll need you to pay a boy to deliver a note in the morning, to a house on Jermyn Street."

"I shall take it myself." She pulled back the blanket and slipped into bed.

"I'd rather you paid a boy." After everything she'd done for him, he'd not have her wasting time traipsing the streets. "I shall reimburse you for any expense incurred."

"We will need to sleep on our sides," she said, changing the subject. "Do you think you might manage it?"

"I can try." He had slept in many awkward places.

After a few minutes spent shuffling, they settled into a comfortable position. Scarlett pulled the blankets around their shoulders. Their bodies were so close her sweet breath breezed over his neck.

"Wrap your arms around me if you're cold." It was unlike him to be so thoughtful. It was unlike him to share a bed with a woman while both fully clothed.

"I'll be fine. Good night, sir."

"Damian. You may call me Damian or Wycliff, if you prefer."

She swallowed audibly. "Good night, Wycliff."

"Good night, Scarlett."

They lay in silence, for how long he had no notion. When her limbs relaxed and her breathing slowed, he knew she had fallen asleep. He watched her for a while—enraptured by her innocent charm—and drifted off soon after. Numerous times in the night he woke to find a dainty hand pressed to his chest. If she was searching for his heart, she was out of luck. The organ lay buried beneath a mountain of bitterness and hatred. Still, that did not prevent him from wrapping his arm around her and drawing her close. A man would do anything to keep warm.

The morning brought an end to his time in the peaceful haven.

When he finally opened his eyes, Scarlett was up and dressed in a faded blue pelisse. No doubt wanting freedom from her obligation, she reminded him of the note he wished to send, waited patiently for him to scribble the missive and insisted on running the errand.

A man of fragile sensibilities might have taken offence at her sudden eagerness to get rid of him.

An hour after Scarlett delivered the note to Jermyn Street, Benedict Cavanagh arrived in his racing curricle to transport Damian home.

"God damn, Wycliff, you look like the devil." Cavanagh glanced around the hovel that had been Damian's sanctuary for the last few days. "Trent is already making enquiries. We'll find the men who did this, mark my words."

Damian nodded. Knowing Lawrence Trent, he would already have Lord Cockram in a stranglehold whilst dangling him over London Bridge.

"Wait for me outside." He would not have Cavanagh witness a moment of weakness. "I would like to bid a final farewell to the woman who saved my life."

"Of course." From the rakish grin on Cavanagh's face, his idea of saying farewell meant something far more licentious. "I'm sure you're desperate to convey your gratitude."

Left alone with Scarlett, Damian struggled to find the right words to express his appreciation.

"Well, as much as it's been a dreadful inconvenience," Scarlett began, for she had no difficulty speaking from the heart, "I shall miss having someone to talk to."

For a man who professed to have no heart, he wondered why

it pained him to leave her in this godforsaken place. Had he not been party to her thoughts on men who abuse their positions, he might have offered to find her better accommodation, perhaps make her his mistress. She was certainly pretty enough. But he preferred his women with a distinct lack of morals, which made this one strictly out of bounds.

"I shall have firewood delivered, and food to replace what I've eaten these last few days."

Perhaps pride forced her to say, "Replace what you have consumed, nothing more."

He stared at her for a moment, an uneasiness filling his chest. A loaf of bread and a sack of wood in no way covered the debt he owed to this angel.

"Should you ever need anything," he said, retrieving a card from his coat pocket and thrusting it into her hand, "you must seek me out. I swear an oath to offer my assistance."

Scarlett glanced at the script on the card. "Thank you, Mr Wycliff."

The pang in his chest sank like a dead weight to his stomach, urging him to do more. "You took me in when most people would not." He stroked her cheek, the soft caress conveying the depth of a foreign emotion he had no desire to dissect and analyse.

Scarlett placed her hand on top of his, and her eyes remained closed for a time. "Your plea to your mother touched my heart. It is the reason I risked bringing you into my home."

Before logic intervened, he untied his cravat and removed the gold chain from around his neck. Maria Alvarez would have placed the cross in Scarlett's palm and kissed her forehead.

Lost in a rare moment of vulnerability, that's exactly what he did. "Take this as a token of my pledge. It belonged to my mother. Sell it. Use the money to buy something you need."

"No!" Scarlett shook her head, her conscience refusing to accept such a precious gift as he knew she would. "I cannot take—"

"I insist." The uncomfortable sensation plaguing his body subsided.

She looked up at him as if he were a respectable gentleman, a deep appreciation swimming in her eyes.

It was the most perfect moment of his life.

As he said goodbye and left Scarlett alone in the cold, shabby room, he questioned why he'd given her the necklace. Numerous answers entered his head as he climbed into Cavanagh's curricle. Some too ridiculous to contemplate. He settled on the one suitable for a heartless rogue—Damian Wycliff always pays his dues.

CHAPTER TWO

London
Three years later

Nerves pushed to the fore as Lady Scarlett Steele climbed down from her carriage and studied the facade of the three-storey townhouse on Theobolds Road. Raucous laughter tumbled out onto the street. Music, singing and feminine shrieks told every passerby that this was the place for frivolous entertainment, a place to indulge one's wild fantasies, one's carnal whims. It was a place of excessiveness, too, for the golden glow of candlelight blazed from every window.

The demi-monde took pleasure in being indiscreet.

They made no secret of their sexual promiscuity. But for all their blatant disregard for propriety, they were loyal to their own kind. Unlike the pompous cowards in the ballrooms who plotted and schemed, there wasn't a person in this house who would dare cross the notorious Damian Wycliff.

"I'll turn the carriage around and wait across the street, milady," Alcock said. "You only need blow the whistle, and I'll barge the door and knock every one of them prancing pheasants on their arse."

Scarlett couldn't help but smile. "It takes a great deal to shock the jaded members of the demi-monde, but I suspect they might raise a brow once they realise you've breasts beneath your greatcoat."

The coachwoman, built stronger and sturdier than any man of Scarlett's acquaintance, doffed her hat. "Aye, and it will shock 'em even more when they discover I punch harder than any of them whelps at Jackson's."

"You'll have no need to fight tonight. These people thrive on pleasure, not pain." Still, knowing her servant would brawl in the street to protect her proved comforting. "I shall be twenty minutes, no more." Unless, of course, her quarry was engaged in lewd activities or lay sprawled on a bed, hugging an empty bottle of brandy.

Keeping the hood of her red cloak raised, Scarlett approached the front door. A succession of rhythmical raps on the wooden panel—a code given to a select few—resulted in her coming face-to-face with a young and incredibly handsome majordomo. Trying not to gape, she handed him the calling card given to her by the owner of the house, the scandalous Mrs Crandell, along with the ten-pound fee required from all newcomers and novices.

The majordomo's emerald gaze journeyed over her partially hidden face, perused the entire length of her body. Upon noting the black dress beneath the vibrant cloak, the servant said, "Ah, the Scarlet Widow. My mistress wondered when you would come." He stepped back, and with a dandified wave gestured for her to enter. "Enjoy your evening, my lady. You're certain to find something here to suit your tastes."

Stepping into the house of the debauched was akin to stepping into a den of wild dogs. Danger lurked in the shadows. Soon, the hungry would be out roaming the plains, ready to chase their prey into a quiet corner, to nip, lick and bite.

But she was the infamous Scarlet Widow.

A lady who had inherited the surname Steele and the same metal rod for a backbone. A lady who wore black to insult her husband when he was alive and breathing, who wore red in celebration as he lay solid and stiff beneath the soil. One sharp glance from her and the pups would scamper back to the safety of their pack.

With a straight back and an arrogant gaze, Scarlett sauntered along the dimly lit passage, past the bucks and rakes who tore their mouths from their scantily clad companions to leer at the new bit of skirt.

Wicked whispers reached her ears.

Every man with immorality flowing through his veins wanted to be the first to bed the Scarlet Widow. A group wager had been made by the members of White's. An amount large enough to keep every downtrodden actress in firewood for more than a few cold winters.

In the crowded drawing room hedonists were dancing, telling bawdy tales, downing wine straight from the bottle. One frolicking couple lay sprawled on the chaise, so overcome with lust that they writhed and bucked for their audience. Smoke, thick and heavy, lingered in the air like Satan's sinister mist. Hell's fire blazed in the hearth. The pungent smell of tobacco and some other woody essence clawed at her throat. Devilish laughter rang loud amid the singing and sighs of pleasure. Honing her gaze, she searched this party of sinners, looking for her elusive quarry.

She did not find Damian Wycliff there, nor was he amongst the drunken sots playing hazard in the study. Lord Merrington grinned at her with his wine-stained lips and invited her to roll the dice. Only when she noticed the lord's bare legs did she realise the stakes were clothes, not money.

Making a quick exit she moved to the billiard room, relieved to find naught but coloured balls rolling around on the green table. Two gentlemen were playing, one she recognised as the golden-haired Adonis from Jermyn Street who had ferried the injured Mr Wycliff home.

Both men studied her, leering at her figure as she stepped closer to the table.

"I'm looking for your friend," she whispered to the gentleman who had once looked upon her measly lodgings with a sneer of disdain. "The one who once brawled in a dank alley off Drury Lane."

He did not reply but glanced behind him to where Mr Wycliff lay stretched on a red velvet sofa, minus his coat and cravat and with his shirt hanging open at the throat to reveal a dusting of dark hair. The buxom lady straddling his thighs moaned and rubbed against him in such a provocative way one could not mistake her intention.

An image of Mr Wycliff lying wounded on Scarlett's bed burst into her mind. She had run her hands over those thick, solid muscles, felt the power beneath her quivering fingers. Lord Steele's legs were pale and puny spindles that struggled to support his ever-increasing paunch. Never had she met a man who possessed the same raw, rugged masculinity as the one currently tugging down the bodice of his eager lover's dress.

The dark-haired man playing billiards cleared his throat. When Mr Wycliff failed to tear his gaze away from the lady's breasts, the gentleman said, "Wycliff. You have a visitor."

With his mouth but two inches from the woman's protruding pink nipple, Mr Wycliff glanced in Scarlett's direction. Dark, hooded eyes observed her with such intensity a shiver shot from her neck to her navel. His mouth curled into an arrogant grin and he moistened his lips as if he had just picked out his next dessert should his current one prove unsatisfying.

Lord, he was as sinfully handsome as she remembered.

With her eyes screwed tight, she had thought about his wicked mouth and cocksure grin many times while performing her wifely duties. It was never Lord Steele's hands fondling her breasts. It was never her husband's body squashing her into the mattress.

"You're not an easy man to find, Mr Wycliff," she said softly, teasing him from the depths of her hood. Judging by the empty wine bottles discarded about the floor, his memory might not be so sharp. "Do you remember me?"

"Should I?" The words rang with conceit.

"We met a few years ago."

"A man cannot remember every woman he's kissed."

"Oh, we did not kiss. Well, not that I can recall."

Damian Wycliff's mocking chuckle rent the air. He sat up, forcing the woman on his lap to shuffle backwards and drag her bodice up to cover her exposed breasts.

"Trust me, had you experienced the rampant sweeps of my tongue, the moment would be seared into your memory."

"Perhaps you proved to be a disappointment."

"A disappointment?" Mr Wycliff glanced briefly at his friends, who seemed to find the comment just as amusing. "Then I highly doubt we've ever met at all."

This was not the man who swooned while she stitched his leg.

This was not the man who cradled her to his chest to banish the cold.

This brash beast lived up to his rakish reputation.

Scarlett skirted around the two men using their upright cues as leaning posts as they watched the exchange. She came to stand in front of the man she had spent a month trying to locate. "It is difficult to have amorous thoughts for a man when he is bleeding to death on one's bed."

He drew his brows together in a look of curious enquiry. "And yet *I* never fail to rise to the occasion."

Scarlett couldn't help but smile. "And I would not swoon after the third jab of a needle."

Recognition sparked in his eyes. Maintaining his calm, unruffled composure, Mr Wycliff swung his legs to the floor and rose to his feet. "Lower your hood." The command carried a dangerous undertone that would make the most hardened criminal obey.

Excitement fluttered to life in Scarlett's chest.

He would remember his promise.

He would remember the precious gift.

"As you wish." Scarlett lowered the hood of her cloak to reveal her face.

Mr Wycliff sucked in a sharp breath.

A tense silence filled the room.

Long seconds passed as he stared into her eyes, studied every facial feature as if comparing it to a fading memory. His hard, stone-like expression relaxed as his gaze moved to the long braid draped over her shoulder.

Marta, her maid, had complained about the style, insisting it made her look young and naive and lacked the sophisticated elegance people expected from the Scarlet Widow. But she had to dig down deep if she hoped to unearth this man's conscience.

"You're alive?" Damian Wycliff's dark eyes grew as warm as his tone. A softness settled around his features, the same softness she had witnessed the day he'd thrust the gold cross into her palm, the day he'd stroked her cheek and made the promise that had brought her to this iniquitous den tonight. He exhaled a relieved sigh and shook his head numerous times. "When you moved, your landlord said you'd left no forwarding address."

No forwarding address?

He spoke as if she had been a lady of quality, not a downtrodden actress desperate to secure her next meal. They had parted knowing their paths would never cross. And yet many times he had returned and knocked on her door, always left food parcels—bread and cheese and wine—when she failed to answer.

To answer would have been a disastrous mistake.

Damian Wycliff possessed a natural charisma, a boyish charm, a powerful body, hard and expertly sculpted. A needy woman would easily grow to love him. But a rumbling stomach and cold bones were easier to live with than a shattered heart.

"I left that life behind." While she had secretly fled to Gretna Green with Lord Steele, her heart had remained in the wretched lodging-house where he had caressed her with his dark eyes during one perfect moment of bliss. "Though I must thank you. Your generous gifts made those last months bearable."

Every week for two months after she had sewn his wound and tended to his fever, a sack of firewood arrived at her door. The chandler called to deliver candles, always beeswax never tallow.

Mr Wycliff inclined his head. "It was the least I could do under the circumstances."

Ah, there he was. The gentleman she had imagined taking into her body to turn the nightmare of the marriage bed into a dream.

They stared at each other for a moment, their deep breathing the only sound in the room, until one rogue standing at the billiard table chuckled.

"Damn it all, Wycliff. Do you know how many men would trade places with you right now? I knew I had seen the Scarlet Widow before."

Scarlett winced. A fake persona proved useful when dealing with degenerates, those eager to make a mockery of marriage. The name came with the power and strength of a Viking army. The name surrounded her, followed her everywhere with raised shields, painted faces and vicious snarls. She bore the scars of her many battles with Lord Steele, emotional and physical scars that had earned her a reputation for being fearless.

The lady on the sofa jumped to her feet. "It seems I am wasting my time here and shall look for sport elsewhere." She straightened her dress, waited for Mr Wycliff to protest. When he ignored her attempt to gain his attention, she strode to the door, skirting nervously around Scarlett as if anticipating a Norse attack. "If anyone can win the wager it is you, Wycliff."

After a moment of confusion, Mr Wycliff's stone-faced

expression returned. "Would someone care to speak in plain English? What widow? What blasted wager?"

The golden-haired god stepped forward. "Ignorance comes from spending too much time abroad. Ignorance comes from refusing to mingle in society, from refusing membership to your father's club. You must be the only man alive not to have heard the gossip."

"Gossip!" he spat. "I'm a man who deals in truths, not petty lies."

Scarlett squared her shoulders. "Then the truth is, Mr Wycliff, that I left my lodging-house because I married Lord Steele." A man old enough to be her father. Not a day passed when she did not regret her decision. "The truth is that since my husband's death I am known throughout the *ton* as the Scarlet Widow. The first man I take to my bed will win a ridiculous amount of money from the members of White's." She inhaled deeply. There wasn't a lord left in London who hadn't tried his hand at seduction. "Now, before you swoon, might I suggest you sit down?"

His formidable glare turned as cold and as black as granite. Wearing a look of contempt, Mr Wycliff scanned her from head to toe.

"The Scarlet Widow?" he mocked. "Who thought of that name? You?" He dropped onto the sofa, lounged back and folded his muscular arms across his chest. "How inventive." Arrogance oozed from every fibre of his being as he stretched his legs and crossed them at the ankles. "So the actress lacked morals after all. As a cynical man, I am not surprised."

His bitterness snapped at her like a rabid dog.

Did he honestly believe she had wanted to marry a disgusting debaucher? A filthy philandering foyst?

"You would say that. You're a man who wants for nothing." Anger surfaced. He'd be dead if it weren't for her. What right had he to judge? "Some of us must bow and scrape to survive."

Hatred—dark and menacing—flashed in his eyes. "And some

of us would rather die than submit to those who get a thrill from manipulating the weak. What was it that finally tempted you? Gold? Diamonds? The finest Parisian silk?"

There was an air of vulgarity about his tone that made her want to sink into a steaming bathtub and scrub her skin red raw. No one could despise her decision more than she did.

"I married Steele because—" The answer would not help her cause, but after three years of betrayal and deceit, she needed to feel clean again. "I married him because someone tried to kill me and I needed his protection."

Panic flashed in Mr Wycliff's eyes.

Two blinks, and it was gone.

The devil reappeared.

"Did I not thrust my card into your hand?" His mouth twisted into a sneer as if the words tasted foul on his lips. "Did I not tell you to call on me should you ever need assistance?"

"You did."

"And you went to Steele instead?" Disgust dripped from every word.

"Yes." The pain of regret threatened to destroy her calm composure.

It was a matter of self-preservation. One more act of kindness and she would have fallen under Mr Wycliff's spell. After all those cold, lonely days in the seminary, those bitterly cold nights spent alone in the lodging-house, she would have welcomed a soft touch and a warm embrace. He might have made her his mistress —a temporary arrangement which would have tarnished the dream.

Mr Wycliff jumped to his feet. "Then what the bloody hell are you doing here now?"

Surrounded by her Viking army, Scarlett was impervious to a man's rage.

She glanced over her shoulder to the men watching their

exchange, hanging on every word. "Might we have some privacy?"

Mr Wycliff considered the men hovering behind and shook his head. "You can speak openly in front of my friends."

"Of course," she replied with a smirk. The man thought nothing of fornicating in front of these men. "Then I am here to call in a debt."

"A debt?"

"*The* debt. You swore an oath. You are a man of your word, are you not?"

The muscle in his jaw twitched. He looked at his friends. "Leave us. Remain on the other side of the door and thrash anyone who attempts to enter."

"Even Mrs Crandell?" the golden-haired fellow said.

"Yes, even Mrs Crandell. The woman is desperate to warm your bed. I am sure you'll find a way to keep her out."

Both men inclined their heads. They placed their cues in the mahogany rack on the wall. One rolled a red billiard ball, sinking it into the pocket before they both left the room.

A thick, oppressive silence descended.

Damian Wycliff observed her for some time before stepping closer, so close heat radiated from his body, warming her as it had done on that cold night three years ago. He was so broad, so tall, so commanding. Most women would feel helpless and fragile in his presence.

But she knew how to deal with domineering men.

And yet she couldn't help but feel nervous of this one.

"I come to hold you to your promise, sir." Her insides churned. Her limbs felt too heavy to lift. Not because she was frightened, but because it took all her strength not to place her palm on his chest, not to beg him to hold her and never let go.

Mr Wycliff clicked his tongue as a mark of disrespect. "As a woman of some notoriety, I imagine you're used to the crude mouths of men. So tell me this. Why would I help you when you have pissed all over my pride? My promise meant nothing to you before."

"You know why I did not come to you." Because she would have wanted more than food and firewood, and her heart had been too weak then. She would have died inside every time he left her alone, alone and naked in his bed.

"Do I?" He dragged his hand through his mop of raven-black hair. "Feel free to enlighten me."

The Scarlet Widow did not expose her vulnerability.

The Scarlet Widow was cold and cunning and came to the point.

"You stand here today because I saved your life, Mr Wycliff." Scarlett stared down her nose as she did to those in the *ton* who once mocked her naivety. "You owe me a debt, and I'm told the devil always pays his dues."

The corners of Mr Wycliff's mouth curled into a scornful smirk as he braced his hands on his hips. "Then show me your wound, and I shall stitch it. Show me the broken bones and black bruises."

The need to drain every drop of arrogance from his magnificent body burned in her veins. "Very well. But I insist you lock the door."

This was not how she had envisioned their reunion, but she had come prepared to show him the canvas that spoke of years of misery. For months she had stood, stripped bare as the artist did his work. Shame cut sharper than the pain. But despite every harsh stroke, Lord Steele failed to paint an obedient wife.

Lord Steele had painted the Scarlet Widow.

CHAPTER THREE

Damian sauntered past the Scarlet Widow and turned the key in the lock. Mrs Crandell knew the importance some guests placed on privacy, though he suspected he would not glean an ounce of pleasure from whatever he was about to witness. He paused, his fingers still gripping the cold metal, the same fingers his angel had once bandaged and tended with care. The same fingers that ached occasionally to remind him of the only perfect moment in his entire life.

He kept the heavy sigh from leaving his lips.

Disappointment left a sour taste in his mouth.

She was not his angel, not anymore.

She was tainted, spoiled by society's sycophants.

He had lost count of the times he'd dreamed of seeing her again. He'd found her innocent smile beguiling. Purity had shone through the dirt and rags to cleanse his soul, too. That sparse little room was still his sanctuary. The only place he had ever felt an ounce of peace.

Ruined.

Replacing his mask of arrogance, he turned to face this

monstrous creation who could never compete with her benevolent understudy.

"Show me," he said with a level of disdain he refused to hide. Facades were for the weak. "Let me see your wounds so I might judge their severity. Perhaps they are merely surface scratches for I doubt you have ever bled out onto the piss-soaked cobbles of an alley."

She did not turn to face him but hung her head as she untied the ribbons on her cloak. The garment fell to the floor—a red pool around her feet—leaving her standing in her widow's weeds.

"Would you mind unfastening the buttons, Mr Wycliff?"

Damian snorted. "I'm no one's maid, Widow." He felt like ripping the blasted garment off her shoulders, tearing it to shreds.

He expected her to bite back, but she reached behind and fiddled with the tiny black buttons.

It took too long.

His patience wore thin.

Offering a frustrated groan, he stepped forward. "I do not have all night." No, after this he would storm up to one of the bedchambers and plunge long and hard and deep into any willing wench.

The widow dropped her hands, her fingers brushing against his in the process.

Every muscle in his body sparked to life.

Damnation!

Anger surfaced. She was the only person in the world ever to affect him. He yanked at the button, ripping it from its thread and sending the damn thing skittering across the wooden floor.

"Pay it no heed," she said calmly. "I have many others."

He did not know if she meant dresses or buttons. Still, he tore the garment open, drew a sense of satisfaction from the shearing sound until he realised she wore nothing underneath.

It was not lust he felt as he stared at her bare skin.

A hot, murderous fury ignited in his veins.

Damian pulled the material apart to reveal shiny pink welts crisscrossing her back. In that dank alley, he'd vomited on her boots. Now he feared he might do so again.

"Steele did this?"

She nodded. "My husband sought to break me."

Thank the lord the sick bastard was dead, else Damian would charge around to his house, slice him open from neck to navel and serve his innards to his dogs.

"From your infamous reputation, I presume he did not succeed." Talking was the only way to cool his raging blood. "The man deserves to rot in hell."

"They're the scars of a hard lesson learned. They're the evidence of my grave mistake, but they are not the only ones."

He wasn't sure he could stomach seeing any more. But he had taunted her, belittled her cause, had insisted she plead her case.

She turned to face him, pushed the black silk off her shoulders down to her waist to reveal rosy nipples and spectacular breasts.

Every man in the world would admire her full, round bosom were it not for the scar running from her collarbone to the delicate pink areola. It was not the mark of a whip but one left from a cut with a blade.

"Have you seen enough?" The widow stood there, every ounce of pride she possessed stripped from her body and discarded along with the morbid material. "Hardly surface scratches," she added to punish him for his foolish comment. "Had I been fighting against Napoleon, I might have received a medal for my injuries."

He stared into her blue eyes. The white flecks made them look as cold as ice floating on an Arctic sea. "If not a medal, you would have earned every man's respect."

"I am only interested in earning your respect, Mr Wycliff."

He stepped closer, struggled to fight the urge to draw her into his arms and offer comfort.

Hellfire!

This woman was dangerous.

Unable to soothe her pain, he pulled the sleeves of her dress up over her shoulders without once admiring the softness of her lush breasts, without dipping his head and feasting on her flesh. Only then did he notice the green bruises marring the skin at her throat.

The sight forced him to gasp and step back.

"They're not black," she said, sounding far too composed, "but they're bruises all the same."

"Your husband couldn't have done this." Having recently returned from Paris, Damian knew nothing of the lord's demise. But if there was a wager at White's, his death must be fairly recent.

Had she killed the blackguard?

Is that why she sought his help?

The widow snorted. "No. My husband died six months ago, his puny manhood still buried inside his mistress. But someone stole into my house in the dead of night and sought to squeeze the last breath from my lungs. Thank the lord for a chamber pot. I walloped the culprit hard enough to send him running."

Numerous questions flooded Damian's mind. Not least to ask if the pot was empty. The most pressing one was what she expected him to do about it.

"What do you want, Widow?" Whatever it was, he should inform her she was wrong about him. He never kept his word. Forever made false promises.

"Isn't it obvious?" she said, pulling up the high neck of her dress to cover the ugly marks around her throat. "I saved your life. I ask that you save mine."

"You want me to find this felon?" He was not a damn errand boy.

"I want your protection."

Those were the words she should have used three years ago.

He would have bedded her, given her every luxury. He would have drained every drop of goodness from her innocent body, ridding himself of the deep ache he had long since suppressed.

"You want me to make you my mistress?"

"Of course not." She gave an exasperated sigh. "No man shall ever put his hands on me again."

Now there was a challenge.

One too tempting to resist.

"But for my own purposes, I will have society believe we are lovers," she continued. "During which time you will help me discover who wants me dead."

"I'm a scoundrel who lives life to excess, not a Bow Street runner turned enquiry agent." Then again, the marquis would be disappointed to hear Damian kept company with such a notorious widow. That was worth the effort alone.

"And I was an actress, not a surgeon or seamstress."

"Of that, I am aware. I still bear the evidence of your inferior sewing skills." Though women loved his jagged scar.

"You would have died," she countered.

"A blessing some might say."

The widow glared. "You may wave your indifference like a celebratory flag, but I know honour flows in your blood."

With his defences already raised, he wanted to prove her wrong. He hated that she knew something about him. Something real. Something true.

Damian plastered a sinful grin, and in the husky voice of a skilled seducer said, "Lust is the only thing flowing in my veins, Widow. Perhaps you might tempt me to accept if you sweetened the deal."

She did not smile or mock him.

She did something far worse.

Pity flashed in her eyes. "Your mother would be ashamed of you," she said, and the words hit harder than any punch. "You called to her in the alley, and she answered your prayers. She sent me to save you. You held her cross, and you made a vow. A solemn promise. And in Maria's name, I hold you to it now."

Maria!

Damian swallowed hard. "You remembered her name."

When the widow attacked, she cut to the bone.

"You gave me her most treasured possession. How could I ever forget?"

The ache in his heart returned. Giving her the cross was a mistake. With every passing day, he'd grown to regret his rash decision.

"I trust the money bought you some comfort." Had she used the funds to buy new boots, dresses, more books? "My mother would have given you everything she owned in gratitude for saving her son."

No one would love him that much again.

A weak smile touched the widow's lips though it in no way reminded him of the angel who had slept peacefully in his arms in bed. "The necklace brought me more comfort than you could ever know."

Wycliff nodded as he silently accepted his fate, accepted that this woman knew how to read his thoughts, knew how to press his back against the wall and cut off all means of escape.

Releasing a weary sigh, he said, "If I am to save your life, Widow, I need to know everything about your situation. I want to know every intimate detail. No lies."

She raised her chin and inhaled deeply as her eyes misted. "You have seen me stripped to the bone, Mr Wycliff. You have seen my truth. Other than the blackguard who created them, you're the only man ever to gaze upon my scars."

For some reason, the thought pleased him.

"And you understand that being associated with me will only add fuel to the fire of your notoriety. There is a reason I spend so much time abroad."

He had shot Lord Cockram in a duel after discovering he was responsible for the beating in the alley. He had shot two other dishonourable devils since. And he would put a lead ball between Lord Steele's brows were he not rotting beneath the ground.

The lady arched a brow. "I am counting on it. You may call at my house in Bedford Street tomorrow, and I shall tell you anything you feel pertinent to my case."

A man need not be an intelligent enquiry agent to know it was better to meet on neutral ground. When he entered her house, he would have full knowledge of the situation.

"No. Have your coachman bring you to The Cock and Magpie in Drury Lane at noon."

She seemed to find something amusing. "I'm sure my *coach-woman* will ensure I arrive at the appointed time."

Damian smirked. "A woman drives your carriage? No wonder you need my protection."

The widow arched a brow. "I advise you to have a care when in her company, Mr Wycliff. She tends to hurl a fist before asking questions, and has a thorough dislike of arrogant, controlling men."

"Ah, a woman scorned?" They were the worst kind.

"She served her time in the underground boxing dens in Whitechapel before buying her freedom."

Hell's teeth. The women who fought there were ruthless. Savage.

"Then I shall mind my manners," he said, for he could never hit a woman regardless of how hard she attacked.

Laughter and loud voices from beyond the locked door reached his ears. No doubt people had heard that London's most scandalous rake was alone in a room with the Scarlet Widow. Come the morning there would be an amusing and bawdy carica-ture in the broadsheets involving a billiard table, cue and two balls.

The widow glanced at the door, though she did not look the

least bit anxious. "Well, I shall take my leave, but will meet you at noon tomorrow."

Some fool rattled the doorknob, made loud groaning noises and shouted, "What the devil's going on in there?"

"Just the childish antics of the demi-monde," he said, wondering why—for the first time in his life—he felt a little ashamed. Whoever it was would need to call a doctor to reset his impending broken nose.

"Actually, it rather works in my favour as there is something I must do before I leave. As a man with a scandalous reputation, I hope you have no objection."

"Objection?"

It was then that the Scarlet Widow drew on her experiences as an actress. She came up to him, dragged his shirt out of his breeches and ruffled his hair before proceeding to make the amorous moans of a woman being thoroughly ravished. Such was her skill that every fake pant made the muscles in his abdomen clench.

"Carpe diem," she said, unwinding the braid to let the soft ebony waves drape over her shoulders. "I trust you will use your winnings wisely."

The widow scooped her red cloak off the floor and draped it around her shoulders. She unlocked the door and yanked it open to find a host of excited guests lingering in the hallway.

"Wycliff proved most satisfactory," she said in the breathless, husky voice of a woman descending the dizzying heights of her climax. And then she disappeared down the crowded corridor.

Damian felt as though he'd been whipped up into a whirlwind, his ragged emotions tossed aside with all the other debris. The Scarlet Widow knew how to leave a lasting impression.

"Well?" Trent said, a wicked grin stretching from ear to ear. "How was she?"

Noting Damian's flagging equilibrium, Trent offered his lit cheroot.

Damian snatched the cigar and drew deep. He blew a puff of white mist into the air before flopping down onto the velvet sofa. "So damn good I needed this smoke."

CHAPTER FOUR

"There is no need to accompany me into the tavern," Scarlett said to Alcock, who had climbed down from her box to play escort. "Stay with Kemp. The streets are so busy today, no doubt someone will complain that my carriage is blocking their way." She took hold of Kemp's outstretched hand as the groom assisted her descent to the cobblestones of Drury Lane.

Alcock tugged her greatcoat firmly across her body and shook her head. "When those drunken sots catch sight of a woman, they forget they're suppin' in a tavern and think they've come to grope in the apple dumplin' shop."

Scarlett pressed her lips together to stifle an amused snort. "I am certain Mr Wycliff will be an adequate chaperone."

Alcock sneered. "Men are all the same, milady. Smile in the wrong way, and they think they've the right to take liberties."

Having witnessed the ugly marks on Scarlett's body, she doubted Mr Wycliff would want to gaze upon them again. Still, she couldn't help but get a thrill from goading the man, and Alcock was particularly candid when dealing with scoundrels.

"Very well," Scarlett conceded. "You may accompany me inside and deposit me safely into Mr Wycliff's care." She raised her hand to silence the woman should she have a mind to make further demands.

Alcock nodded. She barked instructions to Kemp and told him to blow the horn should he encounter any trouble.

With Alcock pressed to her side, Scarlett pushed past the bustle of people crowding the narrow street, skirted around unruly dogs and vendors desperate to sell the apples they'd polished to perfection. The stench of manure and rotten vegetables permeated the air. It was a smell she welcomed for it spoke of hard work, of a time when only the simple things like food and shelter mattered.

Despite a severe lack of funds, she had not been unhappy.

Not until the first threatening letter arrived.

Not until a dark stranger followed her home one foggy night.

Not until circumstances forced her to make other choices—to become the Scarlet Widow.

Oh, how she longed for anonymity. How she wished she was just another nameless face going about another mundane day. No one in this part of town cared that she wore a scandalous red pelisse over her widow's weeds. No one cared that she wore a bright red bonnet with a large black bow as a mark of disdain.

Alcock cursed at a drunkard slumped against the doorjamb and pushed the fellow aside so that they might enter the premises. A lady did not visit a tavern without a male escort. But with her cropped brown hair and square jaw, most people mistook Alcock for a man.

The coachwoman barged through the crowd. Some patrons stood around crude wooden tables in a room where the beamed ceiling was so low they had to stoop. Some occupied chairs near the open fire, their half-closed eyes suggesting they swilled liquor from dawn till dusk. The oak-panelled walls cast the room in an orange glow that made the inn feel welcoming, but Scarlett knew better than to judge anything on first impressions.

Damian Wycliff sat on a long oak settle, his muscular legs stretched out to the side and crossed at the ankles. A thick lock of ebony hair hung rakishly over his brow. The two men from the billiard room sat on the bench opposite, gripping their tankards while deep in conversation.

All boisterous chatter ceased as fifty male heads shot in Scarlett's direction. If only they could see her Viking army, then they might lack the courage to gape and stare. Still, Scarlett drew on the imagined warriors' strength, raised her chin and feigned an air of hauteur.

It was unnecessary, of course, because Alcock insisted on making a spectacle. The woman braced her hands on her hips and said with some frustration, "Ain't no one seen a lady before?"

With the comment spoken in such a high-pitched tone, it caused some confusion amongst the patrons. They spent as much time perusing Alcock's person as they did the newcomer in the vibrant hat. No doubt their minds were engaged in determining whether Alcock was a man with an unusually high voice or something far more threatening.

"Get back to your drinks, gentlemen." The deep, masculine voice powered through the room. "Else I might feel inclined to defend the lady's honour."

To further make his point, Mr Wycliff stood, his dark eyes sending a threatening message. He had teamed his midnight blue coat with a crimson cravat. On some, the combination might look foppish. On Mr Wycliff, it conveyed an air of illicit danger.

All the men in the room quickly averted their gazes, keen to resume their previous conversations before the handsome rogue stripped off his coat and flexed his fists.

Alcock took umbrage at Mr Wycliff's intervention. On a muttered breath she cursed all men to the devil. In her experience, the helpful ones proved just as wicked.

"That is Mr Wycliff," Scarlett said once the noise in the room returned to its previous pitch. "Be polite, as I am in dire need of his help."

Alcock snorted as the gentleman in question sauntered

towards them. "Men like him make promises they can't keep. Men like him serve no one but themselves."

"And you can tell that from the way he walks?"

"I know his kind. Wronged men who want to make the world pay."

Alcock did not have the chance to comment further.

Mr Wycliff inclined his head. "It seems you create a stir wherever you go, Widow."

Scarlett winced at his derogatory use of the name. The tension in the air grew palpable. Her coachwoman was like a loyal dog who thought nothing of sinking her teeth into the flesh of the disrespectful.

Alcock snarled. "Speak to milady like that again, and I'll be the one defending her honour."

"I am capable of dealing with Mr Wycliff," Scarlett said to defuse the situation. "He might fool the world with his arrogance, but he does not fool me."

No, she had seen him at his most vulnerable.

Mr Wycliff arched a brow. "And though you feign the confidence of the Scarlet Widow, beneath the bravado you are still the struggling actress."

Alcock took a step forward, the tip of her booted foot pressing down onto Mr Wycliff's toes. She raised her chin. "I've beaten men black and blue for less."

Mr Wycliff's amused gaze slipped slowly to his feet before fixing on his prey. "And I've blown a lead ball into the chest of men with half your insolence. Perhaps your mistress needs to learn that the stocks are the place for outspoken servants."

"Raise a hand to me, and you'll be pickin' your teeth out of the gutter."

"That is quite enough," Scarlett said, eager to put an end to this uncordial standoff. "If we are to work together, you will learn to get along. Now, allow me to present my trusted coachwoman, Alcock."

"Alcock?" Mr Wycliff's dark eyes scanned Scarlett's burly servant as he dragged his foot out from under her boot. "How apt."

Clearly, he referred to her servant's overtly masculine appearance.

"You may wait for me outside, Alcock, while we tend to business." Despite Alcock's penchant for violence, respect for her position meant she always obeyed her mistress.

"I have taken the liberty of hiring a private room," the rogue said, winking at Alcock and flashing her a wicked grin. "We don't want any ill-timed interruptions."

A muscle in Alcock's jaw twitched, but Scarlett arched her brow, and the woman turned on her heel and marched from the tavern.

The gentleman chuckled. "I sense a little hostility."

"She has spent most of her adult life being verbally abused by men. I've yet to find a way to calm the bitter rage within."

"Ah, the pugilist from the dens in Whitechapel," he said as if recognition had suddenly dawned. "Forgive me. After downing three bottles of claret last night my memory is somewhat hazy."

Scarlett's heart skipped a beat. Please say he recalled the moment where she bared more than her soul. The man had probably gazed upon a hundred pairs of naked breasts. But she could not have those sinful eyes look upon hers again.

"I trust, Mr Wycliff, that you remember some things with clarity. A lady might struggle to expose herself in such a candid way a second time." Indeed, it had taken every ounce of strength she possessed to let the garment fall.

His dark eyes grew warm as he scanned the front of her red pelisse. "Some things a man never forgets." The velvet tone of his voice slipped over her like a soothing caress.

Confusion rendered her momentarily speechless. She had expected his top lip to rise in disdain at the memory, expected to see disgust mar his fine features. She had not expected a look brimming with insatiable lust.

Had he not seen the ugly scars?

Had it not made him feel sick to his stomach?

"Of course, once we're nestled inside a private room," he continued, "you might like to remind me."

The thought of being alone with him again sent her pulse racing. "I suspect one scar is pretty much like another."

"Scar? I thought we were talking about something else entirely."

Scarlett breathed a heavy sigh. She had more important things to do than exchange quips with him all day. "Perhaps we should skip the pleasantries, Mr Wycliff, and get to the matter of your oath."

"You speak of the foolish promise made in the heat of the moment."

The comment hit like a stray arrow, too quick for her shield-maidens to defend. "Nevertheless, you gave your word."

Mr Wycliff inclined his head. "Then I suppose you had better follow me."

With his usual arrogant swagger, he cut through the crowd, grinning at his friends as he moved past their table. The door at the far end of the room opened into a small hallway. Scarlett presumed he had commanded use of a parlour, but he mounted the stairs two at a time, climbed two flights before leading her into a room with a low-beamed ceiling and no furniture other than a bed.

Once inside, he locked the door behind them. "One cannot be too careful. I doubt either of us wants someone bursting in at an inopportune moment."

Nerves rattled in her throat.

Damn him. This man's behaviour often vacillated between gentleman and rogue.

Unpredictability was his middle name. She had learnt to deal with evil devils, and yet Mr Wycliff unsettled her composure at every turn.

Did he feel threatened because she knew too much about him?

Did his hostility stem from the fact she outranked him?

"Sit down." Mr Wycliff gestured to the bed, and her heart smacked against her ribs. He shrugged out of his coat and hung it on a hook on the back of the door. "Kick off your boots and make yourself comfortable, Lady Steele."

He spoke her name as if it were a common joke. At least he'd not called her Widow.

"We have the room for an hour. Best not waste precious time." He dropped down onto the mattress, the bed groaning beneath his weight, and proceeded to tug off his boots. "As we're beginning this partnership with honesty, I would like to thank you for saving my life."

"I did what anyone with a conscience would do."

He shuffled to the top of the bed, propped himself against the pillows and folded his arms behind his head. "It took courage, courage which you now have in abundance."

"One must have fortitude in this wicked world if they hope to survive."

He studied her for a moment. "Sit down else I shall have a devil of a crick in my neck."

Every fibre of her being fought against his request. Perhaps because it sounded like a command. "I prefer to stand."

He shrugged. "As you wish. Now, tell me your story. I must know every detail if I am to offer assistance."

So many images flooded her mind. Vile scenes. Cruel pictures. There was so much to tell she didn't know where to begin. Either way, she would need to hold her resolve. The next hour was guaranteed to be unpleasant.

"I don't know what you've heard about Lord Steele, but—"

"Start from the beginning." His sharp interjection only added to the tension. "Tell me why you moved from a seminary in Bath to a hovel off Drury Lane. Tell me why an educated woman chose to grace the stage."

She had mentioned the seminary in passing three years ago while tending to his wound. How was it he remembered something so insignificant?

"Is it relevant?" No one knew her true identity. Her father insisted she kept it that way. Scarlett hadn't the faintest notion why and could only imagine it stemmed from embarrassment about the nature of his business. "What possible bearing could that have on my current situation?"

"Well, I won't know unless you tell me," came his blunt reply.

"It is personal." Not something one mentioned to a man one did not fully trust.

"Then this is a pointless conversation." He sat up and swung his legs to the floor. "And a complete waste of my time."

"Are you leaving?" Panic surfaced.

There had been too many threats against her person for her to tackle the matter alone. Somewhere, in a tiny part of her heart where hope lay weak and undernourished, she had cast this wicked scoundrel as her hero. She remembered the tender caress, the moment he had thrust his treasured cross into her palm in the only true act of kindness she had ever known.

Mr Wycliff grabbed one of his boots, ready to thrust his foot inside.

"Wait!" Surrender did not come easy. Perhaps she need not give him a full explanation. "My mother died when I was ten. Between the ages of ten and twenty, my father paid for me to attend numerous establishments keen to educate females."

He paused. Keeping a firm grip on his boot, he said, "Why did he not keep you at home and hire a governess?"

It was a question she had pondered on many a cold, lonely night. The answer given seemed logical, and yet it had left a gaping hole in her heart. "His home was his business. A business considered an unsuitable place for a lady."

But she had always sensed it was more than that.

Love did not come easy to Jack Jewell.

Mr Wycliff glanced over his shoulder and narrowed his gaze. "A brothel?"

"No!" she said far too quickly. "Not a brothel but one might call it an establishment for the wealthy and dissolute. My father made me swear never to mention our connection."

Something she said must have piqued his curiosity, pricked his conscience. He dropped his boot, shuffled back onto the bed and resumed his relaxed position. "And he paid for you to live away at a seminary?"

"At numerous seminaries. I rarely stayed in one place for longer than a year."

The memory made the hollow space in her chest seem cavernous. Such instability made it impossible to forge friendships, to nurture relationships. She never belonged, was always the outsider.

"How often did you see your father?" His dark eyes shone with intrigue. Scarlett suspected the question stemmed from more than an interest in her childhood.

"Not often enough." The intolerable ache in her heart throbbed.

Mr Wycliff rubbed his chin as he contemplated her answer. "Regardless of his reasons, I daresay you felt abandoned."

Was he determined to twist the rusty blade further into her chest? Scarlett raised her chin. "Abandoned, and dreadfully lonely."

Good Lord! She would rather bare her scarred breast than her tortured soul.

"I presume your father is dead, hence the reason you left the seminary and took to the stage."

"Yes." She should mention that he took his own life, that the coroner proclaimed *felo de se*—suicide—rather than cite an unstable mind as was common practice. Consequently, everything the man owned went to refill the Crown's coffers.

"So what prompted you to marry Lord Steele?" His intense stare fixed her to the floor. Where she had previously heard a faint softness hidden beneath his words, now she heard a ruthless arrogance, a blatant disregard for women who married for money and status.

"It might have something to do with the fact a stranger followed me home every night for a week. That a cloaked fiend throttled me in the alley and only fled because Lord Steele intervened."

Now she suspected that Steele's arrival was not a coincidence. The devious blackguard was besotted, besotted with the notion of marrying another weak woman who would cower to him in grateful servitude.

Mr Wycliff's mouth twisted with disdain and he arched a mocking brow. "How convenient. Did it not occur to you that it was all part of his depraved plan?"

At the time, rational thought had abandoned her, too. "Have your emotions ever plagued you to the point you long for a moment's peace?"

"Indeed." He inclined his head. "Though from the scars littering your back, peace is the last thing you found in your marriage."

No, fighting for survival had pushed her to unimaginable limits. "Oh, but for the wisdom of hindsight." It was her turn to sound cold and cynical.

"Did you kill your husband?"

"No."

"But you thought about thrusting a blade into the bastard's chest."

"Every day."

"Remind me how he met his end."

"His heart gave out while wedged between his mistress' thighs midthrust."

The corner of Mr Wycliff's mouth curled up in amusement. "A delightful way to go."

She would rather swing from the gallows than suffer the weight of Steele's paunch or the stench of his rancid breath. "That depends upon one's partner."

He crossed his hands behind his head and lounged back on the pillows. "Or upon one's position. I'd prefer to be on my back, gazing up at my mistress' bountiful breasts."

Scarlett swallowed her surprise. She had heard he favoured no one special. "You have a mistress?" The question brought an uncomfortable lump to her throat.

"It was a figure of speech. Why would I want the responsibility of a mistress when I can bed any woman I choose?"

The conceited devil!

"Not any woman," she challenged.

His eyes grew warm and wide, and he laughed. "You think you're immune to my charms, Widow?"

"When it comes to me, arrogance is your downfall."

He sat up, rose to his feet with predatory grace and closed the gap between them. Capturing her chin between his fingers, he stared into her eyes.

"What would it take to seduce the Scarlet Widow?" His sinful mouth was but an inch from hers, his muscular thighs pressing her back against the wall. "I imagine an ounce of tenderness, a kind gesture, a slow, passionate melding of mouths and you would fall into bed as easily as any jaded member of the demi-monde. Am I right?"

He was so right it pained her to admit it.

Craving love would always be her weakness. That's what happened when one sat at the window waiting for a father who never came. One genuine act of kindness meant more than a chest of priceless gems.

44

"Your plan to seduce me has one major flaw," she said, for she had learnt to rely on nothing but her steely defences.

"Do you think I give a damn about your scars?" His rich, liquid tone washed over her, threatened her resolve. A man could not look upon her body without staring at the savage lines. The fact he had mentioned the ugly marks supported her theory.

"You forgot the first rule in battle, Mr Wycliff." Scarlett stroked her hand down her red pelisse, drawing strength from her costume. "In planning your attack, you have failed to consider your defence."

Perhaps he had forgotten that she'd glimpsed him at his most vulnerable. Affection had flashed in his eyes when reunited with the lowly actress who had saved him from death's door. Disdain quickly replaced it upon discovering she was the scandalous Scarlet Widow.

He released her chin and braced his hands on the wall above her head, trapping her in his masculine cage. With his broad shoulders and muscular arms blocking her view, she wasn't sure if it was a move to entice or intimidate.

He bent his head. "Why would I need to form a defence when you are desperate to surrender?"

"Surrender? Are you so certain? Might a sign of weakness not be a planned tactic?" She gave a mocking snort as she was beginning to enjoy this game. "In that first tender touch, I would have you on your knees. The real you—the man who longs for affection just as much as I do—not the fake construction used to create mischief and mayhem. Your kind gesture would leave your heart as open and as exposed as mine. And as for your passionate kiss, well, there is every chance you might taste the truth."

"The truth?" His dark eyes looked almost black as he pinned her to the wall. All she need do was raise her lips to feel that hungry mouth on hers.

Scarlett smiled. "That you wore red today because your persona is as fake as the Scarlet Widow's."

He pushed away from the wall as if the plaster had burnt his hands. "You think you know me. You don't."

Perhaps not, but she fought the desire to know him in every way a woman could know a man.

In the blink of an eye he was sitting on the bed, thrusting his feet into his boots with such force he was likely to cause himself an injury. "But rest assured, Widow, we will rectify the situation tonight."

"Tonight?"

"When you accompany me to the Marquis of Blackbeck's ball."

"A ball? I heard you refuse to speak to your father let alone attend functions at his house." She'd heard that Damian Wycliff avoided respectable gatherings.

He stood, snatched his coat from the hook on the door and shrugged into the garment with some impatience. "Perhaps I am willing to make an exception in light of the fact Joshua and Jemima Steele are attending. They think you are somehow responsible for their father's untimely death and are, no doubt, eager for revenge."

Anger surfaced. "I did not secretly administer medicine that might make his heart give out." Jemima openly conveyed such suspicions. But she was too weak to plan the numerous attacks on Scarlett's person. Mr Wycliff would know that if he bothered to ask more questions. "While you know about the intruder, you know nothing about the other attacks."

"Don't I?" He folded his arms across his chest in a display of superiority. "Something spooked your horse in Hyde Park forcing the beast to rear and cast you from your saddle. Word is you should have broken your neck."

"Through my many trials and tribulations whilst married to Lord Steele, I have learnt how to fall."

His arrogant grin faltered, but only long enough for him to

mutter a curse. "A carriage mounted the pavement in Piccadilly and almost took you under its wheels."

"Thankfully, I have developed quick reflexes."

"There was the wild dog incident in Green Park."

Scarlett arched a brow. The animal had darted from the bushes, teeth bared, ready to attack. "The key with all vicious dogs is not to show fear." And to bribe them with the sweet biscuit she'd retrieved from her reticule. "And you learnt all of that since last night?"

"Well, I have not spent the morning supping ale and fondling the serving wench."

"Then the poor girl must be sobbing into her apron. You forgot to mention the attempted poisoning, though my house-keeper will take great pleasure in telling the story. She so enjoys playing the victim."

"Then I shall call for you fifteen minutes earlier this evening." He pulled his watch from his pocket and inspected the time. "The hour is up." He replaced his watch and unlocked the door. "This is the first time I have left a hired bedchamber feeling wholly unsatisfied."

"If you plan on spending time in my company, Mr Wycliff, you should become accustomed to the sensation. I am the only woman in Christendom opposed to the prospect of warming your bed."

"Liar," the devil on her shoulder shouted.

Amused, Mr Wycliff placed a guiding hand at the small of her back and led her from the room. "If you knew me, Widow, you would know not to offer such a tempting challenge."

CHAPTER FIVE

Damian tugged on the cuffs of his black evening coat and brushed imagined dust from his lapels. He stood on the stairs leading down to his father's ballroom, surveying the lavish spectacle. The crystal chandeliers created an air of opulence. Candlelight glistened in the tall gilt mirrors. The orchestra on the balcony wore matching gold damask coats as they played their instruments with a skill worthy of royal patronage. Liveried footmen in powdered wigs wandered through the room carrying silver trays laden with flutes of champagne.

Damian's gaze settled on his host.

The man he had spent a lifetime hating.

The Marquis of Blackbeck liked nothing more than to bathe in extravagance. Wealth oozed from every fibre of his being. Confidence sparkled as brilliantly as the huge diamond pin decorating his cravat. The marquis conducted his personal liaisons with the same nonchalant indifference he gave to his excessive expenditure.

Heads turned in Damian's direction long before the major-domo made his announcement. Ladies gaped in shock. Some stared with lust lighting their eyes. By the time he reached the bottom step, he would have more than one invitation to join a private party in a lonely lady's bedchamber tonight.

But he wasn't the only newcomer being ogled.

Men in their droves—dissolute and respectable, old and young—eyed the beauty standing confidently at his side wearing a vibrant red dress.

He could hardly blame them. From the moment the Scarlet Widow slipped out of her wrapper, he had fought the urge to run his horny hands over the smooth silk hugging her curves. Delicate lace covered her shoulders. The high collar hid the bruises and scars. She did not need to display mounds of creamy white flesh, for the material clung to her body like a second skin.

The widow touched the sleeve of his coat and whispered playfully, "Something has captured the guests' attention. I wonder what it could be."

It wasn't the comment that created an odd flutter of excitement in Damian's chest. The widow spoke as if he were the only man privileged to hear her inner thoughts, and that fed his vanity.

Damian offered his arm, and the widow slipped her hand into the crook. "Shall we set the ballroom ablaze?" he said, relishing the prospect of causing his father embarrassment. "The gossips' tongues will be so hot every word spoken will sound like a sizzle."

The widow looked at him and arched a brow. "While I take immense pleasure in causing a scene, that's not why we are here."

No, he'd come to settle the debt, to prove Joshua and Jemima Steele had conspired to commit murder. Naturally, the motive was money. By his estimation, he would have their confession within the hour. Then he would set about seducing the beguiling creation at his side until she begged him to bed her, before relegating the whole event to a distant corner of his memory. Simple.

"Surely you have a plan," she continued.

"Only the staid and sober waste time plotting and scheming. Reckless gentlemen act on impulse."

"It was impulse that saw you left for dead in an alley." An impatient huff left her lips though she maintained her affected smile. "I should have known you would tackle my problem with nothing but devilish joviality. No doubt you brought me here tonight for your own devious ends."

It annoyed him that she was right.

Damian steered her through the throng, who parted as if he were Moses waving a staff of divinity. Parched, he snatched a flute of champagne, swallowed the contents and returned it to the tray before grabbing two more.

"Reckless gentlemen rely on their talents to achieve success," he said, offering the widow a glass. And some rogues were like cats. No matter how far they fell, they landed on their feet.

She wrapped her gloved fingers around the stem. When she brought the vessel to her lips, he noticed the slight tremble that spoke of suppressed anxiety. The mere glimpse of the vulnerable actress raised his pulse a notch.

"When your only talent amounts to whoring, Mr Wycliff, I must say I am intrigued to hear more."

"Whoring has its uses. Indeed, I intend to test my expertise on Miss Jemima Steele tonight." He nodded to the thin lady with rodent features standing near the terrace doors. One hard thrust and the chit would snap like a twig. "While I make a point never to seduce wallflowers, I shall use my talent to weaken her resolve."

The widow's eyes grew wide with alarm. "You intend to bed Miss Steele?" she whispered through gritted teeth. "That is your plan?"

Damian shrugged. "I intend to place her in such a compromising position she has no choice but to tell the truth. The lady is far too prim for her own good. And I'm too much of a devil to let the opportunity pass."

"I doubt Satan himself would stoop so low." She seemed more upset than angry.

"I have sworn to protect you, to put a lead ball between the brows of the blackguard who wants you dead." Damian clasped her elbow to reinforce his point. "Whether you like it or not, you're my responsibility until the debt is repaid."

What did she expect? She was the one who used his love for his mother against him. He'd sworn an oath in Maria's name, and he would not disrespect her memory.

Damian braced himself for an argument, but after a moment's reflection, the widow inclined her head in acquiescence.

He stared at her, trying to understand why she had not fought against his control, until a discreet cough to their left drew his attention.

"Lady Steele," the foppish gentleman began. "Forgive the intrusion."

Before Damian could growl "bugger off" in his most vicious voice, the widow said, "Lord Rathbone, what a pleasant surprise." She batted her lashes, her smile as fake as her warm tone.

Rathbone inclined his head to Damian and then bowed to the widow. "I wonder if I might claim the next dance?"

Did the fool not know he had won the bet?

Did he not know that he hadn't a hope of taking this woman to his bed? The widow sought more than elegant clothes and a handsome countenance.

The lord's curly brown hair accentuated the softness of his features. His high collar failed to hide his weak chin. He looked like the sort of fellow who would rather pander to a lady's whims than seduce her into submission. No doubt he wore a nightcap and shirt to bed, made love to his mistress on a set day of the week, always at nine with the candles snuffed.

Damian made a mental note to seek the lord out at the card table and wipe the charming smile from his lips.

"Thank you, my lord," the widow replied. "But it is such a

crush tonight, and I have yet to pay homage to the host. Perhaps our paths might cross later in the evening. Or we might find an opportunity to converse over supper."

Over Damian's dead body.

The woman who came with him stayed with him.

"Of course." Rathbone accepted the excuse too easily. That said, Damian afforded the man a modicum of respect. He must be keen on the widow to stand before a notorious rogue knowing one wrong word might land him a dawn appointment. "I'm told the supper table boasts many extravagant delicacies."

"Then I look forward to sampling its delights."

That was enough. Damian gritted his teeth. Even though he knew it was all an act, he despised her obvious flirtation.

Without offering a word to the soppy lord, Damian cupped the widow's elbow and steered her away. "If I'm supposed to be bedding you, I'll not have you fawning over Lord Rathbone."

She snorted though did not object to his high-handed approach. "If I am supposed to be bedding you, Mr Wycliff, I'll not have you compromising Miss Steele."

"Any attempt to rouse jealousy is for naught. I am immune." He refused to admit that resentment made him want to throttle the lord. Besides, when it came to Miss Steele, he had his limits and planned to do nothing more than frighten the chit.

"It is not my intention to play games, sir. Lady Rathbone is one of the few matrons to show me an ounce of human kindness. Consequently, I find myself unable to be rude to her grandson."

"Then you should put the fellow out of his misery. His excessive drooling must surely frustrate his valet."

The widow's genuine smile almost made Damian stumble. "Lord Rathbone means well, but his overzealous need to capture my attention leads me to wonder if he's pledged money in the wager at White's."

"Distrusting others is something we have in common." The first strains of a waltz drifted through the room. Damian never danced. If he did, he would whisk the widow around the floor, hold her scandalously close just to annoy Lord Rathbone. "Would you like me to make discreet inquiries?"

She shook her head and wrinkled her nose. "I doubt you have a discreet bone in your body. Besides, Lady Rathbone is keen to see her grandson wed, and not to a notorious widow."

"Marriage is not for the likes of us," he said, drawing her towards the terrace for he needed an opportunity to thrust the note he'd written into Miss Steele's hand.

"Us?"

"The cynical."

"I doubt I would ever trust a man again," she agreed.

"You never told me the name of your husband's mistress." Whoever it was paled in comparison to the Scarlet Widow. "It might be an idea to add her to the list of suspects."

She swallowed her champagne and placed the empty glass on a tray carried by a passing footman. "Madame Larousse."

"Madame Larousse? The French actress?"

"*Oui*," she said with a giggle, and he caught a glimpse of the innocent woman to whom he owed his life. "Though I'm told she has another benefactor and has no gripe with me. If anything, I would like to offer her a reward."

Damian would have liked to watch the widow's expression when she learnt the news of her husband's demise. "The madame's voracious appetite is to be commended."

"Indeed." The widow cast him a brilliant smile.

Somehow it found a chink in his armour and infused his chest with a warm glow. To add to this unsettling sensation, he saw his father striding through the crowd, heading in his direction.

Damnation!

Damian reached into the pocket of his evening coat, removed a silver flask and downed two mouthfuls of brandy. "You told Rathbone you wanted to pay homage to your host." He slipped the flask back into his pocket and tugged the cuffs of his coat. "Here's your chance."

Anger burned in Damian's veins as his father drew closer. Over the years, he'd tried every means possible to eradicate the feeling. Absence. Dismissal. Vengeance. Nothing tempered the ugliness inside, the hostility battling for a voice.

The marquis joined them. A few years had passed since Damian last stood within a few feet of the suave lord. Silver streaked the dark hair at his father's temples, but it only added to his air of sophistication. The marquis' dark eyes shone with the confidence and arrogance of a man who commanded attention.

"I cannot decide what I consider most shocking," the marquis said smoothly, capturing the widow's hand and pressing a kiss to her knuckles. Most ladies melted beneath the lord's sultry stare, but not the widow. "The fact you dishonour your husband's memory by wearing red, or that you're having an intimate relationship with my son."

"Illegitimate son," Damian corrected. Bitterness brought bile to his throat. "Or had you forgotten you refused to marry my mother?"

The marquis' amused gaze drifted over him. "Maria did so enjoy telling her bedtime stories."

Damian straightened to his full height. "Are you calling my mother a liar?"

"Would I do that when you duel with every man who so much as brushes against you in a distasteful manner?"

"Would I call you out when you boast that your skill in every regard is greater than mine?" Damian countered.

A man might hate his kin, but that didn't mean he wanted them dead.

"Greater in all things but one." His father glanced at the widow, a sinful smile tugging on his lips. "You appear to have outplayed most men of the *ton*, though I consider seducing a woman to win a bet rather crass."

"Then you lack my skill on more than one count. The widow seduced me." It wasn't a lie. Being proficient in the art of manipulation, she had found his one weakness.

Your mother would be ashamed of you.

Those words had cut deep. Sliced through the iron casing around his heart. It was one thing being aware of one's own hypocrisy, another to have someone call you out. Indeed, if Maria Alvarez could look upon her son, would she see his whoremonger of a father staring back?

"Then the widow means to use you," the marquis said blatantly as if challenging her to refute the claim, "use you for her own devilish ends."

Damian focused on the stranger who'd sired him, on the hatred that made life easier to bear, and tried to determine the reason for his attack. Had the marquis tried to bed the widow and failed? The lord's languid demeanour gave nothing away.

"For a gentleman with impeccable breeding, you banter like a commoner, my lord," the widow said in the haughty manner of a blue-blooded matron. "You may arrive at the riverside in your gilt carriage, but you seem intent on washing your soiled linen with all the other housemaids."

A muscle in the marquis' cheek twitched.

Before his father could utter a word, she turned to Damian, "I expect no less from you." And the comment pricked his pride. "As you both think it fair game to use me to score points, I shall take my leave in pursuit of finding less toxic air."

The widow thrust her pretty nose high, turned on her heel and headed towards the terrace.

Any other time, and with any other woman, he would have said to hell with it and moved to pastures new. Yet the widow had slithered under his skin. Perhaps he lived in the hope of finding Scarlett—the caring soul lost beneath the hideous disguise. Perhaps he hoped her goodness would cure him of his sickening malaise, too.

Whatever it was, something made him turn to his father and say, "I'm sure you have more important guests in need of your attention." He did not pay the lord the courtesy of inclining his head but merely turned his back.

"Why do you fight against the inevitable?" The marquis caught Damian's coat sleeve, stalling him momentarily. "Parklands awaits its master. You only need marry a lady of my choosing."

And Parklands could fall into rack and ruin for all Damian cared. Thankfully, his mother had been wealthy in her own right and so rarely accepted financial help from the lord.

"With the right alliance, society will forgive you anything," the marquis continued.

Forgive him!

He wasn't the one who had made a mistake. "You created a bastard, and you can damn well live with the consequences. Now remove your hand before I make a devil of a scene."

"The aristocracy are governed by different rules." The marquis' hand slipped from Damian's evening coat. "Complicated rules you wouldn't understand."

Damian glared down his nose, the same blasted nose he had inherited from this man. "If you'd loved her, you would have married her. What is so complicated about that?"

"You know nothing of the situation," the marquis countered, but Damian was keen to put some distance between them and so marched away without a backwards glance.

Before heading out onto the terrace, he barged purposely into Jemima Steele, bowed over her hand and slipped her a note whilst making his apologies.

He found his widow outside, her body stiff and rigid, her palms resting on the stone balustrade as she stared at the rows of lanterns illuminating the manicured garden. No doubt he should offer an apology for his ill-mannered comments. And yet the only question that mattered hung like a ton weight from his tongue.

"How many times has the marquis tried to seduce you?" Damian breathed deeply to calm his racing pulse. The answer mattered more than he cared to admit.

She shrugged but did not turn to look at him. "Perhaps once or twice, but he behaves that way with everyone."

"If he has laid a finger on you, I'm done here."

She swung around to face him, her blue eyes wide. Once, the cyan pools had spoken of hope and honesty. Now, they carried the heaviness of grief, though not for her husband.

"Not that I have to explain myself to you, but I am not in the habit of bedding men to climb the social ladder. I am not in the habit of bedding men at all, let alone one who would do so just to prove his superiority."

Damian stepped closer. "The marquis always gets what he wants." Except for control over his illegitimate son. His only son for that matter.

"Then he will be sorely disappointed."

Not for long. The marquis knew how to manipulate people to do his bidding. "Does your reluctance for a liaison have something to do with your scars?" Did the widow's shame make her immune to his father's charms?

"My scars?" she said incredulously. "Despite my notorious reputation, Mr Wycliff, I still possess an ounce of pride."

And yet she had sacrificed her dignity to reveal the hideous marks.

"And if the marquis makes another attempt to lure you into his bed, will your answer be the same?" He'd once thought he might forgive his angel anything, but he could not forgive that.

"To use your own words, Mr Wycliff, I am done here. The marks on my body tell the story of a woman who refused to cower and pander to a man. Having borne such suffering, I shall not crumble to my knees beneath the weight of your veiled threats."

"You're saying you no longer want my help?"

Panic surfaced.

The uncharacteristic feeling proved shocking.

Confusion followed.

The widow moved to walk past him but stopped level with his shoulder. "You swore an oath while holding your mother's cross. An oath to help me, not to threaten me and attempt to exert control. Help me unconditionally, Mr Wycliff, or do not help me at all."

She had taken two steps towards the glass doors before he clasped her wrist and brought her to a halt. "I made a promise to a downtrodden actress, not a notorious widow." The pang in his chest returned. The same ache that had forced him to offer his saviour more than bread and firewood. The same need to make his mother proud.

How was it no other woman roused those feelings in him?

The widow swallowed deeply. "You will find the actress still lives beneath my disguise if you take the time to look."

"My father has a way of rousing the devil in me," he said by way of an apology. It was the best she would get, more than he ever gave. Indeed, he did not feel at all like himself, which explained why he stroked his thumb over the smooth skin on the inside of her wrist.

She inhaled sharply. "Perhaps working together is not such a good idea."

"I made a vow, so I'm afraid you're stuck with me."

She glanced at the place where his fingers rested on her wrist. "It seems so."

"At least until we prove Joshua and Jemima Steele are guilty of attempted murder and you free me from my oath." He did not want her to think this was a permanent partnership.

"And if they are innocent?"

"That's highly improbable." In their grief, the siblings looked to blame someone for their father's death. And the widow's obvious disdain for the man made her the prime candidate. "But there is only one way to find out."

Indeed, they should head to the library, wait for Miss Steele and put an end to the matter. It would not take much for the chit to crack. Based on what Damian had written in the note, the woman would be desperate for his attention.

CHAPTER SIX

The Marquis of Blackbeck's library carried the same air of grandeur as the rest of his mansion house. An autumn palette of leather-bound books lined the polished oak cases. Sumptuous dark blue curtains trimmed with gold tassels and brocade framed two large windows. Despite the plethora of gilt candelabras and the vibrant red pattern on the Aubusson rug, it was an inherently masculine space. Indeed, Mr Wycliff looked perfectly at home as he lounged in the leather chair, his feet propped on his father's imposing desk.

Scarlett had climbed the spiral staircase to the upper-level housing rows of rare books and antique tomes. From her elevated position in the shadows, she had a perfect view of the seating area in front of the fire, and of the complicated man who had taken a letter opener to prise the lock on the drawer containing a box of cigars.

Mr Wycliff proceeded to light one from the candle lamp he had lit a few minutes earlier. "Do not let Miss Steele know you're here," he instructed before drawing the fumes from the cigar deep into his lungs and blowing them out in his usual devil-may-care manner.

Scarlett gripped the balustrade. "I highly doubt she will come. Jemima is as stiff as a starched cravat. And every woman in Christendom knows you're a scandalous rogue."

"Oh, she'll come," he said, blowing a ring of smoke in her direction. "Besides, the invitation mentioned nothing about an illicit liaison."

"Why? Do the prim ones prefer it when you're less direct?" Damian Wycliff could read from the dinner menu, and it would sound seductive.

Would you care for a sweet cherry jus drizzled over succulent breasts?

He stubbed his cigar out on the red leather inlay covering the desk. "The note merely said that if she wanted to know what really happened to her father, she should come to the library alone on the stroke of the hour."

"So you would rather pander to her suspicions than trust your seductive skills when it comes to tempting an innocent?" Given enough time, Scarlett had no doubt Mr Wycliff could lure the maiden into bed.

He pushed out of the chair and headed for the drinks tray.

"You more than anyone should know not to listen to gossip." The crystal stopper chinked as he pulled it from the neck of the decanter. "Contrary to popular belief, I have grown rather selective about the women I bed."

"But not whose breasts you fondle." Having witnessed his liaison on the sofa in the billiard room, she would call him out for his hypocrisy.

He chuckled as he sloshed the amber liquid into a glass. "Do you want the truth, Widow?"

Scarlett sighed. She hated him calling her that. "As you're a man who professes to deal only in the truth, yes."

Glass in hand, he turned to face her, his gaze fixed on hers as he downed a mouthful of liquor. "The lady's husband is a dear friend of my father's. A few more witnesses to the act and I would have found her wholly unsatisfactory. Everyone would think the worst, of course, including the marquis."

Scarlett did not know whether to feel sad or disgusted. Could he not see that his disreputable actions hurt no one but himself? Was he able to see everyone's truth but was blind to his own?

"A pretender is not a master of the truth, Mr Wycliff."

He snorted. "Says the person who has personified her pain by masquerading as the Scarlet Widow."

The comment proved her point. Her pain lived as a separate entity. It was the only way to preserve her soul. She suspected Mr Wycliff had a similar agenda.

"Then it seems we have something else in common, sir. The difference is I have put a name to mine."

"I do not need to hide behind a fake name," he said, his tone bearing a hint of frost. "When I score the winning shot in the game, *I* prefer to take the glory."

Winning might soothe his wound.

It would not ease his pain.

"For all our similarities, I imagine your winning prize looks vastly different to mine." Hers involved a house amid rolling green hills, a sanctuary away from the *ton*. A place where she could strip away the weight of her burden and move freely again. A place where she did not have to live in constant fear for her life.

Silence ensued.

The rattle of the doorknob gave neither of them time to dwell on their hopes and dreams. Scarlett darted back into the shadows, while Mr Wycliff collapsed onto the sofa, his arms spread wide across the back, his knees bent, legs open in invitation.

Scarlett held her breath as she heard the creak of the door opening, the click of the lock as it closed.

"Miss Steele, what a pleasant surprise." Mr Wycliff cast a look of cultivated arrogance. "Would you care for a drink? I can recommend the brandy. Fire hits the throat in just the right spot."

"I have n-not come to drink liquor, sir. You s-said you knew what happened to my father." Despite her apparent nerves, the lady had no problem coming straight to the point. "Your note suggested foul play."

"Sit down." Mr Wycliff gestured to the chair opposite. "I won't bite. Not unless you drop to your knees and beg."

"I—I prefer to stand." She stepped into Scarlett's view.

While Lord Steele had taken pleasure in beating his wife, he treated his daughter as if she were heaven sent. It was easier to spot controlling behaviour when it came with a vicious tongue and a sharp hand. Not so easy when packaged as love and tied with a pretty bow.

"My brother is waiting in the hall should you have cause to live up to your reckless reputation."

Mr Wycliff was no fool. Joshua stood outside because fear kept him from entering.

Mr Wycliff smirked. "What gentleman worth his weight sends his sister into a viper pit whilst lingering safely in the corridor? That said, your brother is welcome to pull up a chair and watch me flex my fangs."

"I—I know you like to shock." The lady clasped her hands in front of her body. The gesture made her appear childlike. "Mischief is your middle name."

"Debaucher is my first, but I draw the line at ruining innocent maidens." He stared at the waif-like creature trembling before him. The lady did not know that beneath the bravado was a man capable of kindness, great tenderness. "There is nothing more disappointing than a limp hand and a weak stroke."

Jemima Steele slapped her hand to her mouth.

"Now," Mr Wycliff continued, "tell me what you know about the threats made to Lady Steele's person."

Jemima shook her head. "Lady Steele? But I thought you had information about my father." She glanced around the room. "Is this another of your ploys to unnerve me?"

A devious grin formed on Mr Wycliff's lips. "My plan to

unnerve you involves telling everyone willing to listen that you were surprisingly free with your affections. You'll be amazed what people believe when one tells a story with conviction."

Jemima's frantic gaze shot to the door.

"Your brother cannot help you," the wicked rogue continued. "Best keep him on a tight leash. You wouldn't want to give me a reason to meet him on the common at dawn."

Wringing her hands, Jemima cried, "Just tell me what you want and let me go."

Mr Wycliff jumped to his feet, and Jemima gasped. He prowled towards her, and she shuffled backwards. "I want to know what gripe you have with your stepmother."

Jemima looked up at the imposing figure towering over her. "Don't call her that. She is no mother to me. She's nothing more than an embarrassment."

Mr Wycliff slid his arm around Jemima's slender waist. The girl pushed at his chest in an attempt to escape. "So embarrassing you want rid of her?"

"Remove yourself, sir." Panic infused Jemima's tone. "Before someone comes in and finds us in a clinch."

"Admit it," he persisted, his mouth dangerously close to Jemima's quivering lips. "Admit you paid someone to spook her horse. Admit to the host of other accidents set to rid you from your association with the Scarlet Widow."

"No!"

"The Widow's shame follows you through the ballrooms. You live in her shadow. You cry at night when—"

"Please, say no more." Jemima stopped struggling against Mr Wycliff's hard body. As she surrendered to him, her hands settled on his chest.

"Men don't want you, do they? They want the Widow." His seductive voice was as smooth as the finest claret. "And yet you long to feel desired, loved."

"Yes," Jemima said, relaxing into his embrace.

"You must hate her." His mouth moved to Jemima's ear, his lips grazing against her lobe.

A shiver ran through Scarlett's body. She knew the power of Mr Wycliff's hot breath, had lain awake huddled next to him to keep out the cold, had felt each soft rhythmical sigh breeze over her neck. For the first time in three years, she longed to trade places with her insipid stepdaughter.

"I do," Jemima breathed. "I despise her."

"And you would do anything to get rid of her, to be free."

"Anything."

"Tell me your secrets. Who did you hire to stage the accidents?"

"Accidents?" Jemima's dreamy voice was almost inaudible.

Scarlett had underestimated the rogue. A few more whispered words and the waif would be hiking up her skirts and perching her bare buttocks on the edge of the desk. Indeed, she suspected the scoundrel might even possess the wherewithal to crack the Scarlet Widow's walnut shell.

A sudden commotion in the hall stole everyone's attention.

Mr Wycliff's dark gaze drifted to the door. The woman in his arms came quickly to her senses and tried to push out of his embrace.

"What's the hurry?" he drawled, clearly unconcerned by the prospect of being caught in a compromising embrace. "We were getting on so well."

Jemima shook her head vigorously, but with her hair scraped back in a severe knot, barely a wisp was out of place. "You were trying to trick me."

The corners of his mouth curled into a wicked grin. "Trick you?"

"Like Satan, you cast your sinful spells." She broke free and brushed her skirts.

"Ladies do say my fingers work the devil's magic."

"And I suspect your mouth is equally devious."

Mr Wycliff's tongue grazed his bottom lip. "What a shame you'll never know."

Two people conversed loudly in the corridor—Joshua Steele and Lady Rathbone. Hell's bells! The matron was forever turning up in the most unlikely places and was not one to linger outside when there was gossiping to be had. But then another voice joined the *tête-à-tête*—the sophisticated tone of the Marquis of Blackbeck.

"Damnation!" Mr Wycliff glanced up to the balcony, to where Scarlett stood in the shadows with her back pressed to the row of cases. One jerk of the head was her summons to descend the spiral staircase and join the party.

"Quick," Jemima said, suddenly panicked. "Lock the door before they all barge in here."

"Have no fear." Mr Wycliff sounded amused. "You're not alone with me. Your stepmother is in the wings waiting to save your fall from grace."

Jemima's head shot around upon hearing the patter of footsteps on the stairs. A scowl formed. The girl's top lip curled into something of a snarl.

"You!" Jemima snapped. "I should have known you were behind this debacle. One word to your lapdog and he scampers to do your bidding."

"Lapdog?" Mr Wycliff put his hand to his heart as if mortally wounded. "I take great umbrage. No one tells me who to lick or bite."

"Mr Wycliff is not the sort of gentleman one offends," Scarlett said. "One wicked word from him and you will find yourself barred from every ballroom in London. Now, if you are behind these ludicrous attempts to cause me harm, I suggest you stop."

There was nothing ludicrous about murder. But Scarlett would be damned before letting Jemima know she was terrified out of her wits. And while Jemima's bitterness was carved into every frown lining her brow, Scarlett doubted the girl had the courage to hire an assassin.

The door to the library flew open, and the marquis sauntered into the room, his stoic gaze fixed upon his son. Lady Rathbone and Joshua Steele traipsed behind.

"Admiring my books?" The marquis moved to the drinks tray and poured himself a glass of port. The large diamond and onyx ring on his finger clinked against the crystal. "Perhaps you're interested in the first edition of Gilles Ménage's *Poemata*. Or I have a rare copy of Plautus' *Comoediae Viginti* that is two hundred years old."

"Latin is not my forte," Mr Wycliff replied in a less arrogant tone now they were in company. "Your brandy and cheroots are more to my taste."

The marquis' languid gaze slid to the open mahogany box on the desk, to the ash and discarded remains of Mr Wycliff's smoke. With his usual impassive expression, he turned to Jemima. "And what brought you here, Miss Steele?"

"Erm … I …" The girl's cheeks coloured beneath his stare. "I—"

"Miss Steele came to speak to me regarding a personal matter," Scarlett interjected.

The marquis raised a dubious brow. "No doubt she is tired of hiding in your shadow and begs you grant her a spot in the sunlight."

"It would not be a personal matter if I divulged our secrets."

The marquis turned his attention to Lady Rathbone. "And might I inquire as to your reason for concerning yourself with what my son does behind closed doors?"

"Me?" Lady Rathbone's droopy eyes bulged. She looked more shocked than offended. "I happened to be passing and noticed Lord Steele loitering in the corridor."

"She asked if I had seen Lady Steele," Joshua said, though he failed to make eye contact with anyone other than his sister.

"Well, yes," Lady Rathbone mumbled. Like his son, the marquis possessed the ability to unnerve those in the room without uttering a cross word. "My grandson mentioned she was here, and I thought she might like to accompany me at the card table."

Lady Rathbone's kindness touched Scarlett's heart, even if at times it proved a tad excessive. "And I would have graciously accepted."

The matron managed a smile while struggling beneath the weight of the marquis' scrutiny. "I am sure we're not too late."

Mr Wycliff stepped forward. During his brief silence, Scarlett had been aware of the power radiating from his arresting countenance. The air sparked with a vibrant and equally volatile electricity. From the moment his father entered the room, Mr Wycliff's striking dark eyes had watched her intently.

"Perhaps Lady Steele has forgotten we have another engagement this evening." Damian Wycliff's commanding voice sliced through the air, ready to slap anyone who offered the smallest protest.

He had made no mention of attending another soiree. And they had learnt nothing new this evening. Jemima made no secret of her hatred. She blamed Scarlett for every scar, every hideous mark inflicted by the cruel lord. Her wicked stepmother roused the devil in all men. Why else would a loving father behave like such a beast?

"Forgive me," Scarlett said, for she had a sudden urge to support Mr Wycliff in a room full of those who looked upon him with fear. Fear tinged with disdain. "It slipped my mind."

He had been so confident of gaining Jemima's confession. So quick to discharge his vow. But it would take more than a feigned seduction to absolve him of his debt. There would be another attempt on her life. Soon.

The thought roused a deep foreboding in her chest. Jemima would not rest until the Scarlet Widow was no more. Joshua had his own secrets. She had spurned numerous advances from powerful men. Forceful men. Men with a right of entitlement.

Lord Steele had once frightened her into marriage.

Did another man hope to do the same?

Everyone was a threat.

Panic surfaced as she scanned the faces in the room. Dishonest faces. Untrustworthy faces. Faces that roused doubt and suspicion.

Loneliness swept up on her like an icy breeze from the north. The coldness made her shiver. Frost coated the barren emptiness within. She was back at the window in the seminary, her inner turmoil a reflection of the wintery scene outside.

Lady Rathbone's comment about staying for another hour and Jemima's complaining echoed in the distance. Both failed to pull Scarlett back into the room.

But then Damian Wycliff appeared in her field of vision. His firm hand at her elbow forced her to blink. "We should leave," he whispered. The heat from his palm flooded her body, thawing the ice in her blood. "Before I punch my father and give Miss Steele the most cutting set-down of her life."

Scarlett met his gaze. Damian Wycliff had a fake face, too. But his mask looked like hers—sharp lines and bold colours. The eyes appeared hard and shallow, for neither wanted anyone to see the soft depths beyond.

"So, you're not staying to hear Señora Garcia's aria?" the marquis taunted. "Spanish opera singers rarely venture this far north."

Mr Wycliff gritted his teeth. "Perhaps that's because we English lack the heart for their music. Or perhaps it's because their hosts suffer from boredom and are quick to move to the next mode of entertainment."

The marquis' mocking laugh rent the air. "An amusing thought though wholly inaccurate."

Scarlett noted the hard line of Damian Wycliff's jaw. What

was he thinking? Was his heart racing? Was he sitting at the window—just like her—knowing no one would come, feeling just as lost and lonely inside?

"We will leave you to ponder the thought, my lord." Scarlett touched Mr Wycliff lightly on the shoulder in a gesture of solidarity. "We have somewhere more important to be."

The marquis' impenetrable gaze bore into her. Perhaps he might join the ranks of those wanting her dead, hire thugs from the rookeries who would do anything to earn a few shillings.

Bestowing those in the room with his usual arrogant grin, Mr Wycliff offered Scarlett his arm. She slipped her hand into the crook, and they made a move towards the door. Scarlett took a moment to stop and invite Lady Rathbone to tea.

Perhaps fearing what her wicked stepmother might do, Jemima had moved to stand next to Joshua. The siblings were opposites in every regard. Fury filled Jemima's eyes, while fear marred Joshua's vapid countenance.

"Joshua Steele is a damn coward," Mr Wycliff said as he retrieved Scarlett's silk wrapper from his father's purpose-built cloakroom. "I doubt he has the courage to mention the word *murder* let alone hire someone to do the job."

"Looks can be deceptive." She permitted Mr Wycliff to drape the garment around her shoulders. She tried not to sigh when his fingers brushed against the high collar of her gown. "His fear stems from a personal matter and has nothing to do with a weakness of character."

Mr Wycliff seemed puzzled. "And yet he looked at you as if you might flex your jaw, inflate your lungs and breathe hell's fire."

"He fears I will reveal his secret."

"His secret?"

Realising that Damian Wycliff was the only person in the world she might remotely trust, the time for honesty was nigh.

"That I might inform his sister of his attempt to step into his father's role."

Recognition dawned. Mr Wycliff took a step forward, an action that left the tips of their toes touching. He grasped her elbow again, and in a rather irate tone said, "Are you trying to tell me your stepson attempted to bed you?"

"He was in his cups," she whispered, wishing she could not recall the amateur fumbling with any clarity. "After a night spent drinking with friends, he became obsessed with bedding the Scarlet Widow."

"A widow who happens to be his stepmother. Where the hell are the man's morals?"

"Morals? Says the man who made a foolish girl believe he had an interest in her." One wiggle of his tail feathers and poor Jemima had slipped off her haughty perch with ease.

"You hired me to save you, not play the pious priest waiting for a confession."

"I did not hire you," she snapped as he led her down the steps of the grand house. "The only reason you're here at all is because I took pity on you in the alley."

"I don't need your pity, Widow." When they reached the street, he threw a barefoot boy a shilling and pointed to the carriage parked on the opposite side of Hanover Square.

Scarlett sighed. "Still, you took it, and the debt makes you mine—at least for the time being." A small part of him had been hers since he handed her the gold cross.

The corners of his mouth formed a sensual smirk that sent her stomach flipping. "You want me, Widow, admit it. Every minute spent in my enthralling company makes you want me all the more."

Oh, Damian Wycliff spouted drivel. She wanted the invalid with a swollen eye and a bandaged leg—the man who knew how to express his gratitude—not the ingrate wearing the devil mask.

The boy came charging back and pointed to the carriage

making its way towards them. Mr Wycliff removed a few more shiny coins from his pocket, thrust them into the boy's dirty hand and ruffled the urchin's unkempt hair.

Perhaps the scoundrel only had a heart for the downtrodden.

As the carriage rumbled to a stop, Mr Wycliff signalled to his groom that he would open the door.

Scarlett drew her red wrapper firmly around her shoulders, for protection as opposed to keeping out the cold. "I presume you lied, that there is no prior engagement and you're taking me home."

"Indeed. While I would have liked to bring the matter to a hasty conclusion, it seems you'll have the pleasure of my company for a few days."

"Tonight has been an utter waste of time and effort." She grasped his fingers as he assisted her into the carriage. Whenever they touched, she was transported back to the moment he caressed her cheek and made a vow, to the moment she knew what it meant to have a dream.

"Not a total waste," he said as he followed her inside and settled into the seat opposite. "Your information about Joshua Steele is most helpful."

"Joshua? Why, because you can use it to blackmail him?"

"No, though the idea has merit. Because it means he has a good reason for wanting you dead."

CHAPTER SEVEN

"J oshua has other reasons for wanting to get rid of me," the widow declared.

She held her hands demurely in her lap as she stared out of the window at the passing street lamps. Her voice carried a nervous edge, one she never showed in company, one that suggested she had been lapse when divulging important details.

"And if he has confided in his sister," she continued, "Jemima will do everything possible to protect him. After all, she has little chance of marrying, and will be clutching his coat-tails well into spinsterhood."

"What other reasons?" Had Damian known of them earlier, had he known Joshua Steele tried to seduce his damn stepmother, he would have cornered the degenerate in the library, instead of his twiggy sister.

The widow dragged her gaze from the window. "I trust I have your full confidence in all matters?"

"If you're asking me to swear allegiance, there is no need." No one had ever asked for his loyalty. It was a burden he wasn't sure he wanted. "I take no pleasure in gossip. I take no pleasure in betrayal."

"And everyone knows you're a man who lives for pleasure." Her quick reply rang of condescension.

"In my experience life has little else to offer," he said, both relieved and disappointed she did not know that he lived only to feed the hatred festering within.

Silence descended as she studied him in the dimly lit confines of the carriage—a penetrating stare that attempted to burrow beneath the rugged landscape.

Her intense blue gaze fixed him to the seat. She leant forward, her outstretched hand finding his to give a reassuring squeeze. Heat crept up his neck as his pulse quickened. Heat flowed through his fingers and journeyed up his arm to bathe his chest in a comforting glow. There was only one way to rid himself of the sensation—drag her into his lap, ravage her mouth and slake his lust. But despite her widow status, he could never treat her like a common harlot.

"Then tonight, I shall clasp my hands together, Mr Wycliff, and pray life delivers something infinitely more rewarding."

Pray?

The only person to draw rosary beads through her fingers and plead for his happiness had long since departed this world.

A hard lump formed in his throat.

The pressure spread to his tongue until it ached.

"Then in return I shall give you my fealty, Widow," he said, desperate to banish these foreign feelings, desperate to return to the place where arrogance reigned supreme.

When the widow released his hand and relaxed back in the seat, he almost sighed with relief. But then she offered him a smile, a genuine angelic expression that spoke of sincerity, and he was nearly lost again.

"While parading as the Scarlet Widow, I discovered that shrewdness is one's ally," she said, moving the conversation away from talk of redemptive prayers. "When one sits at a table with card sharps, one must know how to protect their hand."

"It helps if you understand the game."

"And yet young men often fall foul of the rules. Joshua Steele's need to find his own means of support led to substantial debts at a gaming hell known as The Silver Serpent."

"A notorious place." Only a fool with a death wish failed to settle his account with the house. The serpent was a symbol of Satan, so it was unsurprising to find that many men sold their souls there.

"It has a certain reputation for attracting the dissolute," she replied.

"I know it well."

"Then you know the proprietor."

Every new patron seeking entrance to the club had to arm wrestle the Irishman with bushy red brows. "Dermot Flannery has a fondness for throwing non-payers into the Thames. Often with a cannonball shackled to one ankle."

"That is a fictional tale used to scare the children." A smug grin formed on the lady's lips. "Even so, he is not the proprietor."

Damian snorted. "Trust me, I have been a patron of that club for years and have met Flannery on many occasions."

"Of course you have. Dermot Flannery is paid handsomely to play his part."

Intrigued, Damian straightened. "Then who the hell owns the club?"

"I do."

It took a few seconds for the words to penetrate.

"I beg your pardon?" Perhaps he had misheard.

"I own The Silver Serpent."

"If this is a ploy to impress me—"

"Why on earth would I want to impress you? The details of ownership are irrelevant. But to satisfy your insatiable curiosity, know that my father purchased the club in my aunt's name. The conditions of her will stated that Mr Flannery would act in my stead until I came into my inheritance on my twenty-first birthday."

Damian dragged his hand down his face as he tried to absorb the shocking information. One pressing question burst forth. "Then why marry Steele when you had only to wait to claim your inheritance?"

"Because I knew nothing about the club until Mr Flannery found me a year ago."

"How is that possible? Surely your father informed you of your legacy. Surely he left financial matters in the hands of a solicitor."

The widow sighed. "My father trusted no one other than Mr Flannery. He went to great lengths to keep the information from me. Upon my father's death, Mr Flannery was instructed to retrieve me from the seminary, but that is where things get far more complex."

By all accounts, his life wasn't the only one based on secrets and lies.

"And it did not occur to you to tell me all this during our meeting at the inn?"

"What? While locked in a bedchamber with you half-dressed? Forgive me if I struggled to concentrate on the matter at hand. Besides, you seemed so confident in your desire to act impulsively, and I needed to know I could trust you."

For the second time since reacquainting with the widow, the pang of shame returned. She was right. Arrogance was his downfall. He had made too many assumptions, presumed there must be a certain element of exaggeration when it came to the mounting death threats.

"And you trust me now?"

"More than I did when we met at The Cock and Magpie."

He wasn't sure what had changed since their meeting at the inn. Indeed, he hadn't made things easy. Anger and frustration—that she hid her true nature behind this ridiculous disguise—still gnawed away inside. Needles of guilt pricked his conscience, too. Perhaps he should have offered the poor actress more than food and firewood. Made a noble gesture to help her, one that did not involve making her his mistress.

"And so Joshua Steele knows you own the debts he incurred at The Silver Serpent?"

"Yes, but he thinks I purchased his vowels from Mr Flannery. Society believes the Widow can do anything she sets her mind to."

"Why did Joshua not repay the debts upon gaining his inheritance?" Surely when Lord Steele died, he left his son a reasonable sum.

"Because he inherited his father's sizeable debts. And there is little he can do with the entailed property."

"That gives him a strong motive for wanting you dead."

It occurred to him that Dermot Flannery had a motive for murder, too, and things suddenly became far more complicated than a wallflower's need to steal attention away from her stepmother. And to think he had practically nuzzled the chit's scrawny neck to gain a confession.

"Not only that," she began, and Damian wondered if there would be an end to these constant revelations. "My husband was a patron. In exchange for persuading Mr Flannery to wipe his debts, he gave me the house in Bedford Street. A house unentailed, but one previously promised to Joshua."

Despite this sudden outpouring of facts, something told him the widow still withheld information. "And who inherits should you meet your demise?" The answer might lead them to the culprit.

"Joshua inherits the house in Bedford Street as per my agreement with his father. And for his loyal service, Mr Flannery inherits the club."

So both men would gain from the widow's death. If Damian were betting on the guilty, he'd place his odds on Flannery. He had means, motive, the wherewithal to kill a person with his bare hands.

"I know what you're thinking," she said, staring him in the eye. He didn't doubt it. She had a knack for reading his mind. "Mr Flannery is not responsible for the crimes committed against me. My father trusted him, as do I."

Truly? So why did her actions imply otherwise?

"Then why seek me out when Flannery is the perfect person to act as your protector?" There wasn't a man in the *ton* who would cross the Irishman, nor a man in the rookeries based on what Damian had heard. Or were they just fairy stories, too?

"Because Mr Flannery cannot move about in society. Because I do not want anyone to know I am associated with the club." She paused, a pink blush staining her cheeks. "Because if I told you the real reason I sought you out, where would the fun be in that?"

Curiosity burned in his chest.

"If it is fun you want, Widow, you've hired the right man."

A chuckle escaped her luscious lips. "I did not hire you, Mr Wycliff, but I own your debt until it is repaid."

He pasted an arrogant smile, but it occurred to him that the owner of The Silver Serpent must hold many men's vowels. That this task to find the rogue responsible for the attacks might prove impossible.

The carriage rattled to a halt, dragging him from his reverie.

Damian peered out into the night and noted they had arrived in Bedford Street.

"Would you like me to escort you inside?" he said, not because it was part of his role as enquiry agent and protector. Not because he had a reputation for being a man who could seduce most women into bed. But because he cared about her welfare more than he dared to admit. "Perhaps we could both use a drink to lighten the mood."

A nervous smile played on her lips, similar to the one he'd witnessed on the night in the lodging-house when she had asked to share a bed. "I do not wish to keep you from an evening filled with frivolity."

"At least permit me to check the house for intruders."

She shook her head. "There is no need. The locksmith changed the locks, and I dismissed the two staff hired from Mr Truman's registry."

An uncomfortable sense of trepidation almost made him insist, but he was not a man who pleaded or begged. "Then shall we continue our conversation tomorrow? I should like to hear of the complicated events that prevented Flannery from collecting you from the seminary."

Her breathing suddenly came a little quicker, and she drew in a deep breath. "Can we not focus our efforts on persuading Joshua to confess? Perhaps I should hire a runner to track his movements. Equally, Jemima despises me to the depths of her soul. Perhaps she knows more about the situation than we think."

Damian narrowed his gaze. What was she hiding?

"Yes, we will do all you said, but the Steele siblings are not our only suspects."

"Mr Flannery is not a suspect."

"He is a suspect with as much to gain as Joshua Steele," Damian argued.

"No."

"No?"

"My father treated him like a brother."

"Jealousy and rivalry see brothers striking their kin with the speed of a rearing cobra." The flaw in her logic became suddenly apparent. "You knew nothing of their association until Mr Flannery found you a year ago. How do you know they were close?"

Her bottom lip quivered, and the lines between her brows grew prominent. It took her a few seconds to replace her widow's mask. "I have become quite adept at reading men, Mr Wycliff. I would know if Mr Flannery were insincere."

"Some men are good at hiding their true feelings."

"Like you?" she countered, for this lady was exceptional in defending an attack. "You are not as inscrutable as you would like to believe."

He found the observation both amusing and terrifying.

A gnawing unease settled in his chest, but that did not prevent him from sporting a grin and saying, "It's unwise to taunt the devil."

"Even when the devil is a monster of your own creation?"

"Even then."

Their gazes remained locked. No doubt his eyes were as dark as the unburnt coals in hell. Her heavenly blue eyes held an unexplainable power capable of cutting through his facade. Both refused to back down from this standoff. She had found a way to crawl under his skin, those cunning hands caressing away every objection, smoothing out the hard edges, jagged planes.

The need to shake free from her intense stare saw him shoot across the carriage to sit at her side, so close their thighs touched.

"If I am so easy to read, what am I thinking now, Widow?" he snapped, every word filled with contempt.

A smile crept into her eyes, and he'd be damned if he knew what she was thinking. "You look like you want to murder me, Mr Wycliff. Murder me and make love to me at the same time."

Damnation!

He might change her name to the Scarlet Witch!

"Fighting and fornicating are the only things I know." The need to drag her onto his lap and do the latter thrummed in his veins.

"That's the devil talking. Attempting either will merely prove my point."

Anger flared.

Without further contemplation, he rapped hard on the roof. The carriage rocked on its axis as the groom scampered down from the box seat, opened the door and lowered the steps.

"I'll wait here until you're safely inside," he said, the words tinged with the arctic frost of a man who wanted not to care. "Vauxhall or a gambling hell?"

As soon as the lady's feet touched the pavement, she whirled around and said, "I beg your pardon?"

"Where would you like to go tomorrow evening? Dancing at Vauxhall to spy on Joshua Steele, or would you rather play hazard at The Silver Serpent so I might observe Mr Flannery?"

"Dancing?" She raised her chin. "You strike me as a man who rarely takes to the floor. I imagine your hardened heart is immune to the power of a passion-filled melody."

The widow was right on the first count, wrong on the second.

Music reminded him of what he had lost.

Powerful melodies always tugged at his heartstrings.

"I am sure you will have no shortage of partners," he replied, and yet he had a sudden urge to call out any man who dared offer.

She smiled. "Vauxhall it is, then. Will you call for me at eight?"

"We'll take supper, so I shall call at seven."

"Very well. Good night, Mr Wycliff. I imagine it is relatively early for you. I'm sure Mrs Crandell will have some form of exotic entertainment planned."

"Good night …" For a reason unbeknown, he stopped himself from adding the word *widow*. "Mrs Crandell is hosting a harem party tonight. There are to be bare-chested footmen in turbans and scantily clad dancers who shake their generous hips while jingling bells."

Her amused expression faded. "Well, don't let me keep you. Like the rest of the demi-monde, I am sure you're eager to indulge your wild fantasies."

"Indeed," he agreed, though his wildest and somewhat reluctant fantasy involved stripping the widow bare and using his tongue to trace every scar.

Damian watched her enter the house, spent a few minutes staring at the closed front door before instructing Cutler to take him home. After the many revelations this evening the only things he sought with any certainty amounted to a stiff drink and his own bed.

He untied his cravat and propped his feet on the seat opposite. The widow's intoxicating scent swamped the air, an expensive perfume with the sensual notes of amber and vanilla. The aroma teased his senses, fed his lust. But it was the smell of cheap soap on clean skin he remembered. Craved. A potent bouquet that with every inhalation had the power to nourish his soul.

Removing his silver flask from his inside coat pocket, he swallowed the last mouthful of brandy while replaying the night's events.

Not being as proficient as the widow at reading minds, he wondered what prompted her decision to choose Vauxhall. Might it be the opportunity to flaunt her infamy, to rouse a pang of jealousy in his chest? That thought dragged a chuckle from his lips. And yet he wished that was the reason. The only other motive drew him back to The Silver Serpent and his widow's many secrets. Indeed, he suspected in choosing to visit Vauxhall, she meant to keep him away from the gaming hell. To keep him away from the notorious Dermot Flannery.

CHAPTER EIGHT

The news of Mr Wycliff's arrival sent Scarlett's stomach flipping. An odd flurry of emotions made her dizzy. It was not at all like the sinking, sickening sensation one experienced their first time on stage. It felt different from those rare times she had peered out of the seminary window to see her father climb the front steps. Then, her heart had swelled, swelled to prodigious proportions. Now, the thought of spending an evening with Damian Wycliff caused delicious tingles to race from her fingers to her toes.

But it wasn't the young woman who tended to his wounds and bathed his brow who arrived to greet him. Good Lord, no! She was liable to smile at him in the tender way that left her heart open. Exposed.

No!

Dressed in a gown of midnight-blue with a neckline that skimmed the collarbone to hide her scar—and wearing her confidence like an extravagant accessory—the Scarlet Widow descended the stairs.

He was waiting.

Clothed in black and with the same inscrutable expression others found impossible to read, he watched her descend as Lucifer might study a newcomer at the gates of hell.

The long-case clock in the hall struck seven as her foot touched the bottom step.

As the last chime faded, Scarlett offered the gentleman her hand. "Mr Wycliff, regardless of the terrible things people say about you, you have impeccable timekeeping."

Wearing a grin sourced from an exotic land—striking, unique and with more than a hint of mystery—he raised her hand to his mouth and pressed his lips to her glove. Dark, devilish eyes roamed over the ruby-encrusted comb in her hair, lingered on the exposed skin at the base of her neck.

"When a man lives life to excess, he doesn't waste a minute." Mr Wycliff released her hand and moistened his lips. "Might I say it's somewhat surprising to see you in a colour other than black or red."

"When a lady lives to cause scandal, she does her best to appear unpredictable."

Their gazes locked. The air thrummed with an intense energy. The sudden rush of desire nearly knocked her off her feet. Heat swirled in her stomach. She cleared her throat, lest he notice the quickening of her breath.

The clip of the butler's shoes on the tiled floor broke the spell. Hanson carried her red silk pelisse, but it was Mr Wycliff who took the garment, held it up for her to slip her arms inside and who smoothed the material over her shoulders with his large masculine hands.

"I'm afraid we have company," he said, dismissing Hanson with a nod. "Cavanagh and Trent will join us this evening. While they will remain nearby, they know to grant us an element of *privacy.*"

The last word rolled so seductively off his tongue nerves

banished her initial disappointment. How long could she maintain the facade? How long could she maintain a sense of indifference?

Long enough to protect her heart, she hoped.

"Are you speaking about the gentlemen who enjoy watching you fondle your conquests?" Veiled contempt worked wonders when attempting to hide one's feelings. "If you have another engagement at Vauxhall you only need say. Lady Rathbone is sure to attend and will invite me to dine in her booth."

Mr Wycliff arched a brow. "You're dining with me, no one else." The possessiveness in his tone should have roused her old fears, should have made her bolster her defences, and yet it only fed her excitement. "Tonight, you have my undivided attention. I'm the only gentleman permitted to stroll with you along Lovers Walk."

"Of course," she began, pressing her fingers more firmly into her gloves. "When a lady takes you as her lover, Mr Wycliff, she has no need to spend time in another man's company."

"Precisely."

A sudden image of his hard, sweat-soaked body flashed into her mind. The tender ache between her thighs stole her concentration. It took every effort not to stare at him and sigh.

"I, too, need to alter our plans," she said, grateful she did not appear as one of those women forced to agree with everything he said or did.

"You are coming to Vauxhall?" The fine lines around his eyes crinkled.

"Yes, but to appease Alcock I have said she might ride atop the box with your coachman."

Mr Wycliff drew his head back. "Cutler will not permit her interference."

"Then you may inform him that he has no choice."

He gave a mocking snort. "You may inform your coachwoman that she is remaining at home."

They stood, battle shields touching.

Scarlett considered her options. Some ladies might use their womanly wiles to persuade him, but she knew that would prove fruitless. Her only option was to retreat and attack from a different position.

"You must understand, Mr Wycliff, Alcock fears for my life. The first three attacks took place outdoors. Vauxhall hosts a wealth of opportunity when one is intent on murder."

"I shall be your protector this evening." Though he appeared resolute, the sharp angles of his face relaxed. "There is little your servant can do from the coach park."

"Please," she said softly enough so he would know she spoke from the heart, "she is the only person in the world who cares for my safety."

"Not the only person," he said but then quickly added, "I share the burden until the debt is repaid."

The last comment was like salt to a wound. Her whole life, she had been someone's burden. "Please. You must know I would not ask were it not important."

The sound of raised voices outside captured Mr Wycliff's attention. "I imagine your coachwoman is attempting to take her seat," he said with some frustration.

Scarlett touched his arm then. "Alcock does not deal well with aggressive men. You don't know how she has suffered."

Mr Wycliff's gaze slipped to where her hand rested. His sigh of surrender sent a rush of jubilation to her chest, but she dared not show it. "Then we should rescue Cutler before she has time to retaliate."

Having dismissed Hanson, Mr Wycliff opened the door, and Scarlett accompanied him outside to find Alcock standing with her hands braced on her hips, and Mr Wycliff's vicious-looking coachman growling back.

"Alcock is riding with you, Cutler," Mr Wycliff commanded.

"You are responsible for her, and she will remain with you in the coach park at Vauxhall. Is that understood?"

"Sir, there ain't room—"

"I don't pay you to argue, Cutler. I pay you to drive."

"As you say, sir," the fellow conceded. He glared at Alcock, and through gritted teeth said, "Climb up, sit tight and don't say a word."

Scarlett knew from Alcock's sudden intake of breath that she was about to say something untoward. "Mr Wycliff has been good enough to permit you to ride atop his carriage," Scarlett informed her servant. "Gratitude is the only emotion one should express."

"Yes, milady." With reluctance, Alcock inclined her head to Mr Wycliff. "Thankin' ye, sir." And then she climbed up to the box and settled next to Cutler.

Mr Wycliff turned to Scarlett and opened the carriage door. "Now, can we proceed to Vauxhall?"

"Of course." She offered him a warm smile. "And might I say you can be quite the considerate gentleman when it pleases."

Scarlett glanced inside the carriage to find Mr Cavanagh and Mr Trent sitting together on the left-hand seat. From her enquiries she knew both were also illegitimate sons of the aristocracy's elite. The three men had formed lasting friendships at school, by all accounts. When Damian Wycliff was not gallivanting abroad, the rogues attended many of the demi-monde's gatherings.

"Yes," Mr Wycliff began, noting her slight hesitance, "I'm afraid you have the misfortune of sitting next to me."

"No doubt I shall endure the hardship," she said as he cupped her elbow and assisted her ascent. She settled into the seat opposite Mr Trent, a brooding fellow with piercing green eyes, a hard, sculpted jaw and a deep cleft in his chin.

"And a hardship it will be," Wycliff replied. "I am possessed of rather wide thighs." He slammed the door shut and dropped into the seat next to her. The sudden movement sent the carriage rocking on its axis. "Having taken a blade to my breeches, I'm sure you remember."

Remember?

How could she forget?

"I have a vague recollection." She had washed the blood off those muscular legs, gripped his firm, powerful thigh while sewing the wound.

Mr Cavanagh smiled, his blue eyes twinkling with mischief. "Tell all, my lady. I imagine Wycliff was a rather surly patient."

"On the contrary," Scarlett said, relishing an opportunity to remind Mr Wycliff that he had the capacity to be kind and charming. "I found him respectful, understanding and extremely considerate under the circumstances."

Mr Cavanagh frowned. He glanced at Mr Trent, who arched a brow and then snorted with amusement.

"I've heard Wycliff called many things," Mr Trent said, "considerate isn't one of them. He must have made a lasting impression. Is that why you enlisted his help?"

From Mr Trent's tone, his question had nothing to do with prying and everything to do with protecting his friend.

Interesting.

Wycliff shuffled uncomfortably in the seat beside her. During their meeting at the tavern, he had made a point of informing her that he kept no secrets from his friends. And yet she sensed they knew nothing about the gold cross given to reinforce his promise.

Mr Wycliff proved her theory by saying, "Tell them nothing, Widow, lest my friends use your words to taunt me."

"Did he act the perfect gentleman?" Mr Cavanagh teased as if there was something distasteful when a man behaved with sensitivity and good manners. "I seem to remember him begging for a moment's privacy. Did he bow over your hand whilst delivering flowery felicitations?"

"Were we not in the presence of a lady, Cavanagh, I would curse you to the devil," Wycliff growled. "Perhaps it did not occur to you that a man would be nothing but respectful to the angel who saved his life."

Lord above!

Mr Wycliff had referred to her as a lady and an angel in two consecutive sentences.

"Hence the reason you're behaving rather oddly," Mr Cavanagh countered, determined to torment his friend. "You asked Mrs Crandell to hire exotic dancers and then failed to show." With amusement filling his eyes, Mr Cavanagh turned to her and asked, "Do you happen to know where Wycliff was last night?"

"Don't answer that," Wycliff snapped. "They both know we went to the Marquis of Blackbeck's ball."

"And afterwards?" Mr Cavanagh pressed.

Mr Wycliff removed his top hat and brushed his hand through his mop of coal-black hair. "That is none of your damn business."

Scarlett pasted a perfect smile, but her stomach roiled. Where had Mr Wycliff gone after he'd left her? Certainly not the extravagant party hosted by a member of the demi-monde. Then again, she had to ask herself why she cared.

An uncomfortable silence descended.

Scarlett thought to say something to defuse the tension but could think of nothing other than the heat from Mr Wycliff's thigh as it pressed against hers. She glanced at Mr Trent, who clearly found nothing amusing in the men's banter. Indeed, with the same brooding look she had witnessed earlier, he stared out of the window in a dream-like state as they headed towards Vauxhall.

"What is it, Trent?" There was a serious edge to Mr Wycliff's tone that hinted at a problem or dispute. "You may speak freely in front of Lady Steele."

Scarlett was almost flattered. But Mr Wycliff knew enough about her secret affairs to silence her for good. Indeed, hearing Mr Trent's revelation would help to even the odds.

Mr Trent glanced at her from beneath hooded lids. Those

sharp green eyes, when cold and glassy, would frighten away the most vicious predators.

"We'll be at Vauxhall soon," he said, avoiding the subject of his odd mood. "You've yet to tell us why you insisted we come."

The gentleman's ploy to move the conversation away from his own dilemma worked. Mr Wycliff relaxed back in the seat, his broad shoulder brushing against her. "You're free to entertain whomsoever you wish. All I ask is that you keep us in your sights. Pay particular attention to those in the vicinity, those who seem to show a specific interest in our attendance."

"Praise the saints, Wycliff. You are joking." Mr Cavanagh snorted. "You draw attention wherever you go. With the Scarlet Widow hanging on your arm, even the musicians in the orchestra will be agog."

"We'd need the numbers of an army regiment to follow those curious about your intimate connection," Mr Trent added with a hint of frustration. "And the marquis is sure to attend. I daresay he will find someone to distract Lady Steele while pushing prospective brides your way."

Prospective brides?

Was Damian Wycliff inclined to marry?

"I thought you said marriage was not for the cynical." Scarlett's teasing tone disguised the pang of jealousy slithering in her chest.

She felt Mr Wycliff's penetrating stare a few seconds before he spoke. "The marquis suffers from confusion and often acts as if I am heir to his fortune. It is *his* wish I marry, not mine. If Parklands was too grand a home for my mother, then it is too grand a home for me."

Perhaps his father wished to make amends. Then again, the marquis had a devious streak. Every action served his own end.

"Then seeing us together at Vauxhall will no doubt annoy him."

"The devil beneath his cool facade will be hopping mad.

Apparently, marriage to a lady of his choosing, a lady bribed to take an illegitimate scoundrel as her husband, is the only thing that can save me from a life of damnation."

A chuckle burst from Mr Cavanagh's lips. "A preposterous notion."

"Preposterous, indeed," Scarlett agreed, for Damian Wycliff need be under no illusion when considering marriage. "Love is the only thing guaranteed to save your soul, sir."

"L-love?" Mr Cavanagh could barely say the word for laughing.

Even Mr Trent found her comment humorous. "It seems you're doomed to roam the fiery pits of hell, Wycliff."

"Better to spend an eternity with debauched sinners than virtuous saints," Mr Wycliff replied. "What do you say, Cavanagh?"

Something in his tone forced Scarlett to turn her head and look at him. It wasn't amusement she saw flashing in his dark eyes. Sadness lingered beyond the veil of contempt. How did she know? Because she had seen the same sorrow in the looking glass too many times to count.

The need to ease his pain—and her own, too—saw her thread her arm through his and say, "Well, you will be in good company, for I imagine we are all heading there."

The muscle in his cheek twitched. He looked at her as if she were a mysterious object unearthed with his bare hands. Heat flooded her body. Butterflies tickled her stomach. The other men sharing the confined space turned to each other and continued a hushed yet private conversation.

"You're mistaken," he whispered, edging far too close for comfort. "But I appreciate the sentiment. While we walk the same path, I fear we are heading in opposite directions."

For some reason the thought proved painful. The sudden rush of emotion forced her to swallow. "You think I am destined for heaven, Mr Wycliff?"

A smile touched his lips, one of the few genuine expressions she had seen since reuniting. It only served to feed these odd cravings within.

"You're not one of the wicked," he said, his rich tone caressing her senses. "You're one of life's survivors. One day you may be rewarded with the peace you deserve."

Others would be astounded to hear a hint of tenderness in his voice. Not her. Still, she drank it in like a woman parched, a woman who longed for love and affection. "That's the nicest thing you've said to me."

"Remember it," he said before slipping his mask back into place. "Such moments are rare for a rake."

She might have argued that there was so much more to him than his licentious reputation. She might have silently chastised herself for caring more than she should. But the carriage jerked to a halt.

Mr Wycliff's outstretched arm prevented her from flying forward in the seat. The coachman's cries of complaint reached their ears. The sound of horns and bells rent the air.

Mr Trent lowered the window and peered out. "They call them the pleasure gardens and yet one has to suffer the pain of waiting in endless traffic just to gain entrance."

"A pin in the eye would be preferable to sitting in a stationary coach for an hour squashed between three such large gentlemen," Scarlett agreed.

"Then we'll walk across the bridge." Mr Wycliff shuffled to the edge of the seat. "Trent, as you have the window open, inform Cutler of our plans."

Mr Trent did as requested, and they alighted from the vehicle onto New Vauxhall Road. Many people had a similar idea. Coach doors opened and slammed. A mild sense of panic thrummed in the air as people struggled to walk along the crowded pavement. A few broke into a jog. No one wanted to stand for too long in the queue.

Damian Wycliff captured Scarlett's hand and placed it in the crook of his arm. Straightening to his full height, and with his usual intimidating bearing, he set the pace—a relaxed stroll over Vauxhall Bridge.

No one barged into his shoulder.

No one pushed them aside to hurry past.

"The air here is so clean it cleanses the lungs." Mr Wycliff closed his eyes briefly as he inhaled through his nose, exhaled through his mouth.

"Fresh air cleanses the mind, too," she said, though at the present moment she could think of nothing but the powerful man playing escort. "Judging by Mr Trent's comment, we'll need our wits tonight. The marquis seems set on making mischief."

"The marquis always makes mischief." His tone conveyed the depth of his disdain. He cast her a sidelong glance. "Do not let your stubborn streak overrule your logic tonight. Remain at my side regardless of what takes place."

Scarlett's heart lurched as a sense of uneasiness took hold. "You think something untoward might happen at the gardens?"

"From the nervous croak in your voice, you fear it, too."

It had been ten days since the intruder near throttled her in her bed. A boy had delivered the arsenic-laced flour two weeks before that. Thank heavens her housekeeper had the foresight to raise a query over the unexpected package.

Would the villain make another attempt on her life?

Fear pushed to the fore.

Where better to commit murder than in the secluded corners of the pleasure gardens? The stewards might not find the body for days.

"Based on statistics," she said, "we should be on our guard."

Every step towards the entrance brought her fears closer. Waiting in line afforded her time to concoct stories, to imagine the host of horrific crimes possible in the dark corners of the gardens.

"You know what people say." Mr Wycliff paid the attendant their four shillings and seven pence entrance fees.

"No, what do they say?" she said, prompting him to reply as they followed Mr Cavanagh and Mr Trent out onto the Grand Walk.

"Anything can happen at Vauxhall."

CHAPTER NINE

I t wasn't the luscious greenery, the grand architecture or the array of marble statues that captured one's attention as they entered Vauxhall, but the stunning illuminations. Thousands of lamps, in various shapes and vibrant colours, lined every avenue, decorated the pavilions and colonnades. People gazed in awe, their breath stolen by the spectacular sight.

And yet tonight, Damian was one of the rare few who found something else more captivating.

"No matter how many times I visit Vauxhall," his widow began as she looked about her with wide eyes of wonder, "the majesty of the place holds me spellbound."

Damian drank in the vision of loveliness, of moist lips parted on a gasp, of long lashes fluttering, of the soft swell of her heaving bosom. He saw her then—his Scarlett—the woman with an innocent smile and a pure heart. No matter how hard he tried to fight the feeling, he was the one who stood in awe … in lust … crippled with longing.

"Yes, it's all rather enchanting." His weary sigh masked his carnal craving.

She turned to him, her blue eyes still glistening with brilliance, and his knees almost buckled. "You do not have to be polite, Mr Wycliff, at least not with me. I would much rather you be yourself."

He managed a thin smile. He was always himself. The one half he permitted the world to see.

"And I would rather you called me Damian or Wycliff. I find your formal use of *mister* somewhat grating."

Three years ago he had said a similar thing, and she had called him by the name many men revered. Were he at a gaming table at The Silver Serpent, he would stake his entire fortune on her making the same choice again.

She raised her chin. "I might pay you the courtesy if you agree to refer to me by something other than Widow."

To do that would mean saying the name that haunted his dreams. *Scarlett.* The name his heart had whispered once as he stroked her hair and cradled her from the cold.

"Your point is noted, my lady," he said, breaking into a bow.

She curtsied in response. "Then tell me, *Wycliff*, tell me honestly. What is your real opinion of Vauxhall?"

Damn. Had he placed the bet, he'd be as rich as Croesus.

Conscious that Cavanagh and Trent had wandered too far in front, Damian captured her hand and settled it in the crook of his arm. A mere five minutes had passed, and already, he had lost sight of his motive for attending the gardens.

"You want the truth?" He didn't wait for the answer. "I find Vauxhall pretentious. While it feeds the appetites of many, it does little for me."

Her pretty nose crinkled. "Sir, you are quite the conundrum."

"How so?"

Cavanagh turned to face them and signalled to the large crowd gathered around the orchestra. Some couples danced on the outskirts of the throng. Some watched the military band dressed in their blood-red coats embellished with gold brocade. Damian nodded in response. While he preferred being alone with his widow, they would have to mingle if they hoped to observe Joshua Steele.

"Well," his lady began, "as a man who indulges his desires, who scoffs at restraint, a man with a thorough disregard for the rules, one would think the pleasure gardens were your playground."

One *would* think that if licentious behaviour brought him pleasure. But it only quenched his thirst for power. It was better to command and control than be a pawn on the chessboard of life. Who wanted to be the man people cast aside? Who wanted to be weak and dispensable?

"When a man sups ale day and night, it loses its potency and soon tastes bland."

"Not as bland as eating broth every day for months," she said, amused. "Nothing could be as uninspiring as that."

"That depends on how it is served." Having her feed him the vile concoction, witnessing the care and consideration that went into spooning every last drop into his mouth, had been a moment of pure bliss.

He would have continued the interesting conversation were it not for the numerous heads turning their way. Lord Rathbone whirled around from his group of friends, practically drooled at seeing the woman in the red silk pelisse gliding along the lush green walkway. Joshua Steele met Damian's gaze before quickly turning away. He pushed through the crowd, eager to hide amid the sea of top hats and pretty bonnets.

Damian noticed the Marquis of Blackbeck holding court near the Turkish Tent. The lord commanded the attention of a small, select group of people. Influential gentlemen listened to his pompous drivel. Elegant ladies hung on every banal word. There wasn't a woman in the *ton* who did not aspire to trap the marquis into marriage.

Damian cast the Scarlet Widow a sidelong glance.

Well, perhaps there was one.

"Your father should grace the stage," his widow said. "He certainly knows how to play to the crowd."

"Oh, the marquis is rather skilled at twisting a tale." Bitterness infused Damian's tone. "He repeats the same lines so many times one wonders why the ladies scramble for his attention." The lord was in his fiftieth year. Surely he was tired of playing the juvenile.

"It's not his attention they seek," the widow replied. "It's his money and title."

Damian snorted as he steered her towards the Grove, hoping to avoid another confrontation with his father. "Then theirs is a wasted effort. The man will never marry." No, the lord enjoyed growing his list of conquests.

The widow clutched Damian's arm as they navigated the boisterous crowd swaying along to the music. "Word is the marquis will marry the first mistress to fall pregnant with his child."

The crashing of cymbals made it impossible to hear with any clarity. "I beg your pardon?"

She repeated her comment and added, "The marquis is desperate for a legitimate heir." She leaned closer, so close the seductive scent of her perfume filled his head. "Some say he has developed a problem in that regard. Hence the reason he refuses to take a wife without having proof of her fertility."

Damian came to an abrupt halt amid a swarm of eager revellers. He swung the widow around to face him. "How is it I know nothing of this?" A host of emotions fought for prominence: confusion, jealousy, barely contained rage. Had the marquis married Maria Alvarez, he would have his legitimate heir.

She shrugged, opened her mouth to speak just as the musicians banged their drums and blew their blasted horns. Frustrated by the lack of privacy, he grasped her hand and led her through the Grove to the supper boxes in the Handel Piazza.

"How is it I know nothing of my father's intention?" Damian

repeated now they were free from all distractions. How was the widow privy to such intimate details?

"Perhaps because you have spent an inordinate amount of time abroad these last three years. Perhaps because people know you're a man who despises gossip."

This wasn't gossip. Knowing the depth of the marquis' conceit, Damian suspected this snippet of information bore a remarkable likeness to the truth. And yet that was not the comment he found so damnably intriguing.

"An inordinate amount of time?" he said, drawing her to sit opposite him in a supper box reserved for someone else. He preferred to stare into her eyes when he stripped off her mask. "You should be careful with your phrasing, my lady. A man might think you've taken a particular interest in his whereabouts."

A pink blush stained her cheeks, but she made a quick recovery. "Your vanity leads you to jump to conclusions, sir. I seem to recall Mr Cavanagh mentioning the fact you've spent too much time abroad."

She had been too slow to disguise her initial embarrassment, and so he pressed his point. "You made a specific reference to the last three years. The three years since we parted on a promise." The need to delve into her mind and discover the truth proved overwhelming. All anger at his father dissipated in light of learning this beauty's secrets. "My vanity leads me to conclude that you made it your business to keep abreast of my private affairs."

Noting a flash of panic in her eyes, he reached into his coat pocket, withdrew his flask, pulled out the stopper and offered her a nip of brandy. "It's not rack punch but should suffice."

As she reached out to take the flask, he brushed his fingers against hers—a ploy to unsettle her composure. The mere touch sent a hot bolt of recognition to his chest.

Roles reversed.

He was the one who struggled to hide his sudden intake of

breath. It was his stomach performing a range of death-defying flips.

A smile touched the widow's lips. Amusement turned her eyes a vibrant shade of blue as she sipped the liquor into her mouth.

Damian watched her reaction—the glint of pleasure as the warm liquid slid down her throat, the wide-eyed shock as it left a scorching trail. He took the flask and downed the contents before replacing the stopper and slipping it back into his pocket.

"Well?" he prompted, for he would not let her escape so easily.

She arched a brow. "You're right. But how might I hold you to your promise without knowing where to find you?"

Clever minx.

"Though as a man who acts on impulse," she continued, wearing her champion's smirk, "keeping track of your movements often proved difficult."

And finding her had been downright impossible. "And *you* left the lodging-house like a ghost in the night. After a few months spent searching, I presumed you were dead."

How was it a man could grieve for a kiss he had never stolen? For the loss of a lover he'd never bedded? A wife he'd never wed?

"You looked for me?" She seemed surprised.

Looked for her? People did not simply disappear. He had been out of his mind with worry, far too obsessed with her welfare. Not that he'd admitted his weakness to anyone.

"A bit of bread and a sack of kindling hardly seemed a fair reward for a woman who saved my life. The landlord contacted the supplier when thieves stole the sack left outside your door. Your sudden departure seemed out of character."

She remained silent as her curious gaze searched his face. Suspecting this woman had the power to see beyond the fixed expressions he showed to the world, Damian decided on a tactic to unnerve her.

"So you have thought about me many times during the last three years." His leg brushed hers, his knee coming to rest against her thigh.

The hitch in her breath was unmistakable. "P-perhaps as often as you have thought about me."

He doubted that.

He thought about her whenever he stripped off his clothes to reveal the jagged scar on his thigh, whenever he slid into the bathtub to ease the aching muscle, whenever a woman straddled him and rode him hard. Many times he had breathed her name as his own hand pumped his throbbing shaft. Too many times he had dreamt about her only to wake and experience the same gnawing emptiness within.

The Lord found novel ways to punish sinners.

And yet …

Fate had forced them together again.

It was time to change the subject, to discuss matters of revenge and murder. Something that did not make his heart stretch and beat against the confines of its prison. A topic that did not make his cock throb and ache to push inside her warmth.

But then the supper whistle rent the air, bringing a horde of hungry revellers bursting through the Grove, heading for the boxes. Waiters in tired-looking livery rushed to lay the covers.

The marquis flounced forward like a strutting peacock, his cortege of obedient pets in tow.

Lady Rathbone noticed the widow sitting in a box and waved, while her grandson gaped and stared as if spotting the most delicious thing on the menu.

The Steele siblings were nowhere to be seen. A fact Damian found somewhat disconcerting.

"Are you hungry?" he said, his knee still resting against her thigh. "I find I have lost my appetite." He'd lost his appetite for food but not for her company and certainly not for the need to slake his lust inside her sumptuous body.

But he wanted to make love to the actress, not fuck the widow.

"Hungry?" She looked confused. "I'm famished. You said we were to take supper this evening."

"And we will, a little later." He was aware of Cavanagh and Trent strolling towards them, too, in the company of Mrs Crandell and numerous other patrons from the den of vice on Theobolds Road. "There are too many people here keen to pry into our relationship, keen to spread malicious lies. I'll not have you make a mistake so early in the game."

"Me, make a mistake? I have spent two years perfecting this facade."

The comment gave him pause. "Only two years?" He slid out of the box and offered his arm in the hope the action seemed less like a command.

The lady exited the supper box and gripped his arm. "Like a phoenix rising from the ashes, it takes time for something new to emerge from something so cruelly destroyed."

The last word sent his heart sinking to his stomach.

"You contradict your earlier statement." Despite his previous misgivings, he lived in the hope that his sweet Scarlett had escaped the bonfire. "You said the woman you once were still lives beneath the hard shell."

"I did say that, though I am surprised you remember."

He forgot nothing when it came to the angel who had saved him. "Perhaps where you're concerned, I am keen to learn the truth."

She was about to reply when Lady Rathbone and her grandson came upon them.

"Lady Steele," the matron said with exalted enthusiasm while the lord drank in the sight of the widow's ebony locks fashioned in an elegant coiffure. "As you're sitting in our booth, am I to hope you're joining us for supper?"

The matron offered Damian a strained smile, for few ladies of breeding curtsied to the bastard son even if his father was a marquis.

"Forgive the intrusion," the widow said, all charm and light. "But we've decided to take a stroll before supper."

The matron patted the widow's arm. "Then we will wait for you, my dear."

Lord Rathbone said nothing, though his gaze lingered on the widow's lips. Damian considered stamping on the fool's toe and delivering a sharp uppercut to the chin.

"Please, do not delay your meal on my account. Mr Wycliff kindly agreed to escort me the full length of the Walk."

The matron glanced at Mrs Crandell, who had changed direction and sauntered to a box at the end of the arcade. "Mr Wycliff has *friends* here," the lady said, sneering down her nose as she undoubtedly did when navigating street urchins littering the road. "I am sure he can amuse himself while you dine with us."

Clearly the invitation to sup extended only to Lady Steele and not the rogue out to ravish her in the gardens.

"Thank you for your kind offer." The widow inclined her head graciously. "But I am here at Mr Wycliff's invitation and have promised him my full attention for the entire evening."

Damian offered the Rathbones a smug grin. "Can I help it if the lady finds me irresistible?"

"Then you must dine with us tomorrow," the matron said, ignoring Damian's comment. She seemed most keen to have the widow's company. Perhaps she did want her grandson to marry a woman of notoriety. A woman more courageous than any who graced the ballrooms of the *ton*.

"I shall check my appointment diary and send word in the morning." Without further ado, the widow took hold of Damian's arm, his cue to lead her away.

"I believe Lady Rathbone has designs on having you as a granddaughter," Damian said as he escorted her towards the

Triumphal Arches. "Had she Medusa's power, I would be just another stone statue decorating the arcade."

Sensing the matron's burning gaze boring into his back, he glanced over his shoulder. And yet Lady Rathbone was not the only person whose piercing stare followed them. The marquis seemed just as displeased, while Lord Rathbone looked pained if not distraught.

"Trust me. If Lady Rathbone wanted me to marry her grandson, she would not be so subtle. If anything, I am inclined to believe that she is short of friends and enjoys the attention that comes with playing companion to the Scarlet Widow."

After a brief pause, he said, "Will you dine with them tomorrow?" The thought of her spending time in Lord Rathbone's company roused the devil in him.

"Perhaps," she said pensively as they passed through the arch.

They turned right, heading for Lovers Walk.

"You do not sound eager for their company."

Silence ensued as they strolled the narrow avenue between the bank of trees and the topiary hedge. Away from the orchestra, he could hear the heaviness of her breathing, hear the numerous sighs that told him her mind was troubled.

"Are you not tired of this life?" she suddenly said. "Are you not tired of the games, the lies, the falsehoods?"

No one had ever asked him the question. While his head said no—he lived to bring the marquis misery—he had never considered the other half of himself.

"I take satisfaction knowing my father's life is as vacuous as my own."

"Is that what you truly want? Is that what your heart desires?"

He snorted to hide the uneasiness he always felt when discussing one's emotions. "I could ask the same of you. You seem content to play the Scarlet Widow."

Her fingers slipped from his arm. She stopped abruptly and swung around to face him. "You think this is the life I want?"

Moonlight and the glow from the festoon of lanterns illuminated the pain swimming in her blue eyes. "I want a house with countryside views that stretch for miles. I want a family who picnics in the park, children to love, a husband to adore. But they are the dreams of the foolish and naive, and so I shall settle for the one thing within my grasp."

Damian was too busy forming pictures in his mind to respond. It wasn't that he could envisage the house with remarkable clarity, the children laughing and chasing their dogs, but that he saw himself in the beautiful painting, too.

Foolish was too tame a word to describe the dream.

Ludicrous seemed more apt.

So why had the ice around his heart cracked?

"That is why I came to you," she continued, oblivious to these odd sensations plaguing his mind and body. "You can give me the one thing I want."

Were he a better man, he would give her everything her heart desired. "You should know I will never father a child out of wedlock." He was meticulous about such things, bordering on obsessive.

"Not a child," she said, and somewhere in a place deep in his chest, he felt a pang of disappointment. "You can bring me peace, Wycliff. Peace from the endless nightmares. Peace from this sordid world full of hatred and greed."

He understood the value of a calm mind. During his many sojourns abroad he often pretended he was a different man—one without bitterness writhing like snakes in his belly.

She touched his arm. "Do you know what scares me the most?"

"That the villain will succeed in his attempt to end your life?"

"No, that during the game, I will lose sight of what's important."

Again, the comment made him mentally stumble.

What was more important than vengeance?

"By now you must know that revenge is the basis of my every thought and deed," he said. "The only thing I consider important."

Her other hand came to rest on his upper arm. A vibrant energy flowed between them, brighter than the myriad of lights shining at Vauxhall. "It seems you do many things to annoy your father—drink and duel, bed witless women. What do you do for yourself, to nourish your spirit?"

He arched a brow. "Is that a trick question?"

"What is your heart's desire?"

"I don't have a heart. I traded it with the devil for this impressive body and striking good looks."

But if he did, he would go back to that hovel in Covent Garden and tell the actress her kindness had touched him in a way he'd not thought possible. He would offer friendship, save his angel from the beast hiding in the wings waiting to strike.

"Yes, you do," she said, placing her palm over his beating organ. "Many times while I nursed you, I checked your heart was still thumping in your chest."

"Who's to say I didn't make the deal after you breathed life back into my bones."

"Your argument is weak. You were as handsome then as you are now."

He held her gaze for longer than a heartbeat. "And more often than not, I find you just as endearing." His tone carried the affection he harboured for the woman who saved him. "But if you're asking me what I dream about, let me show you."

Before logical thought persuaded him otherwise, he tugged on the front of her pelisse and pulled her closer. With deft fingers, he'd unfastened the first button from the loop before she had time to object.

"Wycliff?" She swallowed deeply, more than once. "Wh-what are you doing?"

"Responding to your earlier question. My heart desires that I press my lips to your scar."

"My scar? What? No!"

"No?"

"It's ugly."

"We all have scars. For most people they're hidden, hidden away from the world's scrutiny."

She stiffened as he slipped another button free and another but did not bat his hand away or offer further protest. Once all the buttons were undone, he pushed the red pelisse off her shoulders.

"I prefer you in blue," he said, running his finger slowly across the neckline of her gown. She shivered as he eased the sleeve down a fraction to reveal the tip of the mark that began at her collarbone.

"You have made your point, Wycliff." Her breathing quickened as he lowered his head.

He pressed his lips to the silvery line—knew no man had ever kissed her there. Her skin felt warm against his mouth, tasted sweet, surprisingly innocent. Desire burst through his body with the fierceness of a lit firework. He did have a heart, for the damn thing pounded hard against his ribs.

"And what point is that?"

"That you're the only man with the power to unnerve me."

He looked up and cast a sinful grin. "And perhaps the only man you want to bring you pleasure."

His hand settled on her hip, snaked around her back to draw her into an embrace. When his mouth brushed hers, she did not pull away.

The brief kiss amounted to nothing more than the soft touch of his lips, yet the sensation tugged at the muscles in his abdomen, sent a rush of blood surging to his cock. He broke contact, stared at the plump bottom lip he wanted to suck and nip, wanted to feel gliding up and down the solid length of his shaft.

The second kiss might have been just as gentle had the widow not shocked him by tugging his cravat and dragging his mouth to hers.

Passion exploded—wild and fierce.

Nerves appeared to have abandoned her, replaced by uncontrollable need. She was the one who coaxed his lips apart. It was her tongue that delved deep into his mouth in a wanton frenzy. Desperate hands clawed at his waistcoat as if keen to strip him bare.

Their pleasurable moans filled the night air.

A hunger like nothing he'd felt before raged in his veins.

Damian clasped her buttocks, met every delicious stroke of her tongue.

God, he'd lost count of the times he'd imagined this. For once, the reality proved far more satisfying than the dream.

In the distance, the bell rang to announce the cascade. While everyone raced to witness the artificial waterfall scene, he was about to press the widow against a tree trunk, lift her skirts and bury himself to the hilt.

Only, the last strike of the bell sounded closer, more like a gunshot than a clang. The acrid smell of sulphur bombarded his nostrils just as the searing pain ripped through his arm.

"Hellfire!" he cried as he tore his mouth away.

"Wh-what is it?"

Shock made him drop to his knees. He pressed his hand to his arm, pulled it away to see naught but scarlet-red blood. "Some devil shot me."

CHAPTER TEN

I t took a few seconds for Wycliff's words to penetrate Scarlett's fevered brain. She had heard the shot but was so engrossed in the feel of his hot mouth, had cast it off as part of the night's entertainment.

"Shot you?" Panic choked her throat. Anticipating another imminent attack, Scarlett's head whipped left and right as she glanced the length of the avenue but saw no one. "Where?" The crimson blood covering his hand sent a bolt of fear straight to her heart. She dropped to her knees, too. With trembling fingers, she touched his coat and waistcoat but found no sign of an entry wound.

"The ball nicked my arm. The blackguard must have crept upon us, fired through the gap in the damn trees."

Judging from the amount of blood on his hand, it was more than a nick. "I need to get you out of that coat, need to examine the wound."

"Pay it no heed." He squeezed his eyes shut and winced in pain. "Help me to the coach park without drawing undue attention. Cutler will know what to do."

How was it he remained so calm?

"And how am I supposed to do that when your hand is dripping with blood?" The sight reminded her of the night she found him slumped in the alley, though he appeared far more coherent now. That night, she'd feared he would die.

"You'll find a handkerchief in my pocket." He muttered a frustrated curse. "I swear I shall drive a blade through the heart of the man who did this." He gestured for her to help him to his feet.

Scarlett grabbed his clean hand and hauled him up. With no time to rummage around in his coat, she used the lining of her pelisse to wipe away the blood. Then she quickly shrugged into the garment and assisted him back along the Walk and through the arch.

"When Trent and Cavanagh see us heading towards the Grove, they're sure to follow." He took hold of her hand and placed it in the crook of his arm. "Try to make it look as if you're leaning on me not the other way around."

"If we swagger people will believe we're in our cups. Do you feel lightheaded, nauseous?"

He snorted. "I am not about to vomit on your shoes if that is your fear."

"I should hope not. You failed to reimburse me for the last pair."

"You had enough money from the sale of the cross to buy ten pairs of boots."

He sagged against her and Scarlett stiffened her spine to support his weight. "When one is a month behind on their rent," she said, "new boots are rather low on the list of priorities."

"You could have sold your books."

Sell her beloved books?

"Each one carried an inscription from my mother." Sweet messages of love. The only kind she had ever known. "Nothing would have prompted me to part with something so precious."

The heaviness in her heart returned.

"Don't I feel like the heartless rogue," he said, steering her far enough into the Handel Piazza for his friends to notice their return. "I thrust my mother's necklace into your hand when a few pounds would have sufficed."

He pasted an arrogant grin for the benefit of those still seated in the supper boxes, though the crinkles around his eyes told a different story. Surrounded by a large group of admirers, the marquis still occupied his box, but Lady Rathbone and her grandson had vacated their booth.

Mr Trent and Mr Cavanagh observed them with keen interest as they approached the Grove. Obscured by a few trees, Wycliff stopped and exhaled a weary sigh before straightening his shoulders and pressing on.

"A minute ago, when you spoke about your books," he said, leaning some of his weight on her again, "you used the past tense. It implies you no longer possess these treasures."

"No," she said, fighting back the sudden urge to cry. "Steele made a bonfire and forced me to watch them burn." He had pushed her face so close to the fire, the flames had singed her hair, scorched her cheeks.

Silence descended.

At her side, Wycliff's body grew rigid. "God, how I wish I'd been the one to snuff out his light. I fear the need to eradicate the man's bloodline thrums in my veins."

"There is little point dwelling on what was." From her experience that only made living unbearable. "It changes nothing."

"No," he said with a sigh as they navigated the Grand Walk back towards the entrance. "I'm sure you don't need to read words in a book to know your mother loved you." His voice lacked the usual air of confidence.

"You're right. True love lives forever in the heart." Scarlett cast him a sidelong glance, shock banishing her sadness when she noted his pallid complexion. "You're not well." Heavens, she had been rambling on about books while his strength waned. "We must hurry. We must get you home and send for a doctor." She quickened the pace, aware that his steps grew cumbersome, that he was in danger of tripping over his feet.

"Home," he mumbled. His body shook as if the cold had penetrated his bones. "I'm so tired … so tired I could sleep where I'm standing."

A wealth of emotion pushed to the fore.

"Oh, please don't die on me now." Not after she had found a way back to him. Not after that bone-shattering kiss. If her mind wasn't occupied with more pressing matters, she would replay every delicious second.

Wycliff stumbled, and Scarlett caught him by the elbow. The few people passing turned their heads, pointed and chuckled at the lady struggling to help the sotted gent.

They managed to reach the lane leading to the coach park, had walked a few feet when Wycliff closed his eyes, and his head lolled forward.

"Wycliff." Scarlett nudged him, but his knees buckled, and he dropped to the ground. Hot tears sprang to her eyes. "Wake up. We're nearly there. I see the carriage." It was a lie. In the dark field the vehicles were packed as tightly as fish in a monger's cart. "Alcock!" She had no choice but to cry out. "Alcock!"

Oh, where was the woman when she needed her?

Footsteps pounded the ground.

"Alcock!" she shouted again, but it was Mr Cavanagh and Mr Trent who happened upon them.

"What the devil's wrong with him?" Mr Trent barked, his voice carrying an accusatory tone.

Scarlett gulped for breath. "He's been shot, shot in the arm." Tears trickled down her cheeks. It had been some time since she had licked her lips and tasted the salty dew of her pain. "The fiend crept up on us, fired through the trees."

Mr Cavanagh dropped to his knees. He touched Wycliff's sleeve, cursed at the sight of blood on his fingers. "I'll race ahead and find Cutler. Can you carry him, Trent?"

Mr Trent raised a brow. Without a word, he scooped Wycliff up as if he were as light as a child and hauled him over his broad shoulder.

Mr Cavanagh cast her a look filled with pity. "Fear not. Wycliff has nine lives and has used but six. Cutler knows what to do."

Scarlett forced a smile. "Please hurry."

Together, they raced through the field. Cutler—clearly aware that his master was prone to reckless behaviour and knew to be on his guard—bounded towards them with Alcock in tow.

"What is it this time?" Cutler did not look the least bit panicked, yet Scarlett felt sick to her stomach. "Knife wound? Mass brawl? It would take more than one man to put him on his arse."

"Shot to the arm," Mr Cavanagh said, unperturbed. "Based on the amount of blood, I imagine you'll need to remove the ball and stitch the wound."

Cutler nodded and ushered them all towards the carriage.

"He'll not die, milady," Alcock said as she walked at Scarlett's side. "Death takes the good ones. The devil protects his own."

Had they been alone, Scarlett would have chastised her servant, corrected her misconception. For all his bitterness and bravado, Wycliff was ironically dependable. In his company, she felt safe—something she had not experienced since before her mother's death.

"Alcock, you more than anyone should know that outer appearances bear no true reflection on a person's character." Try as she might, Scarlett could not hold her tongue.

Upon hearing her comment, Mr Cavanagh glanced back over his shoulder and grinned. His angelic good looks masked a sinful devil. Of that, she was in no doubt.

Upon witnessing their approach, the groom scampered from his perch and opened the carriage door.

"Climb inside, Lady Steele," Mr Trent demanded in his usual assertive manner.

Scarlett did as he asked and settled into the seat.

"Wake up, Wycliff." Mr Trent slapped his injured friend on the back, and Mr Cavanagh hurried around to the opposite door. With one man at Wycliff's head and the other at his feet, they managed to lie him down on the seat occupied by Scarlett.

"Your lap will act as a cushion," Mr Trent said, though showed no sign of amusement. "I'm sure Wycliff would rather gaze upon your face when Cutler is sewing his wound."

Cutler barked orders to Alcock, instructed her to take the reins —much to his chagrin—to keep the vehicle steady and drive them to Bruton Street.

"Bruton Street?" Scarlett said, almost to herself. Numerous attempts to discover Mr Wycliff's address had come to naught. "How is it no one knows he has a house in such a prominent place in town?"

"Wycliff owns several prestigious houses though he prefers not to live in any of them." Mr Trent climbed inside the carriage and dropped into the seat opposite. "He rents the house in Bruton Street. A short-term tenancy."

How odd.

"Is that because he prefers to spend time abroad?"

Mr Trent eyed her suspiciously. "You will have to ask him."

Cutler climbed into the conveyance. While he was not as broad or as tall as Mr Trent, it was impossible not to feel cramped. Thankfully, Mr Cavanagh took a hackney to the doctor's house to ferry him to Bruton Street.

While Alcock took the reins and directed them through town, Cutler removed scissors from a leather bag in the cupboard underneath the seat. He cut the sleeve of Wycliff's coat and that of the black linen shirt that made him look like Satan's servant.

Feeling somewhat useless, Scarlett brushed the errant lock of ebony hair from Wycliff's brow. His skin was as cold and as damp as the night she had rescued him in the alley. As he slept, he looked just as handsome, just as peaceful. She remembered the hours spent sitting at his bedside, enthralled by the rise and fall of his chest, by the long dark lashes fanning his cheeks.

Cutler's mumbled groan drew her out of her reverie.

The coachman handed her a brown bottle to hold while he opened a wooden box of implements and then set about cleaning the wound with alcohol and a swab.

Mr Trent placed his hat on the seat and shrugged out of his coat. "From the way Wycliff held his arm, I assume the ball missed the bone, and there is no fracture."

"Aye, there's no permanent damage. Hand me the small knife and tweezers."

Scarlett glanced at the surgical set in the box, relieved the coachman hadn't asked for the saw. To calm her fears, she cupped Wycliff's cheek and said a silent prayer until Cutler instructed her to pour the liquid out of the bottle onto the implements and then over the wound in Wycliff's upper arm.

Wycliff jerked awake as soon as the liquid touched the damaged skin and torn tissue. He writhed and cursed the devil.

"Hold him still, milady. Talk to him," Cutler cried as he prodded and poked Wycliff's arm with his ghastly tools. "Help her out, sir."

Mr Trent knelt on the carriage floor and held his friend's legs still with his large hands.

Wycliff groaned.

Pain distorted his features as Cutler dug into his flesh.

Scarlett cupped his cheek firmly and forced him to look at her. "Do you remember when I helped you into the lodging-house and had to rip open your breeches?"

He did not answer though his breathing settled a little.

"I shall never forget the look on your face when I jabbed you with the needle." She would never forget the wild thump of her heart against her ribs. "When you swooned, I thought you'd died."

Beneath heavy lids, his dark eyes focused on her face. "You … you'll not get rid of me … so easily."

"No," she said, forcing a smile. "I cared for you then, and I shall care for you now. At least until you have made a full recovery."

"No broth," Wycliff said with a weak snort.

"No, I wouldn't dream of punishing you with the foul concoction again."

Wycliff closed his eyes, and she continued stroking his face, running her fingers through his hair. All the time, she was aware of Cutler dropping the ball into the surgical box, of him pulling the thread through skin, of Mr Trent's intense gaze as he watched her comfort his friend.

"Reckon the ball's from a muff pistol," Cutler said as he packed away the implements while Mr Trent returned to the opposite seat. "From the size of the wound, I'd say the shot came from a distance of more than twenty feet, and from an inexperienced hand."

"A muff pistol?" Scarlett had considered purchasing one herself. "You mean the shooter was a woman?" And to think she presumed Jemima lacked the courage to commit a crime.

"Now I didn't say that. In a place like Vauxhall, a man would find it easier to hide a smaller weapon."

Guilt flared.

"This is all my fault." Scarlett sucked in a breath as tears burned her eyes. "No doubt I was the intended victim."

"You don't know that." Mr Trent's tone lacked the powerful punch usually delivered. He paused, arched a brow at Cutler, who had finished bandaging Wycliff's arm and had stored the leather bag beneath the seat.

Understanding the silent message Cutler rapped on the roof, and the carriage rumbled to a stop. "If we plan on making it to

Bruton Street tonight, I'd best rescue the reins from that woman." He exited the carriage and closed the door.

Mr Trent remained silent until both drivers finished exchanging quips and the carriage wheels were rolling again.

"Wycliff has his enemies," the gentleman said, "and the marquis is often keen to make a point."

Shocked at the suggestion the marquis might be to blame, she said, "What sort of father shoots his own son?"

"One determined to get his way."

Scarlett shook her head. "I am more inclined to believe it was another bungled attempt on my life."

Mr Trent shrugged. "Either way, it will be impossible to prove."

"Then I shall b-beat every suspect until I gain a confession," came Wycliff's weak reply.

"There is no need to concern yourself with that now." Scarlett placed a comforting hand on his chest. "You'll likely catch a fever and must rest for the next few days, at least."

"Then g-give me an incentive to remain abed, else I shall be on my feet come the morning."

Hearing a hint of his suggestive banter eased her anxiety, until he breathed a pained sigh and closed his eyes.

"He will be all right, won't he?" she whispered. "Tell me you've seen him in worse states."

Tell me this is not all my fault.

"Much worse," Mr Trent confirmed.

"So why is there a solemn edge to your tone?"

The man frowned at her directness. "It has nothing to do with my concerns for Wycliff and everything to do with a private matter."

"Oh." Heat crept up her cheeks. "Forgive me. I did not mean to pry."

A tense silence descended.

Mr Trent stared out into the night for a while before saying, "Do you ever visit your husband's grave?"

The odd and somewhat startling question gave her pause. "No, but if I did, it would be to dance and sing and give praise. I suffered greatly at his hands, Mr Trent, and can only celebrate his passing."

The gentleman rubbed his chin. "And what would your thoughts be should you arrive at his grave to find fresh flowers, a cross fashioned from willow, a letter filled with poetic verse tied with a pretty pink ribbon and left in a decorative box?"

Having created such a vivid picture, evidently, Mr Trent spoke from personal experience and cared nothing for the condition of her husband's final resting place.

Scarlett absently stroked Wycliff's brow as she deliberated her answer. "Then I would presume whoever left them there cared a great deal for the person who had passed."

"Not merely a kind parishioner or a dutiful neighbour?"

"I might say yes, had they only left flowers."

Fascinated by this strange line of questioning, she thought to probe Mr Trent further, but the carriage slowed to a halt. A quick peek out of the window told her they had arrived at their destination.

"Should you ever have cause to seek my opinion on this matter again, Mr Trent, feel free to approach me at your convenience."

The gentleman inclined his head. "I will remain in Bruton Street for a few days and will send word to you regarding Wycliff's recovery. Cutler will see you home. Perhaps Wycliff might send for you tomorrow."

Gracious Lord. Did he think to dismiss her so easily?

"Oh, I am not returning home, sir." On the contrary, she refused to leave Wycliff's side until confident he was well. The devil himself wouldn't drag her away, let alone a man skilled in domination. "Feeling somewhat responsible for Mr Wycliff's condition, I intend to nurse the patient back to full health."

"He won't want you here," came the terse reply.

"Then he can tell me so himself in the morning."

Mr Trent sat forward. "Wycliff never entertains women at home."

She smiled. "I have no intention of asking him to recite poetry or dance a jig, Mr Trent. I seek only to bring comfort. Besides, while the doctor is in attendance, I should like a private word with you and Mr Cavanagh."

Having spent their time in a supper box, they must surely be able to vouch for the whereabouts of certain suspects.

"A private word?" Mr Trent snapped. "On what matter?"

"On the matter of attempted murder."

CHAPTER ELEVEN

D amian inhaled the amber notes of Scarlett's perfume. He felt the intense vibration in the air that warned him of her presence long before the cold linen brushed his cheeks and brow. The ache in his arm failed to draw his attention away from the hunger pangs growling in his stomach. Had he not been so stubborn, had they taken supper in a booth, he would not be in this predicament.

Upon hearing the patter of footsteps move away from the bed, he opened his eyes.

The room was dark but for the lit lamp on the table in the corner and the fire blazing in the hearth. A day had passed, if not more. He knew because he had awakened hours before to find the sun's rays streaming in through the gap in the curtains. And now night was upon them again.

Everything about this moment reminded him of his time spent in her lodging-house. The difference being this room was warm, not icy cold. The poster bed was large enough to sleep four people as opposed to the small cot fit for one.

Beneath half-closed lids, he watched Scarlett as she crossed the room to sit in the chair beside the table. She picked up a book, flicked to a particular page and began reading beneath the light of the lamp. Mere seconds passed before her attention waned. Exhaling a weary sigh, she placed the book back on the table, returned to the washstand and wrung out the linen cloth.

The desire to learn more about the woman beneath the disguise led him to close his eyes and feign sleep. His heart raced in anticipation when she stepped up to the bed, though he suspected she would wipe his brow, not straddle his naked body and end three years of mindless misery.

"Where are you, Wycliff?" she whispered, pushing her fingers gently through his hair, training the unruly locks off his brow. She caressed the strands as if they were silk. "Is it peaceful there? I imagine it is."

When she wiped the cold cloth over his bare chest, not his brow, it took every effort to maintain his steady breathing. The muscles in his abdomen clenched when she placed her palm over his heart.

"Don't leave me here alone in this godforsaken place." The heartfelt words breezed over him, tugging at other muscles he did not know existed.

She began to caress him, the tips of her fingers gliding softly over every muscled contour, grazing his nipples, running circles in the hair on his chest. There was an innocence to the movements that made it the most erotic experience of his life.

It crossed his mind to deliver a line—a comment that if she delved lower, she might find something solid to grip—but that would destroy the beauty, shatter the magic.

A moan left his lips, a signal he was stirring from slumber. She snatched her hand away, and the loss hit deeper than any stab with a blade or ball from a pistol.

He opened his eyes, met her concerned gaze. "Scarlett."

She inhaled deeply at his use of her given name. The word had left his mouth before he had time to hide behind his disguise.

"In calling for Scarlett, are you referring to the actress or the widow?" She tried to sound amused, but the quiver in her voice spoke of a different emotion.

"I am referring to you." The woman who held him spellbound, with or without her mask.

Perhaps losing consciousness had affected his brain. Perhaps the kiss at Vauxhall had messed with his mind. But he knew one thing with sparkling clarity. He had delved into the widow's mouth and tasted his angel.

"Are you still plagued by a fever?" She placed the back of her hand on his brow. "You do feel hot."

"Every part of me is desperate to turn your comment into a lewd joke." And yet he did not. "Instead I shall ask you the same thing I asked the first time you played nursemaid."

"Three days," she blurted as if she already knew his question. "You've slept for three days."

"Three days!"

Good God. The coincidence left him a little in awe.

Had the Lord granted him a reprieve?

Had the Lord given him another chance to do what he should have done three years ago? Three was the number of the Trinity, and so there had to be an element of Divine intervention.

"Please tell me Trent and Cavanagh have not been keeping a bedside vigil." The men loved gathering information to taunt him. Had he dreamed of his angel and whispered her name? Had he muttered lascivious comments about the widow?

"I sent them away as soon as I finished my interrogation."

"And yet you stayed." He had servants to tend to his ablutions, a doctor to administer medicine and change bandages. Indeed, he would be interested to know who stripped him naked.

"I told you I would care for you and I am not one to break an oath."

"Did playing nursemaid remind you of the last time I lay bleeding in a bed?"

He would sell his soul—if he had one—to know what she'd

been doing in his room while he lay helpless. Where had she slept? Where had she changed her clothes for she wore a simple green dress, not the exquisite gown he'd yanked from her shoulder so he might kiss her scar?

"This time I am the one to blame for your injury," she said, avoiding his question. "You took a lead ball meant for me."

"We don't know that. I have enemies, too."

He had ruined many a fool at the card table, though he never squandered the money as people presumed. Due to his investments in industry and shipping, hundreds of men had steady work while a few pompous prigs lost a little more than their monthly allowance.

She drew a chair up to the bed and sat down. "Cutler said the ball most likely came from a pocket pistol, shot from a distance of more than twenty feet. If we consider the fact it was dark, it is fair to assume the culprit didn't care which one of us he hit."

"Or fair to assume the shooter was Joshua Steele. The fellow cannot stop his hands from shaking." Equally, he did not wish to discount the sister. Many people used timidity as a disguise. The chit had certainly shown her temper when conversing with her stepmother. "Did Trent or Cavanagh offer an opinion?"

"Lady Rathbone and her grandson argued during supper. Lord Rathbone stormed out of the booth first, but they both headed for the Grove."

The Rathbones were not suspects so he could think of only one reason why she might mention them. "You think Lord Rathbone might want to kill the competition?"

Any fool could see the lord was desperate to bed her.

She shrugged. "Anything is possible. It would be rather naive of me to discount any suspects."

"Even Mr Flannery?"

"Mr Flannery is not a suspect."

He was near the top of Damian's list.

"And what of the marquis?" he said with some reservation.

Had his father hired someone to dispense with the widow, to further his desire to see Damian wed?

"While he remained in the booth, one or two from his party left before the bell for the cascade."

"And the Steele siblings?"

"Never made an appearance."

Was that because they were secretly stalking their prey, waiting for an opportunity to strike? Or had Steele scampered away like a terrified rabbit, fearing his sister might discover the truth?

"Mr Trent followed us as far as Lovers Walk," she continued, "and then, assuming we required privacy, returned to the piazza. He saw no one else in the vicinity."

"It seems you have been rather thorough in your questioning." Pride filled his chest. How odd when he felt nothing but indifference for most people. "Though there is one topic you've yet to broach."

"Oh. And what is that?"

"You've mentioned nothing about the incident before the gunshot." The need to know her thoughts regarding that scorching kiss burned in his chest. The need to explore her mind and her pretty mouth proved overwhelming, too.

She lowered her gaze as a blush stained her cheeks.

"Well?" he prompted when she failed to reply. "You devoured my mouth with a passion one rarely sees in a woman." The mere memory of the wild melding of mouths sent blood rushing to his cock. With nothing but a few sheets covering his modesty, he wondered when the actress would notice the curtain rising. "Did the sudden release of emotion have something to do with me pressing my lips to your scar?"

"You must be hungry," she said, coming to her feet. "Shall I send for supper? I can assure you it won't be broth."

"Scarlett." That got her attention. "Have you nothing to say about what occurred at Vauxhall?"

She paused. "Only that it does no good to complicate matters. Perhaps we should remember that this partnership stems from a need to repay a debt."

"Perhaps." After the way she'd thrust her tongue into his mouth, he could not continue as if nothing had happened. That kiss was like a spark to lust's hay barn.

"You do not sound convinced."

"As a scoundrel, I'm more inclined to suggest we strip off our clothes and sate the desire raging in our veins. I imagine we would find an affair mutually advantageous." Exciting and pleasurably exhausting, too.

She did not seem shocked at his suggestion. "What would you have me do, Mr Wycliff, hike up my skirts and straddle you in your sickbed?"

He gave a half shrug. "It's a start."

She returned to the washstand and rinsed the cloth in the bowl. "As you prefer honesty, I shall tell you that my experiences of conjugal relations have left me cold to the prospect."

"I beg to differ. A connection exists between us. I felt it three years ago, and I felt it again last night."

It was always the same in her company, even when guilt and disdain for her circumstances roused the devil within. Perhaps once they had satisfied their craving—and it was a mutual attraction whether she chose to admit it or not—they might both find peace.

She walked back to the bed and offered him the damp linen square. "You should wipe your brow. I fear such talk will only raise your temperature."

"My brow is not the part of my anatomy ready to combust."

She cast a wary eye on the bedsheets. "Is there a school rakes attend to master salacious banter?"

"Certainly. I graduated with a distinction after the local tavern wench vouched for my skills in the practical task."

A delightful laugh burst from her lips. "How is it you have an answer for everything? Tell me, Wycliff, are you ever left speechless?"

"On rare occasions." And only with her.

Her kiss had robbed him of the use of his mental faculties. He'd struggled for words when gazing upon the scars criss-crossing her back. Dry mouth proved a problem when she lowered her hood in Mrs Crandell's house, and he realised his angel lived.

"Oh, Mr Cavanagh said to remind you that you need to collect your winnings."

"Winnings?"

"From White's."

"I make a point of only taking money I have earned." It needn't be through honourable means. Most people considered gambling fair sport. "I'll not claim to have knowledge of your body when it's a lie."

She could make whatever claim she wanted. He would not degrade her by openly revealing details of an imagined affair.

"Not even for fifty thousand pounds?"

"Not even then."

Fifty thousand?

Stone the crows!

The members of White's had more money than brains. No wonder Joshua Steele turned from stepson to scoundrel. Then another thought occurred to him. A desperate man, one who hoped to win the funds and settle his debts, might be aggrieved to have lost out to a worthless bastard. So aggrieved the fellow might ease his frustration by firing a pocket pistol.

Perhaps the shooting at Vauxhall had nothing to do with the widow. Perhaps it had everything to do with her. Either way, they were making little progress and something needed to change.

After a moment spent staring at him curiously, she said, "I shall leave you to rest." She returned to the side table in the corner of the room and retrieved her book.

As the only person able to read his mind, clearly she noticed his flagging equilibrium. "Where will you sleep tonight?"

She cast a semblance of a smile. "I have been sleeping in the room next to yours. Mr Trent insists you prefer privacy and so I am happy to return home now you're through the worst."

Trent was right. Damian shared nothing with no one. That way a man was not disappointed. And yet the need to keep the widow close overrode all else. He wanted her to intrude, to disturb his solitude.

"You being here adds a certain credibility to our story. And if you find the room too cold, the bed too lumpy, there is plenty of room in this one." Indeed, he might cry out in the night, find some excuse to have her settle beside him beneath the bedsheets.

"I have managed so far," she said. "After years spent in the cold, draughty halls of a seminary, I'm sure I shall cope sleeping in a plush bed with a mound of blankets."

A picture formed in his mind of a young girl with ebony hair, living without kin and sleeping in morbid dormitories. Those who knew her now would assume she was the strong one. The one who took charge. The one who accepted her fate with the same confident disdain as the Scarlet Widow. But strength came from suffering. Aside from her scars, this woman had suffered more than most.

"Before you race from my bedchamber, tell me why Flannery failed to collect you from the seminary."

She stood between the bed and the door, clutching her book to her chest as if it had the power to ward off the evil spirits who came to haunt her in the night. Ghouls named Loneliness and Despair. The ones who visited him, too, when he forgot to raise his defences.

"Mr Flannery could not collect me from the seminary in Bath because I had left a week earlier. No doubt it proved a shock when he arrived. The house mistress usually waits a week before writing to a parent or guardian."

"No, I suppose one's family pays to know their offspring are safe, not gallivanting about town."

"During my time in various establishments, I only ever wanted one thing." A sad sigh left her lips. "To go home. But despite many attempts, my requests were denied. I'd grown tired of wondering why."

The powerlessness of childhood affected people in different ways. "Some parents believe education guarantees a long and successful life. That it matters above all else."

"And yet I cannot help but think that was not the reason I was there." She swallowed deeply and said, "My father struggled to love me. Perhaps I reminded him of my mother. Maybe he saw a child as a burden."

The throbbing in Damian's arm was replaced by a new and shocking sensation—an ache in his heart. Surprisingly, it had nothing to do with his own misfortune, and yet the similarities were undeniable. Were he not stark naked beneath the sheets, he might have climbed out of bed and pulled her into a comforting embrace.

"Whatever the reason, it is not your fault. From your vague description and your association with Mr Flannery, I assume your father owned a gaming establishment."

She nodded. "He owned The Jewell."

The Jewell?

The club catered to the upper echelons, to the wealthy who could afford to lose thousands, to the second sons who chose gaming as an occupation. Many aristocrats had lost their fortunes there until the club closed abruptly and news of the owner's suicide spread. It explained why she resorted to living like a pauper in Covent Garden.

"Your father was Jack Jewell?" He would wait for her to broach the delicate subject of suicide.

"Indeed. Hence the reason he placed me in the seminaries under the name of Scarlett Hawthorne."

Hawthorne? Yet another fake identity to add to the confusion.

"Then it is clear to me that he placed you there for your own safety." Did she not say that she rarely remained in one place for longer than a year?

"An opinion Mr Flannery shares. One he reiterates whenever I mention the subject of my unconventional upbringing."

It seemed the time had come to learn more about the Irishman with forearms as wide as a normal man's thigh. "While our outing to Vauxhall proved unsuccessful in leading us to the culprit"—though not so fruitless when it came to seduction—"I thought we might visit The Silver Serpent tomorrow night."

Her eyes widened, and she blinked rapidly. "But you're not well enough to venture out into the cold and must remain abed. Dr Redman said—"

"What?" He propped himself up on his elbows. "That I must rest until the wound has healed? I know my limitations. This isn't the first time I've recovered from a life-threatening injury." Did her reservations about accompanying him to the gaming hell stem from something other than concerns about his health? "But if you think bed is the best place for me—"

"I do for the time being."

"Then would you mind grabbing the pot and assisting me with my aim?"

She responded to his comment by raising her chin to disguise the blush. "You have servants more equipped than I to handle the task."

"How is that so when the skin on your palms is soft and callous free? One must treat the precious parts of a man's anatomy with special care and attention."

When her mouth curled into a sly smile, his heart thumped hard against his ribs.

"Clearly your injury has affected your memory. The last time you stirred and asked to use the pot I held naught but the bowl."

Damian laughed. It was not his usual sound of feigned amusement, but one that brought lightness to his chest.

"Then I grant you a reprieve." He might not ask her to help him piss in a pot, but he would feel her hands on his body soon enough. "A reprieve from your nursing duties, I might add, not from your responsibilities as my partner in this case."

"This case? You make us sound like agents working for the Crown."

"A game of fantasy never harmed anyone."

"I conceive you have a rather wild and vivid imagination, sir."

"Let's just say that spies forced to sleep in the same bed might resort to more than an embrace to keep out the cold." Being a man who did not need erotic thoughts to rise to the occasion, it was best he stopped there. "And out of concern for my health and that of your friend Flannery, you should accompany me when I visit The Silver Serpent lest one of us ends up dead."

She studied him for a few seconds before exhaling a sigh of surrender. "If we are to visit Mr Flannery, you should know he will not tolerate arrogance or disrespect."

"Then we will get along famously."

"Or he will kill you. Both prospects prove terrifying."

"Perhaps I might win him over with my wit and charm," he said to lighten the mood. He wasn't afraid of any man, let alone a thug who only knew how to fight with his fists.

"For both our sakes, I hope you do." She inclined her head and bade him good night. She stopped on the threshold and turned to face him. "While Mr Flannery knows about the minor incidents with my horse and the dog in Green Park, he knows nothing about the intruder. It is best we keep it that way."

Was that the reason for her reservation?

Would Dermot Flannery rip through the *ton* like a whirlwind, bringing death and destruction in his wake? Either way, Damian would discover more about the Irishman most gamblers revered. He would discover if Dermot Flannery was a loyal family friend, or a murderer hiding behind a mask.

CHAPTER TWELVE

Once a coffeehouse where men gathered to converse about politics, their wretched wives and play a few hands of cards, The Silver Serpent had done away with the beverage in favour of potent spirits. Spirits strong enough to affect a man's ability to concentrate on his game. Regular patrons knew the house always won, but that didn't stop the young bucks trying to break the bank.

Only fools and drunken sots believed in rags-to-riches tales.

Sensible men knew when to cut and run.

"Did you send word we were coming?" Damian asked as he took Scarlett's hand and assisted her descent from the carriage.

"Of course," she said, straightening her skirts.

"And did you explain the nature of our relationship?"

"Mr Flannery knows we're not lovers if that is what you mean."

No, they were not lovers, not yet, but a man brought back from the brink of death numerous times knew to have faith.

"Am I to assume that we're standing on Princes Street because you cannot enter the establishment via the front door?"

"Women are not permitted entrance, Wycliff. You know that."

"Not even the owner?"

"If men knew of my association with the club, they would bombard me with pleas for clemency. Desperate wives with crying babes in their arms would accost me in the street. Every devious lord would look for a means to bribe me so that I might wipe his slate clean. Hence the reason we are using the side entrance in the alley."

He glanced at the avenue between the two taverns, where drunken revellers stumbled out into the night to empty their bursting bladders. "Please tell me you don't usually visit the club after dark. These passages are unsafe for a woman on her own."

A smile touched her lips. "Why, Mr Wycliff, it almost sounds as though you care about my welfare."

He cared more than she knew.

More than he dared admit.

"If I am risking my life to protect you, I would rather know my efforts are not in vain." It occurred to him that his reply in no way conveyed the truth. That having nursed him for a second time, she deserved better. "You've suffered enough at the hands of a depraved miscreant. I should not like to see you suffer again."

"I am aware of the dangers." She touched his arm in a gesture of reassurance. "But let me put your mind at ease. Alcock usually walks me to the door. I am not the naive girl I once was. Nothing · would induce me to race into an alley alone at night."

"Not even to save me?"

She exhaled a soft sigh. "You are perhaps the only person I would risk my life to save." She shook her head as if someone else had commanded her mind and spoken the sentimental words. "Dear me." Sadness lingered in her light laugh. "You seem to have caught me at a vulnerable moment."

The yearning ache in his chest returned. "That is the most heartfelt thing anyone has ever said to me."

"Remember it. Such moments are rare for a scandalous widow."

Compelled with the need to see her eyes sparkle brightly again, he captured her hand and brought it to his lips. No doubt she expected a brushed kiss across her knuckles, but he pushed at her glove with his thumb to expose the delicate skin at her wrist.

"I shall do more than remember it." He closed his eyes and pressed his mouth to the sensitive spot. "I shall treasure every word."

A lustful energy sparked between them.

Every muscle in his body tensed.

"I—I like this side of you." Scarlett's vibrant blue eyes scanned the breadth of his chest, ventured up to study his jaw, his face. "The side unafraid to speak the truth."

"I always speak the truth."

"No, you don't. Neither of us does."

They were standing on a dimly lit street, amid the muffled sound of bawdy songs and drunken cheers spilling out into the night, and yet it was as if they were alone in the dingy lodging-house off Drury Lane.

"And what is the truth?" He was determined to know. "Speak it in confidence. Speak it, knowing I won't judge you."

"You judged me the moment I lowered my hood in the billiard room, and you learnt of my disastrous marriage. If we're speaking truths, Wycliff, what was it you found so distasteful?"

To tell her would mean baring his soul, explaining how her benevolence had touched him so profoundly a day had not passed without her entering his thoughts. He had placed her on a pedestal —worshipped the goodness flowing like blood in her veins. He'd fought hard against the urge to claim her, control her, to ruin her like he did everything else in his life. In battling his weakness, he had failed her, left her to the mercy of a man who thrived on torture.

He deserved punishment, not her.

He deserved to have his weak heart ripped out and impaled on a stake as a warning to all men who foolishly believed in the superiority of their position.

"Do you really want to know why I have an issue with the Widow?" He spoke as if referring to a mutual acquaintance.

She shrugged one shoulder. "Because you despise women who sell their souls?"

"No. Because no matter how hard I looked, I couldn't see you. The real you, not some figure constructed to prove a point."

"Not even when I bared my scars?"

"Ignorance is a means of defence. The only way my conscience could cope with the sight of such horrific injuries is to believe they were inflicted on the fictitious character called the Scarlet Widow."

The thought of any man hitting her made his blood run cold. Even now, he could dig up her husband's corpse and take his head off his shoulders.

"And what do you see now?" She seemed both eager and reluctant for the answer.

The truth hung on the tip of his tongue, and he let it fall with shocking ease. "I see you, only you. A woman whose courage leaves me in awe."

Her eyes sprang wide. When her surprise faded, happiness danced there.

What would it be like to have the heaviness of their burdens lifted? What would it be like to wake with her each morning, to live a life of peace and contentment? Live the truth, not a lie?

Magical.

Heavenly.

A dream beyond his wildest expectations.

"And what of your truth?" he said, aware of Cutler's and Alcock's curious gazes upon them. The coachwoman's need to protect her mistress meant she accompanied them on every journey.

Scarlett remained still for a moment before taking a step

closer. "Here is my truth, Wycliff. It is about time you learnt to recognise it."

Her hand came up to cup his cheek. Her lips met his with the same level of tenderness he had shown her when he thrust the gold cross into her palm and kissed her forehead.

The muscles in his abdomen clenched. He fought against pulling her to his chest and devouring her pretty mouth. This was a demonstration of *her* feelings, not his, and so he let her taste him in the soft, sweet way that spoke of affection rather than experience.

She withdrew on a contented sigh, though it took a few seconds for her to retrieve her hand from his cheek. It was like the first kiss of an innocent. Yet he was so damn hard for her, just as he always was in his dreams.

"The temperature is sure to plummet tonight," he said in a tone that did not sound contrived. "A man worries he might not have enough coal to keep warm."

She arched a coy brow. "You forget that I've been living in your house for three days. You have enough coal to keep the whole street warm for weeks."

"But my room is particularly cold."

"So cold, you insisted on stripping off every stitch."

He laughed. "From what I've heard of Dermot Flannery, I may find myself in need of another nursemaid."

"Then I shall send to the registry for they are sure to have one on their books."

"But the women are old and smell of vinegar. I want a nurse who will wipe my brow, run the tips of her soft fingers over my chest, marvel in the magnificence of my muscular body."

"Then it's a brothel you want, not the registry." She shook her head as if he were a mischievous child. "Come, we had better not keep Mr Flannery waiting, and I am returning to my own house tonight, so you may stop with the teasing."

"Who said I'm teasing? The night is still young." He offered a grin full of self-assurance. "And you know what people say about The Silver Serpent."

"No, what do people say?"

"Anything can happen at the gaming hell."

Damian Wycliff was incorrigible. Incorrigible, and the most devilishly attractive man ever to make her acquaintance. There was little point hiding her feelings. He had been awake when she conducted a thorough examination of his naked body. Well, not so thorough, for that would have meant delving beneath the bedsheets, stroking those impressive thighs, fighting against the temptation to caress another part of his anatomy, pressing her lips to his warm skin.

With every passing day, they grew closer.

With every passing day, she caught more glimpses of the man behind the arrogant facade, felt her own disguise slipping more times than she could count.

And then he had gone and made the comment that obliterated her defences. The comment that made her heart ache, even now.

I see you, only you.

Not the actress.

Not the widow.

The woman beneath it all. A simple woman who wanted simple things. A woman with so much love to give it took a wall of Norse shield-maidens to keep it at bay.

"Wait on Rupert Street, Cutler." Wycliff's commanding voice drew Scarlett from her reverie. "When a man needs to make a quick exit, the front door is often the best choice."

"Mr Flannery is not a man who makes trouble." Not unless provoked. "No doubt he will be grateful to you for giving your assistance."

"Grateful?" he mocked. "Based on my reputation, he will think the worst."

Oh, she had met men with exceptional manners, with pure bloodlines, with the grace and poise of princes. Most were devious liars. Indeed, when it came to deception, sincerity was the perfect disguise.

Damian Wycliff was often rude. His tainted blood fed an anger worthy of Ares, the god of war. *Virtue* and *etiquette* were foreign words to him. But while he kept his private thoughts hidden, he never lied. He hated with the devil's passion. And if he ever loved, he would do so from the depths of his soul.

"Mr Flannery can see through men's bravado," she said as Wycliff escorted her to the door at the end of the long, dark alley. "He will learn to trust you, just as I have."

"You trust me?"

"I do. More than anyone else in the world."

She felt the penetrating heat of his stare before he drew her to an abrupt halt and swung her around to face him.

"Scarlett." Her name breezed from his lips as his fingers brushed against her cheek. With a gentleness she was unused to, he captured her chin and pressed a long, chaste kiss to her lips.

Her defences crumbled. Every barrier she'd raised to protect her heart from this man lay like rubble around her feet.

"What was that for?" she said, touching her fingers to her lips when he broke contact and stepped away. Was it because she was one of the few people who believed in him?

"I have no idea. The urge came upon me rather suddenly. And I'm a man who indulges his whims."

"I see."

"Do you wish to raise a complaint?"

"No. I have no complaint." She could still feel the essence of the man on her lips and so resisted the need to moisten her mouth for fear she might lose his taste. "Might I expect more surprises?"

"I imagine so." He cupped her elbow and drew her to the wooden door.

"There is no need to knock." Scarlett delved into the pocket of her black pelisse and removed the iron key.

"So no one knows of your association with Mr Flannery? No one knows you possess a key to the door of a club where a substantial amount of money is kept on the premises?"

"Not to my knowledge." She led him into the narrow corridor before closing and locking the door.

"I wonder if the intruder had another motive for entering your home."

Until now, she had been reluctant to recount the events of that night. Fear choked her throat whenever she pictured the image of a fiend dressed in black looming over the bed.

"Theft was not the motive. He could have stolen jewellery, silver, but took nothing but the breath from my lungs."

"And you're sure it was a man?"

"Other than Alcock, I know of no woman with such size and strength."

"Hmm." Wycliff leant back against the wall, his brows drawn in thoughtful contemplation. "And how did Alcock come to work as your coachwoman?"

Scarlett jumped to attention. "Do not think she had anything to do with what happened. Alcock believes she owes me a debt of gratitude she can never repay."

Wycliff raised a brow. From the glint in his dark eyes, it was clear he had made the logical assumption. "You were the one who gave her the money to buy her freedom."

Yet another one of the horrific situations Scarlett had faced these last three years flashed into her mind. Releasing a weary sigh, she leant back against the opposite wall for support, ready to relay the story.

"One night while travelling home in Steele's coach, he stopped the vehicle in Whitechapel and threw me out. As I was intent on behaving like a disobedient trollop, he left me to spend the evening with my own kind."

Wycliff ground his teeth. "I hope every harlot in hell is dancing on his charred remains."

"The dark streets of Whitechapel are hardly safe for a man, let alone a woman with rubies dangling from her throat and earlobes." Bawdy banter did not hurt. But drunken men— deranged and desperate men—sought to play out their lewd fantasies. "It just so happened that Alcock was using the alley where three men knocked me to the ground and tried to steal my clothes and jewels."

And steal something more precious besides.

Wycliff reached across and captured her hand. The gentle squeeze of reassurance acted like a healing balm to the painful memory.

"I assume your coachwoman offered stern words of caution," he said with a knowing smirk.

"Of course, after she broke their noses and left them with purple plums for eyes. She took me back to her lodging-house, fed me broth, and I spent the night there."

"Did it remind you of your time as a struggling actress?"

Scarlett couldn't help but smile. "No, it reminded me of the time spent with you."

The hot, sensual look in his eyes was similar to the one she had seen moments before in the alley. "Despite my injury, I remember the time with great fondness."

"You look as if you might suddenly kiss me again, Mr Wycliff." A woman could live in hope.

"Perhaps I might, Widow."

The anticipation of feeling his mouth on hers burned in her chest. Every sign of lust, every snippet of affection, drew her deeper under his spell. Having him was no longer an option. She would take him into her body, savour every delicious moment, devour every inch of the man who loved her in her dreams.

A tiny gasp left her lips as he straightened. Every fibre of her being tingled while awaiting his touch. But then a gruff cough brought an end to her fantasy, and she cast a sidelong glance to see Dermot Flannery's large frame filling the corridor.

Dermot ran his hand over his bald pate, drew it down the length of his long ginger beard. He stomped towards them, and Scarlett held her breath.

"It isn't gentlemanly to keep a lady lingering in a cold corridor." Dermot stared down his bulbous nose.

Was it cold? She hadn't noticed.

"Few people would call me a gentleman," Wycliff replied. "Though when it comes to Lady Steele, you should know I would lay down my life to protect her."

Scarlett blinked. No doubt Wycliff exaggerated for effect. A man would have to care a great deal to make such a sacrifice. Then again, Damian Wycliff never said anything he did not mean.

"Glad to hear it," Dermot said. His sly smile faded, replaced with a stone-like seriousness meant to threaten and intimidate. "Because if you hurt my Scarlett, I'll take a knife and fork to your fancy ballocks and serve them for supper."

CHAPTER THIRTEEN

A deathly silence hung in the air. The disturbing sound sought every crack and crevice in the dingy basement room Dermot Flannery used to conduct his business.

As the man stared at Damian Wycliff across the battered oak desk, every long, stretched-out second felt like an hour. The ticking of the mantel clock was akin to a death knell. And while it was Scarlett who paid Dermot's wages, the man's need to play parent in her father's absence left her sitting in the seat next to Mr Wycliff feeling just as anxious. That said, the gentleman at her side did not look the least bit intimidated.

Dermot scanned the ledger laid open on the desk. From the faded ink on the pages, the records were not recent. "In all the time you played at these tables, you've never lost," Dermot said in his faint Irish twang. "Nor have you borrowed from the house."

Wycliff shrugged. "Let's just say some people find it hard to read my expressions. Let's say that having wisely invested in my future, I do not need to borrow from a gaming hell, my father or the bank."

Scarlett didn't find it hard to read him. He wanted to murder the world, ravish her. Damian Wycliff held himself up in an impenetrable fortress and yet somehow she had found the key to the gate. She had seen the look of longing flash in his eyes. She was aware of his growing need to touch her—light strokes on her arm, snatched opportunities to sit close, a tender kiss stolen in a dark alley.

"I can read you." Dermot relaxed back in the chair and drew his hand down the length of his beard. "I can read every unspoken word."

Wycliff snorted. "Then I am thankful I never played you at piquet."

"You'd have lost, so you would," Dermot countered.

"Would you care to make a wager?"

"What I'd care to do is have you tell me why two men bundled you into a carriage at Vauxhall. Why the same two men carried you into a house in Bruton Street, and why Scarlett spent three nights sleeping under your roof."

Good Lord!

Dermot Flannery must have hired men to watch her. Shock rendered her momentarily speechless. No wonder he had been acting strangely since she told him about the incidents with her horse and the savage dog in Green Park.

Dermot turned to her and raised his hand in surrender. "Now, now, I know I never told you about hiring the guards to—"

"Guards!" she blurted, feeling somewhat suffocated by the thought this man had monitored her every movement. "For heaven's sake, Dermot, I am not a child. You had no right—"

"You might be a fancy lady," Dermot replied as he folded his thick arms across his chest, "but your father made me swear an oath, and I'll not go back on my word."

Wycliff cleared his throat. "And while I'd like to tell you to rot in hell, Flannery, for your interference means I must pack my belongings and lease a new abode, respect for the lady at my side prevents me from telling you about our little sojourn to Vauxhall."

"Would you care to make a wager?" Dermot said.

Wycliff arched an arrogant brow. "Don't ask me to betray Scarlett's confidence. But know that I, too, swore an oath. Hence the reason I am sitting here listening to your patriarchal drivel."

Scarlett sucked in a breath. Wycliff promised to mind his tongue.

Dermot's eyes grew large and round. "Listen here, lad."

"I am not your lad. Scarlett is not your daughter."

Dermot sneered. "And she's not your wife, yet you kept her in that house of yours for three days. Yer man doesn't need a Cambridge education to know why."

Wycliff shot forward and gripped the edge of the desk. "Then if you're so adept at reading people, one look into my eyes will tell you the lady nursed me from the brink of death, nothing more."

Silence descended once again.

Beneath hooded lids, Dermot stared into Wycliff's eyes. Seconds passed before he said, "Maybe we should call a truce. Mark it with a friendly arm wrestle." Just as Scarlett was about to object, he added, "Just to appease old Flannery."

As a man who favoured his right hand, a man with a wound to the same arm, Wycliff had no choice but to decline. Nonetheless, Scarlett knew with absolute certainty he would not refuse.

"Dermot, this is ridiculous," she pleaded, hoping to make him see sense. "Mr Wycliff is here as my guest. You have no reason to distrust him."

She would never call rank and play the heavy-handed proprietor with Mr Flannery. The man worked tirelessly to protect her investment. Having lost her once, he lived to ensure he never failed her again. And he was the closest thing to kin she had.

"You can learn a lot about a man when he flexes his fist." Dermot yanked one arm out of his coat, pushed the ledger aside and settled his elbow on the desk. "Come on, Mr Wycliff." A chuckle escaped him as he wiggled his fingers. "Let's see if you're as strong as you look."

When Wycliff leant forward and placed his elbow on the table, Scarlett shot to her feet. "Mr Wycliff is unwell. Are you determined to see him keel over from the strain?"

The gentleman in question cleared his throat. "You may beat me in an arm wrestle but let us see how you fare with swords or pistols."

"Fops fight with swords." Dermot laughed. "Cowards fight with pistols. Real men fight with their fists."

"Make no mistake. I can throw a decent punch. Indeed, I would take great pleasure putting you on your Irish arse."

The loud slap of their palms clashing echoed in the room. Both men bared their teeth as they adjusted their grips. Wycliff— the damn fool—was in danger of ripping open his stitches, of bleeding out onto Dermot's well-trodden rug.

"Stop this at once." Scarlett thumped the desk with her clenched fist though seemed powerless against two such stubborn men. "If only you could see how absurd you look."

"Let's begin on the count of three." Dermot shuffled in the seat, placed his best foot forward and angled his body closer to the desk. "One."

"Mother Mary have mercy on both your poor souls." Scarlett glared at them. "If you hurt Mr Wycliff, I shall never forgive you."

Wycliff cast her a mild look of reproach. "Have faith in your champion, my lady."

"Two."

"No!" Scarlett grabbed their clasped hands. "Mr Wycliff took a lead ball to the arm three days ago. Do you want him to die on your desk?" She sounded dramatic, she knew, but after her experiences with Lord Steele, she never fared well beneath the clawing fear of helplessness.

She waited for what seemed like an eternity before Dermot slapped his free hand on the desk in a sign of surrender.

Something about his expression told her he had no intention

of wrestling with Wycliff, that he had led them down this path purely to pry.

"You were shot at Vauxhall?" Dermot said as he attempted and failed to pull his hand from Wycliff's grasp.

Wycliff kept a firm hold and stared down his nose. "I'd wager you already knew that."

"Yer man noted that your shirt was cut, your arm bandaged. Who shot you?"

"It doesn't matter who shot him." Scarlett was growing tired of being a silent voice. She knew better than most what it meant to be invisible. To have one's thoughts and opinions discarded.

Wycliff's dark eyes glinted with menace. "If I knew who put the ball in my arm, the villain would be dead and buried beneath a hefty mound of soil."

Dermot chuckled again. "Ah, a fellow after my own heart."

Scarlett stared at the two men. Now they had played this odd game of intimidation, perhaps they might converse as adults, might unearth some truth from the past in the hope of bringing clarity.

And yet, the hollow emptiness in her chest made it hard to focus. Not since those terrible nights when her husband's depravity poisoned his mind had she felt so weak, so irrelevant.

Tears pricked her eyes, but she refused to let them fall.

She needed air, at present couldn't bear the company of either man and so turned on her heel and strode to the door. Their questions chased after her, demanding a response regarding her intention.

"Scarlett! Wait!"

She was at the door leading to the alley when Wycliff came up behind her. He braced both hands on the frame, caging her in a hard, masculine prison.

"I had no choice but to play Flannery's game," he whispered, his cool breath breezing over her neck to send shivers down the length of her spine. "Men like him, men like me, we've had to fight our whole lives for our positions."

"I've had to fight, too." Years of untold misery pushed to the surface. Too many times she'd hit back believing she might die.

"I know. And I wish I would have done something to prevent it."

Scarlett closed her eyes in an attempt to rein in her volatile emotions. It didn't help having Wycliff's hard body pressed so close. Part of her knew why people used pleasure to obliterate pain.

"About Flannery," he continued. "It's evident he thinks of you as a daughter, that he thought highly of your father, too. We should tell him the truth about the intruder. If his man followed us to Bruton Street, then it stands to reason Flannery might be of assistance to us in our efforts to find the blackguard."

Perhaps Wycliff knew that refocusing someone's mind worked to banish painful memories of the past. Perhaps he knew that just hearing the smooth timbre of his voice was akin to consuming a calming elixir.

"Don't let our efforts to find the villain come between what is happening between us," he murmured.

Come between them?

Nothing would prevent her from having this man.

Scarlett shuffled around to face him, her body brushing against his in the tight space. "They say the temperature will plummet tonight," she said, surprised at the depth of desire in her voice. "Body heat is the only way to keep the cold at bay."

Eyes, dark and dangerously hot, scanned her face, strayed to her hair, lingered on her lips. She wondered if he experienced the same heavy ache in his loins that kept her awake at night, that plagued her now.

Wycliff brushed a stray tendril from her cheek, tucking it with care behind her ear. "Then we should see to this business quickly.

The anticipation of warming your sweet body makes it hard to concentrate."

His mouth hovered achingly close. She wanted to kiss him, tangle tongues, have him plunge deep into her willing mouth, deeper into her starving body. She might have given in to temptation had Dermot Flannery's voice not disturbed their intimate exchange.

"Most couples are forced to wed when caught in a clinch, so they are."

Wycliff pushed away from the door and straightened his coat. He gazed into her eyes, a look to remind her that honesty was the best way forward.

"Being a widow, the same rules do not apply. Besides, you know only too well that I'll never marry again." She glanced at Wycliff, hoping his expert ears had failed to catch the lie. She would marry for love. But the only man who had ever touched her heart was a notorious rake who rarely settled in one place for longer than a few months.

"Well, Scarlett?" Dermot said in the comforting tone of a caring parent. "Will you be sitting down to tell a tired man how our friend happened to take a lead ball in the arm?"

It was time to stop hiding the truth. The threat had escalated. And she would die inside if anything untoward happened to Wycliff. "Perhaps I should begin by telling you how I first met Mr Wycliff. And then I'll tell you how fate conspired to bring us together again."

"Why do I get the impression I'll need more than ale to calm my nerves?" Dermot gestured for them to follow him back to his basement office.

They all returned to the dimly lit room. Both men sat in silence as Scarlett relayed her tale. Numerous times Dermot cursed and thumped the desk for she had never told him about the scars, or the cruelty she'd suffered at the hands of Lord Steele.

Wycliff's face remained stone-like though she could feel the fire raging within.

After dragging his hand down his face, Dermot said, "Had you not escaped from the seminary, had you but waited a few more days, I could have saved you years of pain and heartache, so I could."

"If life is about learning lessons, then things happened as they ought." Had she not fled from the seminary, she would never have taken work as an actress, would not have ventured into an alley off Drury Lane to save the life of the rogue sitting quietly at her side.

"Had yer man Steele not thrown the miniature of you into the gambling pot, I might never have found you."

That was the first night fate had been kind.

Despite a lengthy argument about where Scarlett should reside while they investigated the attacks, they agreed she would remain with Wycliff, and Dermot's men would watch over the house on Bruton Street.

The conversation turned to the suspects.

"Ever since you told me about the dog attack in the park," Dermot began, "I've had someone spying on yer man Steele. You should never have told him you owned his vowels."

"It was the only way to regain control." The information was akin to putting a noose around her husband's and stepson's necks. She held the rope, knew when to give it a hard tug.

"It's a sure way to end up dead in a ditch," Wycliff countered.

"At the time, I wanted peace from the nightmare." It had given her leverage against her husband—a means to bargain for her safety and security. But Wycliff was right. She had failed to consider Joshua a threat. "In hindsight, I've made many mistakes. Mistakes that may have forced Joshua to act out of character."

"If you die, he gets the house in Bedford Street." Wycliff gave a weary sigh. "He can sell it and relieve his burden."

"I'm certain it wasn't Joshua who throttled me in my bed."

"So you say." Dermot growled. He knew nothing about the intruder, which supported Scarlett's theory that the villain entered the house via the garden. "But I'll have the blackguard by the end of the week. Whoever he may be."

"You think the intruder was a hired thug from the rookeries?" Wycliff said. "Few people have the arrogance to murder someone in their own home."

Dermot nodded. "And I want to know where your cook buys her flour. There'll be a record of the transaction, so there will."

"I have already attempted to extract that information. Marleys have no record of the order."

Wycliff snorted. "Mr Flannery means someone took the order, someone paid to taint the flour with arsenic."

"And by the time I'm finished, someone will tell me everything they know unless they want to take a dip in the Thames." Dermot opened the desk drawer and rummaged inside. Retrieving a leather notebook, he pushed it across the desk, not to Scarlett, but to Mr Wycliff. "Everyone the Steele boy has visited, every place he's been for the last two months, yer man recorded in there."

"I'm sure it will make for interesting reading." Snatching the book from the desk, Wycliff flicked to the last page and then turned to Scarlett. "We should examine it at length. I imagine it will either prove Joshua Steele's guilt or his innocence. The last entry made was three weeks ago and will shed no light on the attack in your bedchamber."

"That will be in O'Donnell's new book. I'll have it sent to you in Bruton Street." Dermot turned to Scarlett, his green eyes brightening. "You're welcome to stay here if you'd rather, you know that, so you do."

Why would she stay above a noisy gaming hell, when she might spend the night in bed with Damian Wycliff?

Lust, tinged with something far more potent, fluttered in her belly. She had waited three years to press her naked body against his. Only in her wildest imagination had she ever thought her dream might come true.

"Thank you, Dermot, but we must examine the notebook as a matter of urgency."

"And if we hope to lure the devil from his lair, *we* must be the bait." Wycliff stretched his injured arm, which still clearly pained him. He had refused laudanum, refused to fill his silver flask with brandy. Perhaps it was a way of punishing himself for failing to anticipate the danger at Vauxhall.

"Well, we won't keep you." Scarlett came to her feet. "Shall we meet again in two days to discuss our findings?"

"Two days it is," Dermot replied. "I'll have news of your intruder by then."

Wycliff stood though he looked a little pale. "Should you need assistance, you know where to find me."

What use would he be? With his arm so weak, he could hardly throw a punch. Then again, one look from those piercing dark eyes and any man would drop to his knees and blurt a confession.

They left The Silver Serpent via the alley and made their way to Rupert Street. While the urge to stop and flick through the notebook proved tempting, nothing stole her attention away from the fascinating man at her side.

Wycliff remained quiet in the carriage. With every revolution of the wheels, the silence grew in length and intensity. The heaviness in the air spoke of lust, of a desperate carnal craving kept at bay by a fine thread. Scarlett wondered if she was the only one to feel the powerful vibration. Was she the only one aware that the thread was about to snap? In a dusty, diffident corner of her mind she made excuses for his reticence, believing it stemmed from a need to control the pain in his arm, and nothing to do with his desire for her.

"You look tired." She kept the prickle of disappointment from her voice. "A dose of laudanum and a good night's sleep will aid your recovery."

He stared at her beneath hooded lids, shuffled restlessly in the seat.

"We can look at the notebook in the morning," she added. "Perhaps it is better to examine it when one has a clear—"

"Sleep is not on my list of priorities." His voice sounded dark and devilishly sinful. The velvet timbre stirred an inexplicable heat in her blood. "Examining the notebook can, indeed, wait until tomorrow. I don't need laudanum. I don't need rest."

Scarlett tried to swallow down her desire, but her whole body ached to feel his touch, yearned to have his hot mouth ravage hers again.

"What do you need?" She was already damp between her legs, anticipating his reply.

"You know the answer." Hunger flashed in his coal-black eyes. "The only thing I need tonight is you."

CHAPTER FOURTEEN

The carriage could not ferry them home quickly enough. Damian was of a mind to inform Cutler he had three minutes to reach Bruton Street unless he wanted his master to spill his seed over the new seats.

Lust clawed at Damian's insides like a starving beast. He jiggled his leg in the hope his pounding heart dispersed blood to other parts of his anatomy.

Two hours he had sat in Flannery's dingy office listening to Scarlett relay her tale, witnessing the bearded Irishman curse in a foreign tongue. For two hours, he had struggled to think of anything other than her tantalising offer to keep him warm in bed.

They say the temperature will plummet tonight.

It might be cold outside, but his body raged like an inferno.

Now he thought of it he'd waited more than two hours to have her. Ever since she'd lowered her hood, and he realised who she was, he'd kept the wild urges at bay. No! Longer than that. For three blasted years, he'd craved her touch.

Damian glanced across the carriage at her face cast in shadow. A glimpse of her white teeth nipping at her bottom lip should have spoken of nerves, yet he saw the erotic in everything she said or did.

This crippling urgency might have seen him drag her across the narrow space into his lap, but his conveyance slowed, and he knew they had turned into Bruton Street.

When Damian flung open the door, the wheels were still turning. As soon as the vehicle stopped, he vaulted to the pavement. He didn't waste time lowering the steps but settled his hands on Scarlett's waist and lifted her to the ground.

She said nothing but allowed him to pull her by the hand into the house. He acknowledged his butler with a curt nod. Determined steps propelled them up the stairs.

Once inside his bedchamber, he kicked the door shut. Every fibre of his being longed to push Scarlett back against the wall, to ravage her mouth like a madman. But even in the faint glow of candlelight and the fire's amber flames, he saw a flash of apprehension in her eyes, a hint of fear.

Overcome by his obsession to have her, he had lost sight of what this meant to her. She had given every indication she wanted him, too. But it seemed evident her precoital experiences had left her terrified of men.

"You've said nothing since I made my declaration." He drew her close, tempered his carnal cravings and brushed the backs of his fingers across her cheek. "Since I told you I am crippled with need."

She closed her eyes.

By God, he prayed she wasn't crying.

"Scarlett." His voice was uncharacteristically tender. "Nothing is set in stone. You may retire to the room next door if that is what you want." The muscles in his stomach wrenched at the thought. "We have plenty of time to examine the connection that exists between us."

Damn, he shocked himself. A master of seduction offering his lady a perfect excuse to say no?

When she opened her eyes, he expected to see them awash with doubt. But the blue gems shone with the widow's self-assurance. "Holding you to your word is not the only reason I sought you out. I hinted at another reason once."

She had revealed so many secrets he struggled to remember. "What other reason could you have for approaching me, other than reminding me of my oath?" He thought he knew the answer but wanted to hear the words from her lips. It wouldn't do to appear presumptuous.

"It's as you said yesterday." She raised her chin and inhaled before continuing. "A connection exists between us. I felt it three years ago, and I feel it now." Her breath came a little quicker. "Oh, Wycliff, whatever it is, it beats so strongly in my breast."

Her honesty proved as arousing as her voluptuous curves.

"I can no longer deny it, either." Having lost her once, he'd be damned if he'd do so again. "But I'll not press you into exploring a physical relationship if you're not ready."

Besides, he was somewhat strict about the way he conducted illicit relations. Never had he spilt his seed inside a woman. For him, the act was about banishing painful memories, finding release. It was never about a shared connection. Never about the deep, abiding affection he had dreamt about for years. Lord, he wasn't even sure he was up to the task.

Scarlett placed her hand on his chest. "Because of fear, I let you leave the lodging-house with nothing more than a goodbye. Because of fear, I accepted Lord Steele's proposal without coming to you for help."

Damian snorted. "I struggle to understand why you did that."

"I was weak and couldn't face another disappointment. I have spent my life waiting at a window, desperately waiting for a man to show he cared." She shook her head. "I lacked the strength to wait by the window for you, Wycliff."

He recognised the truth in her words. "Neither of us knew what we wanted then." He wasn't sure they knew now.

"No, but we have earned the right to explore this relationship, to know if something real exists between us. And I am tired of being controlled by my mind."

All this talk of the past had dampened his ardour. And he wanted to get back to when lust and longing burned in his veins.

"Then we must strip off our masks and agree to be honest. Agree to take a leap of faith." He held out his hand. "Know I won't hurt you."

She slipped her hand into his. "Does that mean you intend to bed me, Mr Wycliff?"

"With your permission, I intend to make love to you until we are sated and exhausted. Come."

Perhaps she thought he might pull her to the bed, but he opened the door, guided her down the stairs and out onto Bruton Street.

"Are you going to tell me where we're going?" She looked somewhat confused when they came to a halt on the pavement.

"The conversation we just shared was necessary, but I would have us go back to the moment we jumped from the carriage, ready to rip each other's clothes in a wildly erotic frenzy."

"Oh. I see." Her provocative smile said she was more than willing to indulge his fantasy. "Then let me say you look tired. A dose of laudanum and a good night's sleep will aid your recovery."

Damian slipped his arm around her back, indifferent to the fact one of Flannery's men might be watching them from across the street. "Sleep is not on my list of priorities. I don't need laudanum. I don't need rest."

He leant forward and pressed a kiss to her cheek, another to the corner of her mouth.

She swallowed deeply as her hand skimmed his chest to grip his shoulder. "What do you need?"

"I need you."

Scarlett willed her heart to settle. If she could pull on her disguise, she might not appear so nervous, so ridiculously naive. Her experience of the *act* went as far as squeezing her eyes shut and praying to God for her husband's quick release. When a woman bedded a man like Damian Wycliff, did she not need a certain skill in the field? Did she not need the confidence of the Scarlet Widow?

But despite her fears, one thought refused to be tempered.

She wanted to love the man who used a facade to disguise his pain. The need to soothe him, to see a hot spark of desire in his eyes, burned in her chest.

Gathering her courage, Scarlett captured his hand. "Then make love to me, Wycliff. Make love to the lost woman who doesn't really know who she is."

"I know who you are." The gentle timbre of his voice stirred the longing within. "You're the woman whose courage knows no bounds. You're the woman with the kindest heart I've ever known. Without your mask, you're stronger than the widow, more benevolent than the actress."

With the tight coil of her nerves relaxing, she decided to tease him. "Then who kissed you at Vauxhall?"

"You did. The woman bursting with passion." He arched a brow and cast a devilish grin. "The woman desperate to rip my clothes from my back and ravish me in the gardens."

The memory brought heat to her cheeks, heat to her aching sex. The same overwhelming lust consumed her now. Indeed, she was in danger of stripping him naked in the street.

"Then take my hand, Wycliff, and don't let go." Without another word, she pulled him to the front door, up the stairs back to his bedchamber.

The time for talking was at an end.

After crossing the threshold, he slammed the door shut.

A mere second later she was in his arms, wrapped in a strong embrace.

His hot, greedy mouth came crashing down on hers as the binds of restraint snapped beneath the weight of their desire. She pushed her hands up over his hard chest, caressed the sculpted muscles before threading her arms around his neck.

Wycliff pressed his body into her, grasping her buttocks and squeezing as his tongue slipped past her lips to delve so deep inside her mouth her legs almost buckled.

The evidence of his arousal pushed against her abdomen—so long, so solid and thick, even through his clothing. Her sex pulsed in response, eager to mate with him, to feel him push inside her body and fill her full.

The sound of their breathless pants, of their moans and murmurs of pleasure, sent her lust for him spiralling. Drunk with these new sensations, she slipped her fingers into his hair, grasped and tugged the ends as her tongue stroked his in a wild and frenzied dance.

"You don't know how long I've waited for this." The words escaped him on a gasp. He captured her chin between his fingers and tilted her head to drag his lips along the line of her throat, leaving a fiery trail.

She knew exactly how long she had waited, to the day, to the hour. "Three years spent longing. Three years spent yearning." Her eyes fluttered closed as his tongue traced a circle on the sensitive place behind her ear. When he drew her earlobe into his mouth, her body melted to liquid fire.

"Then we must make up for lost time."

A lifetime of loving him would be ample reward.

But for now, she had no intention of wasting a second. "Take off your clothes."

Wycliff pulled his head back and met her gaze. "You want to

see me naked?" Mischief danced in his eyes. From his arrogant grin, he had no issue flaunting his toned physique.

She stepped back, felt the loss of his hands on her buttocks but knew she would feel them again soon enough.

With his heated gaze fixed on her, he shrugged out of his coat, unfastened his waistcoat, untied his cravat. Every sleek movement, every slow tug to undo the buttons built the anticipation.

"Now your shirt." Her mouth was dry. "Do it slowly."

Wycliff moistened his lips. The mere sight of his tongue sent a shiver from her neck to her navel. "Expect that I shall ask the same of you."

Grabbing the hem of the fine lawn, he crossed his muscular arms and pulled the garment over his head. He crumpled it into a ball and threw it to the floor to join the rest of his apparel. Then he stood, waiting for her appraisal.

Glorious was the only word to describe every muscled contour. Scarlett had gazed upon his bare chest numerous times, had spent hours watching him as he lay asleep in bed, imagining what it must be like to inhale the scent of his bronzed skin.

He ran his hand over the broad expanse of his chest. "It's nothing you haven't seen before."

"And something I hope to see many times again."

"Damn right, you will." As he tugged off his boots, she looked to the stitches on his arm, to the mottled purple bruising surrounding his wound. Were she of sound mind she would chastise him for not wearing his bandage, but her head was a muddled mess, her emotions a slave to her cravings.

The boots landed on the floor with a thud.

"Shush," she said, a giggle escaping. "If you're not careful, you'll alert the servants."

Wycliff chuckled. "Love, in a moment, you'll be riding my naked body as if leading a race at Epsom Derby. Thankfully, the servants are deaf to most sounds, trained to respond to nothing other than the tinkling of a bell."

The mere mention of lovemaking stirred a quickening deep in her core. It didn't help that Wycliff's hands moved to the buttons on his breeches. With slow, sensual grace, he unfastened the buttons on the waistband, then the top two securing the fall front.

"I imagine over the last few days you must have seen this before, too." Fixing her with a wicked grin, he pushed his breeches down past his hips. "Though I fear it might have appeared less ... rigid."

The sinful devil stripped off his breeches to stand before her like a proud victor in a Roman arena. Power radiated from his broad shoulders, from the rippling muscles in his abdomen. But it was the solid length of his manhood that held her transfixed.

Scarlett gulped. "You're rather larger than expected."

He palmed the length of his jutting erection just to tease. "Have no fear. I've always known we would fit." His heated gaze perused her from head to toe. "You must be hot in those clothes."

Hot? She was ready to combust. But the thought of stripping naked, the thought of revealing her scars again rendered her immobile.

"Can I ask you something?" No doubt he heard the tremble in her voice.

"What? Now?"

"Where did you go after you left me in Bedford Street on the night of your father's ball?" In light of what they were about to do, the answer seemed important. Or was it nerves that made her ask? Had the widow abandoned her and left the naive girl behind?

Wycliff closed the gap between them. He stood so close she could smell the earthy scent of his skin. "Do you want the truth?"

"Everyone wants the truth, even if it hurts." What was it she wanted him to say? Had he not already explained that they shared a connection?

"Would it hurt you to know I visited another woman?"

Hurt her? It would cleave her heart in two. "It would."

How had her defences crumbled so easily?

He stroked her cheek. "I went home to drown my sorrows. I drank alone for an hour and then fell into an empty bed." His fingers moved to the buttons on her pelisse, and he undid them as deftly as he did the night at Vauxhall.

"What made you go home and numb your thoughts with liquor?"

"You did." He pushed the pelisse off her shoulders. "You've held me in your spell since I met you. The night of the ball, I realised I had but two options." He spun her around to unfasten the row of buttons on the back of her dress.

"And what were those?" The brush of his lips at the base of her neck woke the butterflies in her stomach. Scarlett closed her eyes, savoured every second.

"If I had no hope of making love to you, I might be forced to join a monastery."

A smile tugged at the corners of her mouth.

"Now, don't you think you've punished me enough?" he said, placing his hands on her shoulders and easing her dress down her arms to pool on the floor. Her petticoat followed. "I might be standing while I strip you naked, but you've had me on my knees for years."

The comment bolstered her confidence.

"While the position has certain advantages," he continued, "I'm a man who desires equality."

He tugged at the ties on her stays. Every movement released air into her lungs. The little jerks sent her imagination racing as she anticipated the thrusts of his body entering hers.

When down to nothing but her chemise, stockings and boots, she expected him to swing her around, to get to work on the other garments hindering their lovemaking.

But Damian Wycliff was a man who defied expectation.

His mouth was on her neck, sucking and nipping.

His hands found the hem of her chemise, and he slid the material slowly up past her thighs to her waist.

A soft breeze brushed over her bare buttocks.

"Tell me you need me inside you," he whispered, burying his face in her hair and inhaling deeply. "Tell me you want this as much as I do."

"You're the only man I've ever wanted inside me."

A growl resonated in the back of his throat. "Then raise your arms."

"But my scars?" How might he love her while looking at the hideous marks?

"Our scars make us who we are. Raise your arms, Scarlett."

She did as he asked, relished the feel of the material gliding up over her ribcage and skirting the outer curve of her heavy breasts. Then he dropped to his knees behind her, bit down gently on one buttock while caressing the other. Beginning at her ankle, he ran his hands up over her stockings, stopping at the top of her thigh.

Her sex throbbed for him to touch her there.

"I know what you want." No doubt he wore the cocksure grin she loved. He untied the laces and yanked off her boot, smoothed his hands over the stocking again from ankle to thigh. The pads of his fingers grazed lightly over her sex, tearing a moan from her lips. "You're so wet for me, love."

Scarlett's body tingled from her head to her toes. "Only for you."

The scoundrel set to work on the other boot, traced a scorching path up her thigh to massage her sex again. He stood, gripped her hips and pressed his erection against her buttocks.

"What about my stockings?" She wasn't sure how long she could stand these teasing touches.

"Leave them on."

His solid manhood pushed through the gap between her legs, slid the length of her pulsing sex. He continued to tease her from behind, to caress her breasts, to roll her sensitive nipples between his fingers until he'd dragged a whimper from her throat.

The sudden thought that he might take her like this—bent over the bed, exposed, her scars on display—forced her to pull away and turn around.

Desire swam hot in his eyes. "There are so many things I want to do to you. My wicked tongue won't rest until I've tasted every inch of your body."

Lust emboldened her to say, "And I intend to ride you like I'm racing for the finishing line at the Derby."

Things turned wild as their rampant emotions took charge.

But she was the one who kissed him as though she might die without his taste, without the feel of his tongue exploring the far reaches of her mouth. The need to protect her heart, the need to control him, found her pushing him onto the bed. She climbed on top of him, devoured every inch of bare skin, though she could not take his erection into her mouth—not after her degrading experiences at the hands of her husband. Instead, she straddled him, eager to feel full. Complete.

The sound of their ragged breathing filled the room.

"Now," he panted. "Take me into your body before the agony of waiting kills me."

"What do you do to prevent a child?" she asked as her fingers settled around his manhood ready to position him at her entrance.

Wycliff blinked, looked so consumed with passion he could not rouse a coherent thought. "French letter—but don't stop now. Let's worry about that in a moment." He glanced at the milky tear weeping from the head of his erection. "I'm crying with need for you, love."

Scarlett rubbed the head over her sex, teased him by taking him half an inch into her body. "Do you need me to take you deeper, Damian?"

"Yes."

She slid down another inch as he stretched her wide. "Deeper?"

He jerked his hips impatiently. "Hell, yes."

Without warning, she sank onto his hot shaft. Took the man who made her heart sing into her needy body, right up to the hilt.

CHAPTER FIFTEEN

"F uck." The obscenity burst from Damian's mouth as he jerked his hips and pushed deeper into the silky channel of Scarlett's body.

God, it felt heavenly.

Divine.

This wasn't the first time he'd been desperate to slake his lust, but the first time with Scarlett satisfied more than his aching cock. What proved most shocking was that he'd been unable to wait, unable to address his meticulous need to wear protection. Delving into a drawer to unwrap the French letter, blowing into it to ensure there were no holes, seemed less important than the need to claim this woman as his own.

Of course, nothing would make him spill his seed inside her.

Nothing, except for exchanging marriage vows and scribbling proof in the parish register.

The minx straddling his thighs was about to come up on her knees, and so he gripped her waist and held her in place. Impaled. His.

"Wait for a moment." His words were a husky whisper.

"Wait? Why?" Panic flashed in her eyes, and she put her hand over the scar above her breast. "Is something wrong?"

"Far from it. I want to feel you, feel your heat surround me." No matter how many times he'd envisioned this moment, nothing prepared him for the stimulating sensation of her muscles hugging him tightly.

"Does this have something to do with your fear of fathering a child out of wedlock? We don't have to continue." Her actions betrayed her words when she splayed her hands on his chest, came up on her knees and sank slowly down to swallow his cock.

"God damn." The need to pound hard, to hear the audible slap that would feed his arousal, came upon him suddenly. Hell, he was always the one in control. He said how. He said when. He took what he wanted, gave little, just enough to maintain his rakish reputation.

"You feel so good, Damian," his bewitching temptress said as she rode him at an achingly slow pace that had nothing to do with nerves. Each delicious slide drew him deeper into the majesty of the moment.

While still riding him, she reached up into her hair, pulled out the pins and shook the ebony tendrils loose. The silken locks danced over the alabaster skin on her shoulders. He wondered if she'd done it to hide the scar. Then she leant forward, thrust her luscious breasts towards his mouth and rode him like she was a few furlongs behind in the race.

"Bloody hell." Never in his life had he been claimed so fiercely. Yet for the first time, he no longer felt the same sense of isolation.

The bed creaked. The headboard smacked against the wall.

The guttural moan from his mouth would awaken the dead, let alone alert the servants. He would explode inside her if he didn't do something quick.

Wrapping his arm around her waist, he rolled her onto her back. Before she could protest, he settled between her thighs and lavished her sex with deserved attention. A man as depraved as Lord Steele did not care about his wife's pleasure.

He lapped the evidence of her arousal as his tongue flicked back and forth. Two fingers mimicking the thrust of his cock brought her to a blinding climax.

"*Damian!*" The sweet cry of ecstasy was like music to his ears. The muscles in her core clamped around his damp fingers.

He did not give her time to climb down from the dizzying heights but positioned himself at her entrance and pushed home. A wave of ecstasy rippled through him. How was it possible to feel sated when he was yet to reach his climax?

Every instinct cried for him to rush, to ram hard, ram deep.

His angel lay there, her hair splayed across the coverlet, her lips swollen, the hazy look of desire swimming in her eyes, and he could not think of a time when he'd seen something so beautiful.

Suddenly, this wasn't about his wants, his need to make love to the only woman he'd ever truly desired. It had nothing to do with a rake claiming the only woman to elude him.

It was about her.

Every remarkable aspect.

Damian leant forward, squashing her breasts against his chest, and kissed her with a passion that went beyond lust. Then he withdrew from her body slowly, almost entirely, before pushing deep inside her again. His pleasure came from watching her lips part on a gasp, from watching her eyes flash hot with excitement.

He continued this slow, teasing torture even when her dainty hands clasped the muscles on his back and urged him to quicken the pace. Even when she arched and writhed beneath him.

"You're mine." The words tumbled out of his mouth as he angled his hips so he could rub against her sex with each thrust.

"I'm yours," she cried, her pants accompanied by pretty moans.

"Never forget it."

A wealth of emotion flooded his chest when she came apart for the second time, when her body hugged him and refused to let go. It took great effort to withdraw, but fear and habit made him finish with his own hand and pump his hot seed over her stomach.

Exhausted, he collapsed on the bed beside her, captured her hand and twined their fingers.

This was a first for him on many levels.

Usually, he would be washing, dressing. Within five minutes he would be at the door, promising another liaison soon, the vow forgotten before he'd reached his carriage. And yet he was ready to gather this woman into his arms and sleep for an eternity.

He stared at her as she lay with her eyes closed, a light sheen of perspiration coating her skin, watched her until her ragged breathing turned light and even.

"Tell me you're not asleep."

A smile brightened her face, but she did not open her eyes. "No, I'm not asleep. I'm floating on a heavenly plane."

Masculine pride made him grin. He drank in the sight of her magnificent body until his gaze fell to the scar marring her breast. Guilt's sharp talons pierced his chest, ready to rip out his heart. It wasn't his fault, he knew, but he would give anything to go back in time and erase her pain.

He contemplated jumping out of bed, locating Joshua Steele and beating a confession from his quivering lips. Instead, he went to the washstand, wrung out a cloth and came back to the bed.

The first wipe over her stomach reminded him of the many times she had attended to his ablutions. "It makes a change for me to wash your body with a cold cloth."

Still wearing her satisfied smile, she looked at him and said, "It's about time you repaid your debt. By rights, I must be entitled to hours of pampering."

He laughed—he never laughed with any of the women he'd bedded. "What do I owe? An hour a day for three days?"

Her eyes grew round. "An hour? I spent the best part of three hours wiping your brow. And it's six days, not three."

"Eighteen hours, then."

"Agreed."

"When shall I begin?"

"You may wash me now, as I should retire to my bed. We must rise early in the morning and focus our attention on examining the notebook."

"You are in bed."

"I meant the bed next door."

The sudden thought that he did not want her to leave stole his breath. He was a man who craved privacy. "Stay here, in bed with me."

I don't want to be without you tonight.

She arched a brow. "I doubt either of us would get much sleep."

His cock jerked to life at the prospect of plunging into her wet body again. "Let's not make any plans. We'll settle beneath the sheets and see where the mood takes us."

She stared at him for a moment, as if the decision had more serious implications. "I have never slept in bed with a man, other than that one time with you."

"And I have never slept in bed with a woman, except for that one time with you."

She bit down on her bottom lip, just like she did on that night three years ago. "Will you hold me in your arms to banish the cold?"

"Will you lay your hands on my chest while you sleep?"

Neither answered the other's question. They did not need to.

They settled into bed, lay huddled together on their sides despite the excessive space.

For an hour, Damian watched her sleeping—just as enchanted as he was that magical night in the lodging-house. Then he drifted off into a peaceful slumber. The first he'd known in years.

Scarlett lay in Wycliff's bed propped up on one elbow, the rumpled sheets wrapped around her legs as she watched her lovable rogue sleeping. She'd lost count of the times she had gazed upon him intently while he was oblivious to her lustful scrutiny.

But lust was not the only emotion she felt when in Damian Wycliff's company.

Since the first time they parted, she had loved him a little.

Since reuniting, that beautiful seed of hope had sprouted roots.

Every day the sapling stretched towards the sun, optimistic yet still so fragile.

She placed her hand lightly on his chest. Touching him always brought comfort. Having him deep inside her body was akin to experiencing heaven on earth. Not once had her nightmares returned to haunt her. Not once had visions of Steele's cruelty interrupted the beauty of the moment.

Where would it all end?

She had no notion.

But her experiences had taught her that life was just as delicate as the first buds of spring.

Wycliff stirred beside her. He stretched his body, his hand edging beneath the sheets to reposition his manhood. Her own sex pulsed at the thought of climbing on top of him and riding him as she had done last night. A frisson of doubt over his feelings for her prevented her from acting.

Oh, her body begged her to reconsider.

Still naked, she turned on her side to face the window. If Wycliff wanted to make love to her again, he would have to make his intentions clear. Excitement tickled her stomach when he stretched, sighed and exhaled a pleasurable hum.

Silence filled the room though she grew intensely aware of his breathing.

Remaining in the same position, she shuffled a little so he would know she was not deep in slumber. Her ploy worked, for he rolled onto his side behind her, pressed a kiss to her bare shoulder, pressed his erection against her buttocks.

She resisted the temptation to arch her back. She would have Wycliff work a little harder to seduce her. When he placed his warm hand on her hip, she released a small sigh. After all, he needed to know she was not opposed to joining with him again.

"Scarlett?" he whispered. "Are you awake?"

"Hmm," came her drowsy reply.

The wicked hand on her hip ventured slowly north to cup her breast. The first brush of his finger over her nipple almost sent her shooting off the bed. Instead, she wiggled her hips against his erection, inviting him to slip between the gap in her thighs.

"You minx." The huskiness of his voice conveyed the depth of his need. "You want me to make love to you, is that it?"

She arched her back in response, and he pushed into her body to fill her full.

Heaven.

The brief thought that he had not sought a French letter, that the scars on her back were so glaringly visible, left her mind the moment he withdrew to thrust inside her again. She could spend every morning like this—close to him, loving him.

This slow, sensual mating didn't feel like the joining of bodies. It felt more like the joining of souls. She might have laughed at her own naivety—for women often confused lust with something more sentimental—but then Wycliff pressed his lips to the scars on her back, told her she was beautiful, and she fought the urge to cry.

Damian Wycliff did, indeed, have fingers that worked the devil's magic. It took naught but his expert strokes to break her into a million sparkling pieces. A whimper escaped her when he withdrew suddenly, and she felt the hot, wet evidence of his climax on her buttocks.

He climbed out of bed almost immediately, yet she would have liked him to remain inside her even when soft and unable to perform.

"Don't think that washing me now reduces your debt," she teased when he returned with a cloth and spent far too long wiping her buttocks. "It doesn't count when it is to our mutual advantage."

"Then I suspect it will take me years to work off what I owe."

If only she could believe that were true. "Years? You rarely remain in one place for longer than a few months. You must repay the debt before your next trip to France."

He returned the cloth to the washbowl and turned to face her in all his glorious nakedness. "I have no intention of leaving London."

The questions she longed to ask danced on her tongue. Instead, she chose a subject guaranteed not to cause her any pain. "Is there a reason you own property and yet prefer to lease a house in town?"

He turned back to the washstand and swirled the cloth in the water. "I like to give my father the impression I refuse to settle." Water trickled from the linen square as he wiped his chest, wiped the extraordinary length of his flaccid manhood. "It annoys him that I won't take a wife, won't accept the ridiculously large country estate gifted to me last year for my twenty-fifth birthday."

"And you live to annoy him."

"It is undoubtedly the only thing that keeps me sane."

She wanted to probe him further, but he threw on a robe and tugged the bell-pull. "I'll have breakfast sent up. What with the loud moans and groans and the violent rocking of the bed, there is little point hiding our relationship from the staff."

Scarlett climbed out of bed, too, aware of Wycliff's heated gaze blazing a trail over her naked body. She rummaged through the pile of clothing, slipped into her chemise, straightened the sheets and returned to the comfort of her lover's bed. By the time she had finished, she looked like a virgin on her wedding night.

"What did you do with the notebook?"

Wycliff looked for his coat amid the mound of discarded garments. "It's here somewhere." He recovered the leather pocketbook and threw it onto the bed.

Scarlett flicked to the first page while Wycliff beckoned his servant to enter and gave instructions concerning the morning meal.

The small book contained a detailed account of Joshua Steele's daily appointments. The notes began not long after Dermot had broached the subject of her numerous *accidents*, tales he had heard from members of the club. Having occurred in broad daylight, many had witnessed her horse bolt and throw her to the ground. Many women had screamed upon seeing the savage dog bounding out from the blanket of trees.

"Found anything of interest?" Wycliff asked as he climbed back into bed.

"Joshua visits his tailor far too frequently for a man riddled with debt." Scarlett scanned the next few pages. "And he visits a place on Russell Street at least twice a week. Always at night." She squinted. The name of the establishment proved hard to decipher. "It reads like Alter Bags."

She laughed and handed Wycliff the notebook.

He perused the pages, flicked back and forth before the corner of his mouth curled into a grin. "It doesn't say Alter Bags but rather Altan Bagnio."

Scarlett wrinkled her nose. "I've never heard of the place. What do they sell?"

"Pleasure." He chuckled. "Well-heeled clientele lounge in the Turkish baths before supping and moving on to more vigorous entertainment."

"You mean Joshua is visiting a brothel?" What would stiff old

Jemima say when she discovered her precious brother entertained prostitutes?

"Altan Bagnio is more than just a brothel. It caters to the more deviant appetites. Restrictive apparatus proves very popular, so I'm told."

"Restrictive apparatus?" It sounded more like something one might find at a science lecture. "Might you speak the king's English, sir?"

Wycliff laughed. "No doubt Joshua Steele enjoys having his wrists tied to the bedpost while seeking his pleasure. And that is me conjuring a rather tame image."

"Surely not."

While she knew men sought a variety of means to satisfy their needs, she couldn't imagine the timid fellow enjoying that level of domination. That said, Lord Steele's need to inflict pain was unnatural. Perverted. And what's in the roots must surely come out in the branches.

Wycliff seemed to find the thought of Joshua's unusual craving amusing.

"Do not mistake me," he said, "you may tie my wrists to the bed, love, and do what you want with me. But at that pleasure house, the lord will be treated like a slave."

Scarlett snatched the book from him. And yet she could not shake the image of Damian Wycliff strapped to the bed while she devoured every delectable inch.

She flicked through the pages, stopping abruptly at one particular entry. "Joshua visited the bank and then took a hackney to a house in Ely Place, off Holborn Hill." She cast Wycliff a sidelong glance. "What if that's where he hired the man to throttle me in my bed?"

Wycliff frowned as he repeated the street name. "I don't suppose O'Donnell noted a description of who he met there?"

"No, only that he stayed for an hour before returning home."

"It could be an address of a solicitor or doctor. Or someone he

173

met at the bagnio who entertains certain clients at home. I'll ask Trent to investigate."

A light knock on the door brought the footman with the breakfast tray. Wycliff insisted on eating in bed, and so Scarlett nibbled on toast while reading the entries in the book.

"When you've finished eating, I intend to lick every crumb off your chest," he said in the sinful tone that stirred the hairs on her nape.

"Had you told me that before, I would have gnawed on the bread like a savage."

He leant over and kissed her shoulder.

It took nothing more than a suggestive comment and one chaste kiss to ignite a fire in her core. "I get the sense we might not venture far from bed today."

"As I'm in debt to you for eighteen hours' worth of pampering, I imagine not."

She turned the page in the book, gazed at the words, but they failed to penetrate her brain. "We must at least attempt to find something useful in this book," she said when Wycliff trailed his finger the length of her arm.

"We have. We will calculate when Joshua intends to visit the bagnio and surprise him there. He can hardly refuse to answer our questions when strapped to all four corners of the poster bed. And I shall send word to Trent and ask him to visit the house on Ely Place today. Flannery has men watching this house, so what else can we do in the meantime?"

True.

But she couldn't help but wonder about Jemima.

"Do you not think we are making a mistake focusing all our attention on Joshua? There are other suspects."

The marquis was on their list, but she supposed neither of them cared to pay the pompous lord a visit. One did not threaten or bribe such a prominent member of the aristocracy.

"Joshua is the one with the most to gain."

"At the time the intruder struck, I was no threat to your father's ambition to see you wed. That does not mean he wasn't involved in the shooting at Vauxhall."

"No, although he finds the thought of revenge utterly distasteful."

"He doesn't strike me as a man who creeps around in the dark, or a man who hires someone to threaten and intimidate on his behalf." And they knew with absolute certainty that he had not left his supper box.

Silence descended.

Scarlett continued looking through the book, knowing that guilt's rigid finger did indeed point to Joshua Steele. But then another entry caught her attention. It took a moment for her eyes to absorb the words. Scarlett flicked frantically through the pages looking for similar listings. She found two more.

"What is it?" Wycliff asked.

"At no point since the death of that abominable creature I married have I seen Joshua in the company of Lord Rathbone. And yet he has visited the lord's house in Portland Place three times in two months."

"Perhaps Steele feared Rathbone was competition. Perhaps he thought that if you grew close to the lord, you might divulge his secrets."

"But they are both members of White's." She knew that, but did not know if Rathbone had taken part in the wager. "Why not conduct their conversation in one of the private rooms? And Lady Rathbone made no mention of the visits."

Consumed with suspicion, she could not shake the feeling that both lords were conspiring to bring about her downfall.

While Wycliff took the notebook and scanned the pages, Scarlett's mind concocted all sorts of villainous plans. And yet Lord Rathbone had appeared sincere in his attentions. Then again, Lord Steele had seemed just as trustworthy when she married him three years ago.

"By my calculations, Joshua will visit the bagnio either tonight or tomorrow night. Cavanagh will visit the madam of the house and use his seductive skills to persuade her to divulge information."

"And what will we do?"

Wycliff arched a sinful brow. "For the time being, I need to work on banishing the fearful thoughts from your head." From the way he moistened his lips, she knew what he had in mind. "And hopefully tonight we will visit a brothel for the dissolute. We will give Joshua Steele the pain he so desperately craves. We will discover the truth."

CHAPTER SIXTEEN

*A*ltan and *bagnio* were not words that rolled easily off the tongue. Translated, they meant golden brothel or something to that effect. No doubt the owner thought the name created an air of mystery. Or was it that with such specialised services on offer, they did not need to attract the usual patrons?

Damian didn't care who saw him entering the establishment, but he cared what the gossips said about Scarlett. "I can speak to Joshua alone if you'd prefer to wait in the carriage."

They were standing on Russell Street, a mere three feet from the door to the house that from the outside looked like any other respectable townhouse. If the walls could talk, they would tell a somewhat different story.

"I'll not sit in the dark while those women try to entice you with their whips and chains. Besides, I'd like nothing more than to drag a confession from Joshua's lying lips."

"Assuming he's here."

A whole day had passed before they received news from Cavanagh that Joshua Steele planned to visit the brothel tonight. Having paid the bawd fifty pounds for the information, Wycliff was to pay a further two hundred to gain entrance. It would have been vastly cheaper to hire a harlot and go snooping around the rooms.

"But the madam assured Mr Cavanagh that Joshua would keep his usual appointment."

Damian arched a brow. "The woman would recite gibberish to earn fifty pounds." He pulled his watch from his pocket and inspected the face beneath the dim light of the street lamp.

"What time is it?"

"A little after nine."

"We shouldn't have too long to wait."

They waited for five minutes. Damian considered knocking on the door, but the bawd had insisted she'd not have her patrons witness such a blatant breach of privacy.

Another few minutes passed before a woman—dressed in a purple gown as fine as anything worn by an aristocratic lady—opened the door and ushered them quickly inside.

"I believe the price to visit our friend in his chamber is two hundred pounds." Damian kept his voice low. "No doubt you seek payment in advance."

"I'll not talk here," the madam murmured. "Follow me." Scanning them both with some suspicion, the bawd—who looked no older than thirty—directed them to a room further along the hall.

They passed a drawing room decorated with sumptuous gold furnishings. Women dressed like innocent debutantes sat playing cards and sipping sherry while awaiting their gentleman friends. One played the pianoforte. Another appeared engrossed in a book.

"Are you certain we're at the right place?" Scarlett whispered.

Damian drew her closer as they followed the madam into the room at the end of the hall. "Deviants like to appear respectable."

Scarlett raised her chin in acknowledgement. "That explains the surprising air of normality."

The bawd gestured to a desk sporting a fancy ink pot and

quill. "Two hundred pounds for the key to your friend's room, and your word you'll not mention my kind act to another soul."

Kind act? The woman demanded an extortionate sum.

Damian flicked his coattails and dropped into the seat at the desk. He withdrew the crisp notes from his pocket and flattened the corners. "And what name shall I scribe?"

The bawd gave a coy grin. "Here, I'm known as the mistress of every manoeuvre, but you can make the notes payable to Iris Blyth."

Damian dipped the nib of the quill in the pot and scratched the woman's name along with his signature. "You may take the notes in good faith. Coutts is a reputable bank."

The madam snatched the notes from the desk. She made sure the ink was dry before folding them neatly, hiking up her skirts and placing them in her petticoat pocket.

"The lord you're looking for declined the use of our basement baths. Heather took him up to the room on the second floor." She reached into the porcelain pot on the desk, retrieved a key and handed it to Damian. "Turn left once you reach the top. Give the key to Heather before you leave."

"How long has our *friend* been upstairs?" Better to interrupt the lord whilst he was restrained in an embarrassing position.

Iris Blyth glanced at the mantel clock. "Half an hour."

"Then it's time we interrupted the party."

They were about to leave the room when the madam called after them. "I have girls free tonight if you find yourselves a little curious."

Damian snorted. "Having had some experience with domination, I must decline." He was not referring to his own need for control. "Three years spent on one's knees is long enough." He turned to Scarlett and whispered, "Though I might need to bow between your legs during the carriage ride home."

Scarlett batted him on the arm as they left the room. "Do you approach every challenging situation with devilish joviality?"

"There is nothing challenging about pleasuring you."

Scarlett breathed an exasperated sigh. "I am speaking of the situation with Joshua."

"Of course."

They mounted the stairs in silence. From the loud splashing emanating from the basement and the painful cries echoing from numerous bedchambers, Damian doubted the lords would hear the cavalry approaching.

There was but one door on the second floor to the left of the stairs. With deft fingers, Damian slipped the key into the lock and turned it carefully. He eased the door from the jamb and peered into the dark room. Heather had drawn the curtains on the near side of the poster bed. Candles flickered in the standing candelabrum, casting an amber glow over the dark wood and burgundy furnishings.

Scarlett clutched Damian's arm upon hearing the whimpering from beyond the curtain. He took hold of her hand, and together they crept into the room and closed the door.

"You think I don't know what goes on in that stupid head of yours?" The woman's harsh voice sliced through the air, the words accompanied by a sudden and rather sharp slap. "You think I don't know what you say about me?"

"I swear—" The man groaned painfully. "I swear, I have said nothing."

"You've been whispering to your friends. Telling little tales."

"No!"

Damian might have found the whole thing laughable, but Scarlett gripped his hand so hard her nails dug into his skin. He cast her a sidelong glance, noted the panic in her eyes even in the faint light.

"Liar!" the woman called as some unseen and undoubtedly violent action tore another whimper from Steele's lips.

"Please, Damian," Scarlett whispered, pressing her forehead to his shoulder. "I cannot bear it. Please, make it stop."

It occurred to him that the setting reminded her of a painful memory. That despite the contrived scene, it drew parallels with her own tortured past.

Damian cupped her head and pressed a kiss to her hair. "Wait here," he mouthed when her troubled gaze met his. The harrowing sight tore at his heart.

She nodded, though it took a moment for her to release his hand.

Feeling the devil's fury in his chest—the need to punish any man with the surname Steele—he strode around the bedpost, ready to pummel the lord for taking pleasure from these repulsive games.

The sight that met him stopped him in his tracks.

Joshua Steele was not spread naked on the bed with his wrists shackled and his jutting erection pointing skyward. Oh, he was naked, but he was on his knees, huddled into a ball while the scantily clad woman at his side gripped a riding crop.

All anger dissipated. Perhaps because Damian saw a vision of Scarlett cowering in the lowly position, not her depraved stepson.

"I suggest you sit up, Steele," Damian said in a voice hard enough to make the devil pause. "Unless you want me to take that crop and teach you a lesson you will never forget."

The lord shot up from his foetal position, exposing the angry pink welts on his chest. He squinted in the dim light. Recognition dawned. "W-Wycliff?"

As if she'd been awaiting her cue, Heather sidled from the bed, taking the crop with her. She held out her hand and Damian dropped the key into her sweaty palm, then she slipped from the room as quietly as they had entered.

Steele grabbed the coverlet and yanked it across his lap to cover his modesty. "What the hell are you doing here?" His cheeks flamed crimson. "Y-you've come to the wrong room. Since when were you a patron?"

"I'm not here to see Heather." Wycliff ground his teeth. "We are here to speak to you about your sudden interest in Lord Rathbone. And to ask why your sister knows nothing about the son you fathered with your mistress in Ely Place."

It hadn't taken Trent long to discover the information.

The lord opened and closed his mouth, but no sounds tumbled out. It was as if an uncontrollable panic began in his toes and took a minute to reach his brain. His limbs started shaking. He rocked back and forth, his teeth chattering before a wealth of suppressed emotion burst from him like a geyser from the ground.

"Lord, please, no! You cannot tell Jemima."

"Tell Jemima what? That you sired a child out of wedlock?" Disdain for all men who failed their illegitimate offspring clung to every word. "You had better hope I find nothing untoward at that house. And you will double whatever you're paying your mistress for the upkeep of your son."

"Double?" The lord gulped. "I'm not even sure it is mine."

"It?" Damian clenched his fists. He was ready to pound Joshua Steele's face. One punch for this pathetic lord. A second punch meant for the damn Marquis of Blackbeck. That said, not once had the marquis denied Damian was his son. "I've a mind to thrash you, yet I fear you might enjoy taking a beating."

Scarlett came to stand beside him. A gentle hand on Damian's arm helped to relax the tense muscles, helped rid him of the need to punish the world for one man's mistake.

"Jemima deserves to know she has a nephew." Pity, not anger or disgust, flashed in Scarlett's eyes when she looked upon the sorry creature cowering on the bed. "It is about time you acted like a responsible gentleman and not a henpecked nincompoop."

Steele stared at Scarlett with round, red-rimmed eyes.

"What is this about?" Scarlett gestured to the marks on Steele's chest and frowned. "And do not say it is about pleasure, not to me."

How could anyone understand the need to experience pain,

least of all a woman who had suffered greatly at the hands of a monster?

"Tell me," she urged when he failed to reply. "Your father is dead. None of us need fear him anymore."

Joshua rubbed his eyes. "Neither of us stood and faced him. Neither of us held him to account for the terrible things he did."

Had the dead lord taken his temper out on his son, too?

"Trust me it would have served no purpose other than to bring more misery down upon us all." She raised her chin. "And so I ask again, when did you develop a need to punish yourself?"

"Can I at least put on my shirt?"

"No," Damian interjected. "You'll tell us what we want to know, and you will tell us now."

He could not lose sight of the fact that this man might be responsible for the shooting at Vauxhall. This man might have orchestrated the accidents in the park, hired someone to break into Scarlett's home to get rid of her for good.

"Tell me when, Joshua." Scarlett took a step closer to the bed. While she might have shown disgust, her countenance spoke of compassion. "Does it have something to do with your father? Something to do with me?"

A tense silence filled the room.

The heaviness in the air proved suffocating under the weight of the lord's burden.

"Do you know how many nights I lay awake listening to what he did to you?" Joshua practically gasped with relief upon speaking the words. "Do you know how many times I heard you crying and did nothing?"

"How could you not have heard?" Scarlett said softly.

Images bombarded Damian's mind. Horrific images of an angel dragged to the depths of hell, of her pale, weak body finding the strength to crawl out of the fiery pit. He felt her pain —the wrenching ache akin to someone slicing his gut and spilling his innards.

"This—" The lord prodded his chest. "This is retribution."

"No, Joshua, this is guilt."

Silence descended once again until Scarlett's voice broke the stillness. "Are you responsible for the attempts on my life?"

"No!" The lord shook his head. Desperate to reinforce his point, he added, "I want to save you, not kill you. I want to take back every dreadful thing my father did."

Was that the reason for his foolish attempt to seduce his own stepmother? Did his need to avenge her mean more than a fear of ridicule and prosecution?

"You cannot change what is done," she replied in the terse tone of the Scarlet Widow.

It occurred to Damian that in seeking to protect her from all scandalous rogues, Joshua Steele had a motive for wanting him dead, too.

Damian stepped up to the bed frame. "Did you sneak up on us at Vauxhall and fire a pocket pistol?"

The lord blinked and drew his brows together in confusion. "Someone tried to shoot you?" he said, concerned only for Scarlett.

"Not her, me!" Damian spat. "Someone shot me in the arm though we are attempting to discover who was the intended target."

"No, I swear you leave me shocked." The lord put his hand to his throat, clearly panicked at the thought. "I brought Jemima home at nine. You may question my staff. Lord Loxton saw us leave. In her grief, my sister seeks to blame someone for the lewd way our father met his end."

"So, Miss Steele is determined to cause trouble for the Scarlet Widow?" Damian asked.

"Jemima is incapable of doing anything more than spreading gossip." The lord glanced at the burgundy coverlet. "May I dress now?"

"No." Damian folded his arms across his chest. "Why the

sudden interest in Lord Rathbone? You've visited his house three times in two months when you've rarely exchanged pleasantries before."

Guilt affected people in many ways. The telltale signs of a man with something to hide always amounted to the same. An inability to maintain eye contact. A weakness in the voice that showed a lack of conviction.

Joshua Steele conveyed neither as he looked at them directly. "Rathbone approached me at White's. He offered his condolences and invited me to dine with them in Portland Place."

"Them? You refer to Lord Rathbone and his grandmother?"

Joshua nodded. "Lady Rathbone dined with us on all three occasions."

"Did you speak about me during your visits?" There was a light air of suspicion in Scarlett's voice. She always spoke highly of the Rathbones, and Damian prayed neither had played her for a gullible fool.

Joshua snorted. "I got the impression *you* were the only reason they extended the invitations. They paid scarce attention to my hopes and ambitions."

Did Lord Rathbone dribble into his soup at the mere mention of Scarlett's name?

Did Lady Rathbone's obsession with the notorious widow dominate every conversation?

Scarlett cleared her throat. "What did you discuss?" One could not mistake the ring of mistrust in her voice.

"They wanted to know how you met my father."

"Everyone knows I was working on stage when we married." She cast Damian a sidelong glance that conveyed a lifetime of regret.

"They were curious about how you came to work as an actress, whether your parents are alive." The lord avoided meeting Damian's penetrating stare. "If you want my opinion, Lord Rathbone has developed an affection for you. I am convinced he intends to offer marriage and is biding his time until you and Wycliff … er … part ways."

Part ways?

Anger flared.

Did people presume their affair amounted to nothing more than physical attraction? That once they had slaked their lust, both parties would look to pastures new? Could no one see the rope that bound them together? Could people not see they were two parts of the same puzzle?

Damian waited for Scarlett to correct the misconception, but she did not. Why would she when he had a reputation for never settling? Why would she presume to know a man's feelings after her experiences with Lord Steele?

"And what did you tell them?" Scarlett inquired. "What did you tell them regarding my parents?"

The lord shrugged. "The truth."

Scarlett's mocking snort told the story of her unconventional upbringing, of secrets and fake names. So how was it this fool had the answers?

"I told them your parents were dead," Steele continued. "That they must have left you destitute, else why would a woman of your gentle breeding take to the stage?"

While Scarlett fell silent, Damian contemplated the information.

Intuition told him Joshua Steele was too simple to arrange complex plots. Judging by the flaring pink welts on his skin, he would rather inflict pain on himself than on the woman who took pleasure in mocking his father's memory. Jemima Steele, on the other hand, openly despised the widow. But that seemed too obvious.

Currently, all the evidence pointed to another conspiracy.

Like Scarlett's first husband—bloody hell, Damian hated the thought of her marrying that devious blackguard—had Lord Rathbone staged the accidents to frighten Scarlett into marriage? Rathbone knew nothing about the oath Damian had sworn three years ago and perhaps presumed Scarlett might seek the aid of her dear friend Lady Rathbone.

Consumed with jealousy, had Lord Rathbone fired the shot at Vauxhall?

But why would a peer want to marry a notorious widow whose bloodline was lacking? A widow whose purse was not robust enough to support an aristocratic family for generations?

It made no sense.

Damian retrieved the lord's clothes from the chair and threw them onto the bed. "Might I suggest you seek other ways of dealing with your cowardice? This odd form of flagellation will only feed your obsession."

The lord dragged his hand down his face. "Is it too much to hope you will keep this matter private?"

"Your son needs a father, not a foolish fop." In all the ways it mattered to society, it was too late for the boy. Still, knowing a parent cared eased the burden of illegitimacy. "Do your duty by the boy, and I'll not breathe a word about what I've witnessed."

"Those terrible marks on your skin remind me of my own weaknesses." Scarlett's voice carried the pain of her experiences. "But I had little choice other than to stand there and take my punishment."

Had she never fled? Had she never thought to pack up her jewels and sail across the ocean? Start a new life? Having spent so long in educational institutions, was it the idea of having a home that she loved?

"If I discover you've revisited this place," Scarlett continued, "I shall make sure the world knows of your predilection for pain."

"And Jemima?" Panic flashed in the lord's eyes.

Scarlett hesitated. She pursed her lips before answering. "I shall say nothing to Jemima, but you will discover if she had anything to do with the attacks on my person. You will meet Mr Wycliff and offer proof that she played no part."

"Proof?" Steele's mouth fell open. "How am I to obtain proof?"

"I have no notion," she replied with the arrogance of the Scarlet Widow. "That is your problem to solve. It will give you something to occupy your mind while you battle these perverse cravings."

Without another word, she whirled around and strode towards the door.

Damian snatched the shirt off the bed and threw it at the lord. "I suggest you dress quickly before temptation strikes. When equipped with the required information, you may send word to Benedict Cavanagh in Jermyn Street." Damian would be damned before revealing the whereabouts of his current abode.

Scarlett was waiting at the top of the stairs when Damian left the bedchamber. She looked pensive, and for the first time in his life he feared what a woman might say.

"I think it's time I dined with Lady Rathbone." She did not look pleased at the prospect. "Something is clearly amiss. While the matron likes to gossip, I cannot fathom her need to pry into my past."

"Can you not?" Did this lady not know how attractive she was to men? "Rathbone wants you. Since that night at my father's ball it seemed evident to me."

"Then why sneak about? Why not come to me directly and convey his intentions?"

Damian shrugged. "Like most lords of the *ton*, perhaps his grandmother insists on choosing his bride. Perhaps his grandmother's need to spend time in your company is a way of discovering your worth."

Scarlett sighed. "I have an open invitation to dine at Portland Place and so shall send word to her tomorrow."

He didn't like the thought of her going alone. "Then I shall accompany you." The words left his mouth before logic intervened. Aristocratic women invited illegitimate sons to their beds but never their dining tables.

"You know she won't entertain you." Her irritation was aimed at the matron and not his foolish remark. "Indeed, I'm of a mind to tell her we are betrothed, to tell her that some ladies care nothing for titles."

Damian tried to muster a response, but his mind had raced from betrothal to wedding. He'd spent three years wishing he'd bedded her, but it was the fact he wanted her in other ways that proved disconcerting.

"If not titles and handsome lords, what do some ladies care for?" he said, desperate to know how he might satisfy all of her wants and desires. "What do ladies seek?"

A rogue with hatred in his heart?

A man who wore a mask?

An illegitimate son who, miraculously, had found the capacity to care about someone other than himself?

Mischief danced in her eyes. "To tell you would leave my heart dangerously exposed. There are only so many times one can deal with rejection."

He might have said that he liked her exposed. He might have said that he would treasure her heart, not break it, but they were startled by the key rattling in the door across the hall. Having promised the mistress of every manoeuvre they would respect the other patrons' privacy, Damian captured Scarlett's hand and escorted her down the stairs and out to the safety of his carriage.

Deep in conversation with Alcock—while huddled together on the box seat—Cutler failed to notice their approach. Damian called his coachman's name, and the man's face flushed for neglecting his duty.

"It's mighty cold tonight, sir."

"Indeed." Damian opened the carriage door and cast Scarlett a sinful grin. "The temperature has plummeted. A man might wonder how he shall ever keep warm."

He wanted her again.

He always wanted her.

"Have you blankets as well as surgical implements beneath the seats?" Scarlett's alluring smile and wanton eyes told him that, despite everything she had learnt tonight, she wanted him, too.

"I'm sure there are a few. In any event, with the blinds closed, things should soon heat up." He turned and addressed Cutler. "We'll take the long route home."

"Along the Strand and St James' Park?" Cutler clarified.

Damian nodded. "Twice around the park."

CHAPTER SEVENTEEN

D elighted at the prospect of dining with the Scarlet Widow, Lady Rathbone had insisted on sending her new carriage to collect Scarlett from her house in Bedford Street. Still feeling uneasy about her attending alone, Damian advised Alcock and Cutler to take his carriage and park close to the matron's house in Portland Place. Should Scarlett wish to make a sudden exit, there would be someone waiting to ferry her home.

Having missed their meeting with Flannery the night before, due to their unexpected appointment at the bagnio, the Irishman agreed to meet them this evening. Damian would explain Scarlett's absence while updating Flannery on the new developments.

While Flannery would no doubt miss the lady's company, Damian experienced a similar sense of loss as he washed and dressed in his bedchamber. Everything he touched carried her potent scent. The energy in the air lacked vibrancy. One look at the mussed bedsheets and passion for her stirred in his loins once again.

He had felt similarly deprived the day they parted ways at the lodging-house. Despite being consumed with gratitude—or that's how he'd chosen to label the emotion—he had walked away, and her memory had plagued his dreams. Now, having parted from her a few hours earlier, the clawing emptiness within mirrored the stark emptiness of the house.

Never had he welcomed the idea of being a husband and father. He was a damn rogue, unsuitable company for anyone aside from the dissolute. So why could he not shake the image of Scarlett swollen with his child? Why could he not shake the need to have her love him for more than the way he satisfied her in bed?

You bloody fool, Wycliff, he said to himself.

Let no one in—that was the rule.

Perhaps being hit with a lead ball had weakened more than his arm muscle.

Dressing quickly to banish these errant thoughts, he raced from the house and hailed a hackney to take him to The Silver Serpent.

He entered the premises by the front door, noted the concerned look on Flannery's face when a steward escorted Damian down to the basement office.

When Scarlett failed to enter the room, Flannery dismissed his employee with a flick of the wrist before honing his sharp gaze on Damian. "By God, you'd better have a good reason for coming alone, so you had. Tell me nothing's happened to Scarlett."

Damian dropped into the chair on the opposite side of the desk. "Had anything happened to her, I would be shackled in chains at Newgate having beaten every pompous lord to a pulp."

"Then where is she?"

"Dining with Lady Rathbone. One of society's matrons."

"Dining?" Flannery frowned. No doubt he knew Scarlett well enough to know she would not cancel an appointment simply to gorge on peacock and loin of veal. "Does it have something to do with your meeting at the brothel last night?"

After swearing the Irishman to secrecy, Damian relayed the tale of their visit to the bagnio, omitting details of the steamy carriage ride home. "It is apparent that Lord Rathbone wishes for more than friendship. Scarlett thought it best to put an end to the man's misery, and she detests their blatant efforts to pry."

"And you let her go there alone?" The wrinkles on Flannery's forehead rippled up to his bald pate. "I didn't take you for a feck-less fool, not at all."

"The dissolute do not get to dine with the aristocracy." The uneasiness in Damian's stomach turned to trepidation. "And surely you know the woman is stubborn."

Flannery dragged his hand down his face and sighed. "Stubborn and too proud by half."

They sat in silence for a moment, disquiet thrumming in the air.

"Did you discover anything about the attacks?" Damian said. Talking was the only way to dispel all anxious thoughts.

"I've got a friend, Maguire, who runs the dog fights at the Westminster Pit. He knows the Turner brothers who work out of The Compass Inn on Rosemary Lane. After exchanging a few vowels as payment, Turner told me a nabob hired a once Bow Street Runner turned enquiry agent who's as bent as a shepherd's crook."

"Hired the runner to frighten Scarlett?" Damian would have the name of this turncoat and put an end to the matter tonight.

"Hired the runner to get rid of her for good."

Damian jerked his head back. Panic choked his throat. "Then why the bloody hell did you not send word to me at Bruton Street?"

"Don't be galloping away with yourself." Flannery held up his hands in mock surrender. "Yer man dived into the Thames and never came out."

Damian wasn't sure whether to gasp or sigh. "While I am grateful the blackguard is dead, did you not think to discover the name of his employer before throwing him into the water?"

"Oh, I didn't throw yer man from the bridge, though my

fingers itched to send him hurling. The fool jumped." Flannery pursed his lips and shook his head. "If the lass had come to me sooner, I could have saved her weeks of heartache, so I could."

Yes, but Damian would still be wallowing in ignorance, wondering what had happened to his angel.

"Perhaps Scarlett's silence was a ploy to keep your neck from the hangman's noose."

Flannery threw his hands in the air. "I'm telling you, let the Lord strike me dead, yer man jumped. But we found his room in Bermondsey, found this letter." The Irishman reached into the top drawer, withdrew the folded paper and pushed it across the desk. "Serves as proof, so it does."

Damian peeled back the folds and examined the neat penmanship. The instructions were clear. The runner must make another attempt to snatch Scarlett from her bed. To take her to a warehouse on the riverbank in Shoreditch and dispose of her there. Five hundred pounds was the fee for accomplishing the task.

"I don't suppose you've had time to discover who owns this warehouse off Tooly Street?" Damian scanned the missive again, looking for evidence as to the identity of the sender. There was something distinctively feminine about the sweeping curls. "And in your efforts to follow Joshua Steele, did you not consider his sister the more likely suspect?"

Flannery rubbed his bald head. "A Mr Johnson leased the warehouse, paid in advance and left no address. And the lass is too free with her tongue to be a threat."

Everyone knew of Miss Steele's disdain for the widow. So much so, she would be the prime suspect in any murder case. But would that be her alibi? Was that part of the chit's plan?

Damian refolded the paper and pushed it back across the desk. "Might we speak openly about your friendship with Jack Jewell?" A niggling suspicion told him that the past held the clue to the mystery. "He must have trusted you a great deal."

Flannery's green eyes flashed with uncertainty.

"We want the same thing," Damian continued. "We want to bring an end to Scarlett's nightmare."

A resigned sigh breezed from the Irishman's lips. "Jack's sister was my— We were— Well, I was married, but my wife remained in Kilkenny."

"And Jack embraced you as a brother instead of beating you for disrespecting his sister?"

"Oh, it wasn't pretty. I can tell you that. But we settled our differences in the end. Scarlett was away in Canterbury, and Bernadette was Jack's only kin."

"Canterbury? One of the many seminaries hired to keep Scarlett far from home?" Damian's tone brimmed with contempt.

Flannery nodded. "Bernadette, she didn't agree with sending the poor lass away. But Jack wouldn't have her in London."

Damian's heart ached for the lonely girl shunned by her father. The marquis was not alone when it came to fathers who lacked compassion.

"Did Jack ever say why?"

"Oh, he loved Scarlett, so he did, called her a gift from heaven and made me swear to protect her until my dying day. But Jack didn't talk about anything other than money."

It made little sense.

Why would a man who loved his daughter send her away for the best part of ten years?

"Was money the reason Jack Jewell took his own life?"

Flannery sucked in a sharp breath. "Did Scarlett tell you that?" He didn't wait for an answer but leant across the table and in a low voice said, "I should have known something was amiss when he gave me a few trinkets for Scarlett and asked me to bring her to the Serpent should anything untoward happen. But a man like Jack Jewell doesn't put a pistol in his mouth and pull the trigger."

"Then you suspect foul play?"

Had a lord sought violent means to regain his vowels? It

seemed the most likely explanation. But hadn't Scarlett mentioned an attack in the alley led her to marry Lord Steele? What if the event had nothing to do with Steele and he simply happened to be in the right place at the right time?

"Let's say I doubt things happened as the coroner said." Flannery paused but then added, "But I beg you not to tell Scarlett."

An icy shiver raced across Damian's shoulders.

What if someone did shoot Jack Jewell?

But what motive would they have for killing his daughter?

Damian tapped his breast pockets looking for his flask but remembered leaving it at home. "And you gave Scarlett these trinkets?" Perhaps there was something valuable amongst the items, an heirloom lost in a game of hazard.

"She has them, just a bible, a shawl and her mother's ring."

They didn't sound like items that might induce a man to murder.

"And Jack gave you nothing else, nothing for safe keeping?" There had to be something else, something of value. The coroner's verdict meant all property was forfeit, confiscated by the Crown. The more Damian thought of it, the more he believed Scarlett's problems had to do with her father.

Flannery shook his head. "Nothing."

Silence descended.

"I mean he left a letter case after his last visit but didn't live long enough to reclaim it," Flannery continued. "There's nothing in it, nothing at all but dockets and receipts."

Hell's teeth!

Did the man not think it an important piece of information?

"Where is the case now? Do you still have it?"

Flannery shrugged. "Somewhere. Most likely the attic. Should you like to see it, Mr Wycliff?"

"I think that would be a good idea." Damian couldn't suppress the hint of sarcasm in his voice. "After all, it may hold the key to this damnable mystery."

While Flannery stomped from the room in search of the letter case, Damian's thoughts turned to Scarlett. Was Lady Rathbone fawning over the widow, trying to establish if she might make a suitable wife for her besotted grandson? Would Lord Rathbone's constant dribbling spoil his dinner?

He could imagine the pretentious babble.

Scarlett did not belong with them—she belonged with him.

Flannery returned some fifteen minutes later, carrying a black leather case under his arm. "This is the one, so it is." He shook the case and brushed off the dust. "I'm surprised the rats haven't nibbled the corners."

The portfolio looked like it had been abandoned in a loft for thirty years, not a little more than three. "And he said nothing to you about storing it for safekeeping?"

"Jack arrived with the case. When he left, it was under his chair."

Damian placed it on the desk, flicked the catch and withdrew the pile of musty papers. The dust made him sneeze. "There must be a hundred receipts here." He snatched the top one and scanned the faded words. "Lord Mulberry's vowel, though it says *repaid*."

Flannery dropped into the seat behind the desk, took a handful of receipts and examined the first one on the pile. "Another vowel repaid. And a bill from that place in Bath."

And so it went on.

More of the same—papers that meant nothing now.

Flannery's groans and grumbles mirrored Damian's frustration. The Irishman slapped another receipt on top of the discarded pile before frowning and snatching it back again. "Who did you say Scarlett was dining with tonight?"

Damian's head shot up. "Lady Rathbone. Why?"

"This one here bears the same name." Flannery handed Damian the note. "But it's an old receipt, twenty years or more."

The note bore a date, although the last two numerals were hard to decipher. It could be 1801 or 1807. Either way, Christopher Rathbone owed the sum of twenty thousand pounds, and Jack Jewell has signed off the debt as paid. On the reverse, Christopher Rathbone had written a declaration transferring guardianship of his cargo to Jack Jewell.

Cargo? Crates of silk, cotton or tea?

And guardianship, not ownership?

It seemed odd.

"What do you know of Christopher Rathbone?" Damian asked.

"Nothing at all. Twenty years ago, I lived in Kilkenny."

They continued reading the other receipts and dockets but found nothing of interest. Still, Damian's thoughts returned to Christopher Rathbone. He could hardly bombard the Rathbones with questions. However, there was one person in the *ton* who kept abreast of the gossip. Perhaps the marquis knew something about the character who had traded cargo for vowels. An exchange so important Jack Jewell had kept the receipt in a case until the day he died.

"As there is nothing else to be done here, I might pay my father a visit." The marquis would no doubt hide his shock, for Damian had only ever called on the man once. And that was to hurl vile abuse a mere week after his mother's death. "The marquis makes it his business to keep abreast of society's affairs."

Suspicion flared in Flannery's green eyes. "So you think this might have something to do with the attacks on Scarlett?"

Damian shrugged. "Who can say? But it is too much of a coincidence to ignore."

"Take the note with you. Speak to Scarlett. Jack may have mentioned this Rathbone fellow at some time." Flannery pushed out of the chair. "I'll send O'Donnell to watch Miss Steele. While the only man who proved a danger is dead, it pays to be cautious, so it does."

Damian bid Flannery farewell and was about to leave when the Irishman decided he had something else to say.

"Oh, Mr Wycliff."

"Yes?"

"A man who kisses a lady in the street might want to think about marriage."

❦

If the Marquis of Blackbeck was shocked, offended or delighted to have his only son escorted into his study, Damian could not tell. At no point during the thirty seconds of silence did a muscle move on the marquis' face.

"Some people believe books contain the devil's magic." The marquis leant back in the chair behind his desk and steepled his long, elegant fingers. The diamonds on his onyx ring glittered in the candlelight. "They speak of fictional stories, of course. Then again, all stories are subjective."

What was it about his obsession with stories? "As always you speak in riddles when a simple greeting would suffice."

"Life is abound with puzzling conundrums."

"Yes, like why you are still intent on fathering a child at your age." Damian dropped into the sofa flanking the fire. He would not sit opposite his father like a young pup awaiting instruction. "Is temperance not said to be the flower of old age?"

While the marquis appeared the epitome of self-control, clearly it was an illusion.

The marquis arched a neat brow. "I may have graced this world for fifty years, but I am as youthful and as virile as you."

"Has it not occurred to you that these empty liaisons only please on a superficial level?" Damian realised there was something hypocritical in his statement. A point reinforced when his father's eyes flashed with mockery.

"An insightful notion, though I am yet to see a sinner preaching to the masses on Sundays."

Damian deserved that. "I'll not deny I've led a less than moral life. Perhaps that's because the blood of a transgressor flows through my veins." He recalled a comment made by Joshua Steele regarding the child he'd fathered out of wedlock. "At any point, did you doubt I was your son?"

"Never."

Sharp and to the point, that one word conveyed many things. Confusing things. It spoke of respect and trust, something Damian never associated with the Marquis of Blackbeck.

The marquis rose gracefully from the chair and moved to the many decanters lining the side table. He did not ask if Damian cared for a drink but poured two glasses of port, regardless. "A rare vintage from Oporto," he said, offering Damian the dainty crystal flute. "Dated the year you were born. A fitting toast considering you've yet to bombard me with the usual string of obscenities."

The marquis dropped into the sofa opposite and raised his glass in salute. "To stubborn sons."

"To fathers who shirk responsibility," Damian countered, raising his glass.

The marquis smirked. "And to men who believe gossip without taking the time to discover the facts."

They drank in silence while Damian resisted the urge to ask his father what he meant.

"Now," the marquis began after savouring and swallowing a mouthful of expensive port. "I doubt you came to tell me you plan to become master of Parklands and take a wife."

"A wife?" Damian should scoff at the notion. But an image of Scarlett entered his mind, and the thought didn't seem as repulsive. "If I ever marry, it will be for love."

"Such sentiment is commendable, although one cannot always guarantee one's affections are returned."

Suspecting the conversation would turn to Damian's mother, he chose to ask the question plaguing his mind since leaving Mr Flannery. "What do you know of a gentleman by the name of

Christopher Rathbone? While I am aware of Lady Rathbone and the current heir, I presume he is a relation."

The marquis' inquisitive gaze drifted over Damian's face before straying to his injured arm. "Does this have something to do with the reason you stumbled like a drunken sot through Vauxhall? If you needed my assistance, you had only to ask."

Damian tried to gauge what his father knew of the shooting, but the lord gave nothing away. "I am assisting Lady Steele in a personal matter. As you're a man with an extensive knowledge of the *ton*, I merely wish to know if Christopher Rathbone is related to the Rathbones who reside in Portland Place."

"You enjoy the widow's company?"

"Immensely." There was little point lying, though Damian prayed his father kept any derogatory comments to himself.

"Christopher Rathbone was Lady Rathbone's youngest son. Uncle to the present Lord Rathbone. A reckless fool to most."

"Was? You mean the man is dead?"

The marquis inclined his head. "He left England some twenty years ago, when you were but a boy, and never returned. I'm told he died in abject poverty in a dingy apartment in Paris. Of course, Lady Rathbone tells a different story, as do most women overly concerned with appearances."

For once, Damian ignored the veiled swipe at his mother. "Different? How so?"

The weak yet knowing expression on the marquis' face spoke of a man well-versed in people's need to manipulate the truth. "To the *ton* reputation is everything. Consequently, the man was a tortured poet, gifted with words yet plagued by the tragic death of his wife and young child. In reality, Christopher Rathbone was a spoilt prig. Jealousy for his older brother led to crippling debts."

"Then he must have maintained control of a business. He used cargo from a shipment to repay one particular debt."

The marquis' eyes glinted with tepid amusement. "Undoubtedly another fictional story. The man was nowhere near as astute as you when it comes to business acumen."

There was a hint of pride in the marquis' tone that proved unsettling. Damian was unaware of his father's interest in his business dealings. During the minimal time spent in the lord's company, the only conversation amounted to verbal sparring.

"A true story in this case. I have written proof."

He would not produce the receipt for that would mean divulging details of Scarlett's unconventional background. And in truth, he did not trust the marquis not to use the information for his own end.

"Then I highly doubt he obtained the cargo by honest means."

Silence ensued while the marquis swirled the port in the glass and took another delicate sip.

"When you spoke of Christopher Rathbone's family, you mentioned a young child. So his wife did not die in childbirth?" Damian wasn't sure why the question seemed important. Equally, he was aware that he did not feel the same anger towards his father when playing the role of inquisitive enquiry agent.

Was that the reason for his improved mood?

Or was it that his heart sang with a different emotion and there was no room left for hatred?

"His wife died in the birthing bed. Rathbone took the child to Paris when she was but a year or two old, and she perished there a month later."

"She? Christopher Rathbone had a daughter?" Numerous thoughts bombarded Damian's mind. When it came to Scarlett, he was a man prone to fantasy, but his current conjecture stretched his imagination to the limit. "You're certain?"

"Your mother took great pity on the man. Had events taken a different turn, I imagine you might have been betrothed to the chit while she was still in the cradle." The marquis placed his glass on the side table and adjusted the cuffs on his coat. "This happened over twenty years ago. I cannot imagine why it should concern Lady Steele."

Damian fell silent.

A warning rang in his head like the clang of a death knell.

Might a human life have been traded as coldly and as dispassionately as a ship's cargo? Might a childless couple be tempted by an offer to raise a sweet babe? God, if his mother's cross still hung around his neck, he would take hold of it and pray his suspicions were wrong. Pray that another man had not discarded Scarlett so callously.

"Lady Steele enjoys Lady Rathbone's company," Damian said, wondering if the matron had planned it that way. "Though having heard rumours about Christopher Rathbone, I am inclined to believe not all is as it seems."

The marquis arched a brow. "Like most women, Lady Rathbone is a chameleon. She may present a sincere and amiable countenance, a beauty of heart and mind that speaks of benevolence, but beneath it all, her skin is an ugly mottled green."

Damian sighed. He wished his father would be more succinct. "You mean she should not be trusted."

"Lady Rathbone would sell her soul if she thought it might benefit her family. She is the sort who would smile and hand her companion a drink whilst driving a blade between the ribs."

CHAPTER EIGHTEEN

"I cannot tell you how relieved we were to receive word from you." Lady Rathbone waited for the liveried footman to pull out her chair before taking a seat and continuing. "We were told you left Vauxhall in somewhat of a hurry."

Scarlett glanced at the multitude of dishes gracing the mahogany table—meat, game, jellies and custards—a feast fit for twenty people, not a guest of one. Aware of Lord Rathbone's heated gaze upon her, she brushed her skirts and sat demurely in the seat.

Scarlett smiled. "Mr Wycliff is a rather impulsive gentleman." Impulsive and dangerously appealing. The mere mention of his name sent her heart pounding. "When it comes to entertainment, boredom sets in rather quickly."

How strange that she feared Wycliff would tire of her more than she feared those threatening her life.

"I understand your need to make a statement to the world, my dear." Lady Rathbone nodded when the footman came to fill her glass with claret. "But if you persist in keeping company with the likes of Mr Wycliff, no serious gentleman will entertain you. The man is a pariah. An outcast to his own kin."

The comment caught Scarlett off guard.

Never had the matron spoken so openly about her disdain for the illegitimate son of the Marquis of Blackbeck. Perhaps Wycliff was right? Perhaps the matron did intend for Scarlett to marry her grandson.

"As a widow of some notoriety, one who openly keeps company with scoundrels, am I not considered a pariah, too?"

"Circumstance has led you to behave as you do," Lord Rathbone interrupted. He seemed most ardent in his opinion. And while the gentleman's handsome countenance made him appealing, her heart did not ache for his touch. "Given another option, my lady, I am positive your choice of companion would be different."

Even if Scarlett had been born of nobility, she would still love Damian Wycliff.

The sudden thought stole her breath.

And while she wanted to bask in the warmth her love evoked, she couldn't help but feel apprehensive about the future.

"No, my lord, I do believe I would be friends with Mr Wycliff, regardless."

Lord Rathbone's hand trembled, and he spilt his soup. He glanced at his grandmother as if dreading her reaction. How odd. Scarlett presumed the matron pandered to the lord. That's the impression she gave.

Lady Rathbone's discreet shake of the head roused a frustrated sigh from her grandson.

The lord shook off his irritation quickly. "Might I say you look splendid this evening, Lady Steele?"

Scarlett dabbed her mouth with her napkin. "Thank you, my lord. As you know, scarlet is a particular favourite of mine."

She had deliberately worn red. Something told her she needed the strength of her shield-maidens tonight. Both people seated at the table hid behind shields, too. The question was whose defensive wall would crumble first?

"Jemima has been stirring the hornet's nest again," Lady Rathbone said once they had finished the first course. "She told Captain Compton-Burnett's daughter that you were working the streets around Covent Garden when Lord Steele came to your rescue."

While Scarlett cared little for gossip, Jemima was a nuisance. If Joshua wished her to keep his secret, he had better do something to silence his sister.

"As I told the gel," Lady Rathbone continued whilst a footman dressed her plate with delicacies, "your father was the youngest son of a country squire, and you fell upon hard times after his death."

To hide the secret of her parentage, Scarlett may have been evasive, but she had never lied. If the matron chose to invent stories for appearance's sake, perhaps it was time to enlighten the lady.

"At no point did I tell you my father was the son of a country squire."

"I'm certain you did." Lady Rathbone glanced at her grandson who froze with his fork midair. "If not the son of a country squire who was he?"

Scarlett straightened—her steel backbone being the only thing she had gained from her miserable marriage. "Did Joshua not tell you when he dined with you last month? My parents are dead. My mother—"

"There is no need to explain," Lord Rathbone interjected. The fellow's Adam's apple bobbed unnaturally, and his growing agitation left him red-faced. "Such things should have no bearing on one's future prospects."

"No bearing?" Lady Rathbone's sharp reply proved out of character. "Place is determined by one's wealth and birthright."

It was then that good manners abandoned Lord Rathbone. He snatched his napkin from his lap and used it to mop the sheen of sweat on his brow. "Can we not simply finish our meal and discuss the weather?"

"You know we cannot." The matron expressed a surprising coldness of manner.

The woman's snobbery came as somewhat of a shock to Scarlett. Why keep company with a notorious widow who once graced the stage when lineage meant everything?

"Perhaps it's time we all dropped the pretence," Scarlett said for she suspected she was more a gullible fool than a Viking warrior. "You'd not find a woman kinder than my mother. But as someone recently pointed out, the good ones are so often taken early."

Lady Rathbone sat rigidly in the chair, every muscle tense.

Lord Rathbone sat with his head bowed, like a man consumed with grief having been forced to take a pistol to his beloved horse.

"And as for my father," Scarlett continued, resolved that they would hear the truth, "his name was Jack Jewell. He owned a gaming hell catering to dissolute lords, lords who would sell their children for a chance to play another hand of piquet."

Lady Rathbone jerked back in horror.

Lord Rathbone blanched and shuddered in fear.

"Jack Jewell!" The matron screwed up her aristocratic nose as if the footman had dropped his satin breeches and fouled the white linen. "That name has been the bane of my existence for nigh on four years." Her jaw firmed, hiding the soft jowls. She glared at her grandson. "I told you she knew and is playing us for fools. Did I not tell you she plans to lure us into a trap? Extort every last penny?"

Lord Rathbone appeared inconsolable. He lacked the energy to do anything other than shake his head.

"Percival!" Lady Rathbone snapped. With an irate wave, she dismissed the servants. "Pull yourself together."

Scarlett watched this odd exchange—talk of traps and extortion—feeling she had missed a vital piece of information. How was it a matron of Lady Rathbone's standing knew Jack Jewell so well?

"Percival." The woman's mouth thinned with disappointment. "Your father would have dealt with the matter promptly. He would not have waited for four years."

"Can we not simply swear the lady to secrecy?" the lord pleaded.

"Secrecy? I'll not wager everything our ancestors worked for on the hope of trusting a woman who's lain with Blackbeck's mongrel."

With a look that said his world was about to come crashing down around him, Lord Rathbone glanced at Scarlett and said, "What is it you want from us? Tell me my grandmother is wrong and that you possess the integrity of my father, not yours."

Scarlett blinked in bewilderment.

How dare anyone suggest Jack Jewell was unprincipled? Yes, he may have lacked the capacity to love her, but he was her father, and no doubt he had tried.

"I must call you to task on your error, my lord. My father was respected amongst his peers. Commitment and loyalty flowed like blood in his veins."

"Loyalty?" Lady Rathbone snorted. Her eyes turned dark with barely contained fury. How was it Scarlett had not seen beyond the matron's mask before? "Your *father* was a cheating, conniving ne'er-do-well who sought to bring this family to its knees."

Scarlett knew little to nothing of the Rathbones' family history. Had Lord Rathbone's father or grandfather lost money at The Jewell? Was that behind their contempt? Then another thought struck her. One that had plagued her mind for years. Had Jack Jewell done something monstrous, something that gave him a reason to take his own life?

"My father owned the gaming hell. You cannot blame him for other men's weaknesses." Every fibre of her being told her to push out of the chair and leave. But the stubborn streak she'd developed in her marriage urged her to stay, to get to the real reason behind Lady Rathbone's fake facade.

"We are not talking about the man who raised you," Lord Rathbone said in a voice weak with nerves.

"No!" Lady Rathbone said. "We are talking about the father who confessed to his sin on his deathbed. The fool who was too blind to see that one silly transaction would see the Rathbone name ruined."

Scarlett's head ached. Her temples throbbed.

They were speaking different languages.

She stared at the untouched food on her plate and tried to make sense of the conversation.

Lady Rathbone continued mumbling as if involved in a secret argument with an invisible opponent. The candlelight cast sinister shadows on her face. Who was this strange woman? Scarlett hardly knew.

Lord Rathbone cleared his throat. "Had my father known you were sold like common goods to Jack Jewell, he would have found you and brought you home." Pity flashed in his eyes. "By birth we are cousins, but my father would have approved a marriage. You must understand we thought you were dead."

"Dead?" The word tumbled from her lips as she sat there, trance-like, lost in a thick cloud of confusion.

"This can all be solved if you agree to marry me." The lord's mouth curled into a weak smile. "We could be happy. We will move from town to my estate in Herefordshire and—"

"No! It is too late for sentimental nonsense." Lady Rathbone surged from her seat. "You cannot take a mongrel's mistress to your bed. She might be with child. I'll not have Wycliff's whoreson raised as a Rathbone."

They began arguing amongst themselves.

But one thought rang loudly in Scarlett's ears.

Jack Jewell was not her father.

Disbelief rendered her speechless. These people were

mistaken. And yet in her heart she had always known something was amiss. Did that mean the sweet woman who raised her until the age of ten was not her mother, either?

Of course it did.

The sudden lump in her throat made it almost impossible to breathe. Tears sprang to her eyes—hot, burning evidence of her pain. Salty rivulets trickled down her face. The loss left an unbearable hole in her chest.

"Are you saying that m-my father was a Rathbone?" How she found the strength to form the words, she would never know.

"A Rathbone and my uncle," Lord Rathbone clarified.

"I see."

She did not want to see.

The man who struggled to love her had paid for the best education. Jack Jewell had seen to it that she had something to call her own, even if it was ownership of a gaming hell. But what of the man whose blood flowed in her veins? He had discarded her as if she were a stone in his shoe.

Did no one want her?

Was she a burden to everyone she met?

A wracking sob caught in her throat and she knew she must leave. She pushed out of the chair, her mind disconnected to everyone and everything. The matron and grandson continued to disagree, but their raised voices sounded muffled now.

"I must go." With an unsteady gait, she navigated the dining table. Through the chaotic haze, she focused on the door.

But Lady Rathbone grabbed Scarlett's sleeve and tugged hard. "You're not going anywhere, dear. You're the only person alive who knows the truth."

The action took Scarlett by surprise. When the matron yanked harder, Scarlett lost her footing. Arms flailing, she tumbled back. The thud as she hit her head on the corner of the table reverberated through her body. A scream burst from her throat and then her world faded into darkness.

CHAPTER NINETEEN

Damian heard Scarlett's scream as he stood at Lady Rathbone's door, about to storm past the snooty butler when he refused to grant him entrance. His blood ran cold. Flannery was right. Why the bloody hell had he let Scarlett come alone?

"Had I been born a gentleman, I might have said excuse me." Damian pushed the butler aside, knocking him back into the console table. "But I'm a bastard by name and nature."

The butler straightened his periwig. "Stop, else I shall send for the night constable." He dashed towards Damian and grabbed the sleeve of his coat.

Damian growled, and the terrified servant let go.

"Send for the damn constable," Damian shouted as he raced along the hall as if the devil were at his heels. "Though I suspect it will be your mistress carted off to a cell."

As Damian burst into the dining room, it took him a moment to absorb the shocking scene.

Fear rendered him frozen.

Scarlett lay sprawled on the Persian rug, pale and lifeless. Her eyes were closed, as if she had already taken her last breath, already said goodbye to the world. Blood? Thankfully, no sign of blood. Lady Rathbone loomed over the body, her mouth twisted in a wry grin. Lord Rathbone sobbed as he knelt at Scarlett's side, his frantic hands patting her arms and chest.

The burning need to murder the one responsible saw Damian charge at the lord, grab him by the scruff of his coat and drag him backwards. "That is not how you check for a pulse."

Damian dropped to his knees and captured Scarlett's wrist. Trembling fingers made it impossible to feel the beat of life. He silently cursed and tried again. Coldness seeped into his bones. A cavernous emptiness consumed him to the point he struggled to breathe, too.

"T-try the base of her throat," Lord Rathbone said in a grave tone as he came to his feet. "Sometimes the p-pulse is stronger there."

Damian tugged at the high collar of Scarlett's dress and pressed the pads of his fingers to the delicate skin on her neck. The weak yet rhythmical pulsing of her heartbeat tore a relieved gasp from his lips. He stared at her chest, trying to focus on the light rise and fall that confirmed she was alive and breathing.

The thought that the only person he treasured might have been taken from him, too, made him lean forward and touch his forehead to hers. A terror like nothing he had experienced before clawed at his mind, concocting horror stories of her waking with impaired memories, with a mind that no longer recalled all they had shared.

Anger surfaced then.

The devil's fury made him jump to his feet and turn on Lord Rathbone. "What the hell did you do to her? Did she spurn your advances? Did she tell you her affections lay elsewhere?"

The lord gaped and raised his hands in surrender. He was about to speak when Lady Rathbone said sharply, "She choked on a fishbone and fainted. Now, get out of my house and let me send for a doctor." The matron glanced over Wycliff's shoulder to the door. "Osmond! Osmond! Throw this miscreant out."

"A choking woman cannot scream."

"Not that I need answer to you, but Lady Steele screamed when Percival thumped her on the back. And it's a good job he did, for the bone might still be lodged in her throat." She sucked in a breath. "Now, remove yourself at once. Osmond! Oh, where is the fool?"

Damian squared his shoulders. "Fear not, I am leaving and taking Lady Steele with me. Then I shall return to discuss the matter of how Christopher Rathbone repaid his debt to Jack Jewell."

The blood drained from the matron's face. Guilt lay in every line and crease. Her arrogance faltered for a few seconds as her eyes flicked nervously back and forth in their sockets.

"My son died four years ago, having spent more than a decade abroad." Lady Rathbone composed herself and stared down her patrician nose. "How might he have run up debts in London when he lived in Paris?"

Few aristocratic ladies knew the name Jack Jewell let alone that he ran a gaming hell in London. "You seem remarkably informed. And Christopher Rathbone's debt to Jack Jewell was repaid before he left for the Continent."

"That was twenty-two years ago! Gossip is twisted to ridiculous lengths over the course of an hour let alone decades. Though I'm surprised a man of your inferior breeding would take notice of tales."

Possessed of a desperate urge to take Scarlett to a doctor, Damian knelt down and scooped her up into his arms. "Tales? I am a man who deals in truths, not petty lies."

"That is hard to believe knowing both your parents," Lady Rathbone countered.

Her reply gnawed at his insides. And yet his father had never lied about his involvement with Maria Alvarez. "You are hardly one to claim the crown for bearing respectable offspring. And your point is moot. I hold proof of the transaction, a transaction that bears your son's signature."

Damian wasn't entirely sure what the term *cargo* meant. Fear had led him to bang on Lady Rathbone's door and demand to speak to Lady Steele. Instinct told him that the woman in his arms was the only thing of value Christopher Rathbone had to sell.

"Selling a person for money is immoral," Damian continued, hoping to draw the truth from the matron. "Selling one's daughter to pay a gambling debt is downright despicable. What would your friends say, Lady Rathbone, if they discovered your son had lied about his daughter's death? The scandal would ruin your good name, tarnish your pristine reputation."

"Be quiet, mongrel!"

"Indeed, one might go to great lengths to keep such a secret."

Lady Rathbone harrumphed. "Leave now, or I shall have you removed. Osmond!"

Damian was about to say he loved a good fight, but Alcock came bursting into the dining room followed by the harassed butler clutching his bloody nose. One look at her mistress lying helpless in Damian's arms and the woman bared her chipped teeth and growled like a ravenous hound.

"I thought I instructed you to wait with Cutler."

"Beggin' your pardon, sir, but you ain't my master."

Damian suppressed a frustrated sigh. The woman was a law unto herself. "Your mistress is alive, Alcock, but if you want to help her, punch Lady Rathbone if she attempts to leave this room."

Alcock stepped in front of the door, her bulky frame making it impossible for anyone to push past. "Right you are, sir. I've no qualms in hitting her ladyship."

A whimper escaped the matron's lips, but she gathered herself and stamped her foot. "You cannot tell me what to do in my own house."

"Have no fear, my lady," Osmond cried from the safety of the corridor. "I have sent for the night constable."

"You fool, there is no need for the constable." For the second time this evening, fear flashed in the matron's eyes. "This is nothing more than a misunderstanding."

"There's every need for a constable." Now he had come this far, Damian would have the truth from this deceiver's lips. "Perhaps he would like to hear how you've spent years secretly hounding Lady Steele. I also have the note you sent to the runner offering a reward once he'd dispensed with her in a warehouse in Shoreditch. An expert will surely verify the handwriting." Or more than likely not. "And the runner's confession will give the magistrate much to contemplate." He omitted the part about the runner's dive to the bottom of the Thames.

Lady Rathbone gulped.

A tense silence ensued while everyone awaited her response.

A faint murmur from Scarlett's lips broke the stillness. Her eyes flickered open, and she looked at him. "D-Damian?"

Regardless of the onlookers, he kissed her forehead and whispered, "Rest, love. This will be all over in a minute. Alcock will take you to my carriage, and we will seek the advice of a doctor."

"Sh-she wants me d-dead." Scarlett raised a limp hand though lacked the strength to point at Lady Rathbone.

"This is all conjecture." The matron gave a weak chuckle. "She simply fell when I reached for her arm and then she hit her head on the table. Ask Percival. He will tell you."

"Was that before or after choking on a fishbone?" Damian said. "You were missing from your booth the night I was shot at Vauxhall. Perhaps you pulled a pistol from your muff intending to kill Lady Steele."

"Preposterous poppycock!" The matron's cheeks ballooned.

Lord Rathbone, who had remained subdued throughout the exchange, was instantly overcome with a surge of anger. "You do possess a pocket pistol. You told me you carried it in your reticule for fear of footpads at Vauxhall."

"Be quiet, Percival! Half the ladies in London carry one when visiting the pleasure gardens." The matron shuffled backwards, her gaze constantly shifting to the door. "Possessing such a weapon is not proof of guilt but merely common sense."

With his injured arm aching from holding Scarlett for so long, Damian turned to Alcock. "Take your mistress to the carriage. I shall join you the moment the constable arrives."

"The constable?" Lady Rathbone scoffed. "He will believe a respected member of the *ton* over a good-for-nothing bachelor's son. Now stand aside. I refuse to listen to these ridiculous tales a moment longer."

"What a shame, as this good-for-nothing bachelor's son won't rest until every member of the nobility knows of your depravity. Indeed, the Marquis of Blackbeck seemed most interested in hearing my theory when he confirmed you were mother to Christopher Rathbone. Imagine his shock when I tell him the truth about why I asked."

Silence.

The deafening sound filled the room. The striking absence of noise threatened like an invisible spectre.

For a moment Lady Rathbone appeared defeated. Years of using devious methods to hide the truth had come to naught. But then the matron's loud gasp tore through the room. Her eyes turned dangerously wild, yet there was a distance there as if she had finally sunk to the dark depths of her depravity.

"You can't tell the marquis!" The matron's high-pitched screech caught them all by surprise. Her body shook with barely contained rage. "You will tell no one, do you hear?"

Damian shook his head. "It is too late for negotiations."

The matron had made the mistake of not approaching her granddaughter years ago. Scarlett had a good, kind heart, and would have embraced the Rathbones had they acted honourably.

"It is never too late." Lady Rathbone cast a menacing grin. "Pariah! I'll not be beaten by a filthy mongrel."

In a sudden and violent attack, the matron raced to the table, grabbed the carving knife from the silver platter and lunged at Damian.

With a need to protect the woman in his arms, Damian swung around and braced himself for a slash across the back.

Alcock charged forward, but Lady Rathbone stabbed at the coachwoman like a possessed banshee. Alcock ducked the first swipe, but in the tight space struggled to maintain a defensive position.

Hell. Damian felt helpless to act.

A scuffle broke out.

Lord Rathbone joined the affray.

Confusion descended.

He protected his grandmother from Alcock's punch but then tried hard to wrestle the knife from the woman's grasp.

"Leave this to me!" Lord Rathbone cried, but Lady Rathbone cared nothing for her own kin. A swipe to the handsome lord's cheek left a trail of blood. "Good God, have you lost your mind?" He clutched his face, seemed somewhat disorientated.

"I have the constable, my—" Osmond almost fainted in shock upon witnessing his mistress wielding the blade like a crazed lunatic.

The constable's mouth dropped open. "Throw the knife to the floor, my lady." He hovered on the threshold, reluctant to enter.

Deranged and consumed with madness, the matron ignored the constable's repeated plea.

"There's no option left but to disarm her, Alcock," Damian said. "Imagine you're back in the fighting pits in Whitechapel."

Alcock nodded. She firmed her jaw and snarled, shuffled her feet, ducking and dodging each slash and slice. One timely hit to the stomach saw the matron fall forward. Alcock grabbed Lady Rathbone's wrist and twisted until the woman yelped in pain.

The knife fell to the floor.

Everyone breathed a sigh of relief.

But the chaos did not end there.

The constable spent the next ten minutes calming the matron, although she tried to lunge from the chair numerous times when Damian revealed the facts of the story.

Bedlam ensued when Lord Rathbone summoned his carriage to escort his grandmother and the constable to the magistrate. Reluctantly, the lord agreed that for everyone's safety, the matron should wear shackles.

Damian would have to wait until morning to explain his version of events to the magistrate. Scarlett was his priority, and he would send for Dr Redman to come to Bruton Street and inspect the patient posthaste.

"Lucky you let me ride atop your coach, sir, else that madwoman might have carved you up like a hock of beef," Alcock said, opening the carriage door and helping Damian to settle Scarlett onto the seat. "Instead of pickin' your teeth out the gutter, you might have been pickin' your fingers."

For the first time tonight, Damian forced a weak smile. "Indeed, a man might overlook your stubborn insolence when you're so skilled with your fists."

"Seems you and Lady Steele are of a similar mind." Alcock gave a curt nod. Once Damian had settled into the seat, she closed the door and climbed atop the box.

When the carriage jerked forward, Damian drew Scarlett onto his lap and cradled her head on his shoulder. "You're safe now, love," he said in a soft, gentle voice that had no place in a rogue's repartee.

Scarlett's eyes flickered open. "Safe," she repeated, raising a limp hand to cup his cheek. "I—I always feel safe with you."

CHAPTER TWENTY

I t was as if someone had taken an axe to Scarlett's head and tried to cleave it in two. The thud drew every muscle in her body taut. Her brows furrowed in pain. The pounding in her temple sent sharp shocks down to her jaw. Having squeezed her eyes shut to ease the blinding ache, it took effort to prise them apart.

Daylight danced around the gaps in the drawn curtains. The hustle and bustle of city life echoed beyond the room—the clop of horses' hooves, the rattle of carts, the energetic thrum of life.

Thank the Lord she was alive, still breathing.

There had been a moment in Lady Rathbone's dining room when she feared she would never see the light of day again. How had the matron duped her so easily? When had the weak, docile woman turned into a crazed criminal?

Scarlett knew the answer.

For four years, Lady Rathbone had known her son's secret. Ever since Lord Steele's death, she had been a kind and supportive friend. But behind the screen of sincerity, the matron had despised Scarlett to the core of her being.

Jack Jewell was not her father.

The sudden thought brought a different pain.

It was the opposite of emptiness. Losing her parents hung like a heavy, heavy weight in her heart. She would never get the opportunity to ask questions, never be able to wrap her arms around them and thank them for taking care of her when her real father shirked his responsibilities.

Heavens, and to think she was related to Lady Rathbone.

Disbelief, along with a hundred unanswerable questions pounded in her head, too.

"Dr Redman advises complete rest for the next few days." The rich, masculine voice drifted across the room. "He said you may experience slight memory loss. May have a megrim for a week or more."

Scarlett's gaze followed the voice to the corner of the room, to where she had sat while waiting for Wycliff to recover from his gunshot wound. Her heart lurched at the sight of the handsome gentleman sitting in the chair. He wore the same dark blue coat as he did the day she met him in the tavern. The coat clung to the bulging muscles in his arms, complemented the Mediterranean look of his dark hair and sultry eyes. He'd teamed it with a black cravat and breeches, the material of which clung to his powerful thighs.

"If there is one thing Blake can teach us about life, it is its fragility." Wycliff gestured to the book in his hand. "That said, I experienced it firsthand last night."

"I can scarce remember much after the fall." Whenever she had found the strength to open her eyes, she was in his arms.

"Please tell me you remember everything until the point you hit your head on the table." His tone conveyed a sense of trepidation. "Tell me everything in this room is familiar to you."

Did he fear she wouldn't remember him?

Did he think she would forget those glorious times when he entered her body and made her whole again?

"Of course I remember." She remembered she loved him.

Loved him more than she had dared admit to herself. "And this room holds many fond memories." Beautiful memories.

His smile deepened.

"Was it you or Dr Redman who stripped off my clothes and left me in a chemise?"

"Do you honestly think I would let another man put his hands on you?"

The warm feeling returned to her chest. Despite her pounding head, she wanted this man to take her in his arms and make all her troubles fade away.

"Dr Redman left a tincture for the megrim on the night table," Wycliff continued, "and laudanum should you have trouble sleeping."

Scarlett glanced at the medicine on the table, but her gaze fell to the pretty vinaigrette bottle with a painted scene of a gentleman pushing a lady on a garden swing.

"And the vinaigrette?"

"Contains an aromatic vinegar made by my housekeeper. The bottle belonged to my mother. She kept it at her bedside, and I would often stare at the painted figures and invent stories. It belongs to you now."

"To me?"

"A gift."

"You seem to make a habit of giving me gifts that represent treasured memories." She would never forget the day he gave her his mother's precious cross.

He fell silent though she could feel the contained emotion bursting to break free.

"Is there a reason you're sitting so far away?" She wanted him to sit next to her, to touch her hand, stroke her brow, kiss her in the way that spoke of something more profound than lust.

"The doctor assured me you need rest. As a man with a raging appetite for you, I thought it best to keep my distance."

"After the terrible things I learnt last night—"

"Two nights ago. You slept the whole day yesterday."

The whole day?

And still her head throbbed.

"After the terrible things I learnt, perhaps I want to feel close to you."

"What we want and what is advisable are two different things. I'll not risk losing you just to satisfy a desire."

Her light laugh triggered the thumping ache, but she was determined in her course. "I am asking you to sit on the bed, not rip off my chemise with your teeth."

"Must you rouse lascivious images in my head?" Wycliff placed the book on the table and came to sit beside her on the bed.

She considered his impeccable attire. "Are you going out?"

He inclined his head. "I intend to call on the marquis. Twenty-six years' worth of questions insist on having a voice."

They were similar in that regard, although she had twenty-three years' worth of questions that would forever remain unanswered.

"It's not too late for you. The only person who can shed light on your father's relationship with your mother still lives. Go to the marquis. Demand the truth." She hoped it might ease his pain, hoped they both learnt to accept they were powerless to change the past.

Wycliff captured her hand and stroked it tenderly. "I met Lord Rathbone at a coffeehouse this morning. It might relieve you—it might sadden you—to know that Lady Rathbone took an over-dose of laudanum last night, coupled with a quart of brandy."

"An overdose? Is she alive?"

Wycliff pursed his lips and shook his head. He explained about the receipts found in the letter case, about the villain Lady Rathbone hired, about the matron taking a pistol to Vauxhall.

"The magistrate who presided over the meeting concluded that there was insufficient evidence to prosecute. No one can attest to the true meaning of the word *cargo*. The mumbled words of a dying man on his deathbed are often inadmissible. And I could hardly mention that the man guilty of the crimes against you is at the bottom of the Thames."

"So you couldn't produce the letter offering payment in exchange for my life?"

"Not without implicating Flannery. Besides, the letter bears no name, signature or seal. No one can verify the identity of the sender. And the magistrate will not commit a member of the aristocracy to trial without substantial evidence."

With her mental faculties weaker than usual, Scarlett found it hard to absorb the information. "Did the constable not witness her wielding a blade?"

"The magistrate suggested time in an institution, one capable of treating female hysteria."

"It beggars belief that she may have been free to wreak havoc again." Scarlett shuddered at the thought. "Had a maid behaved so abominably, she would have swung by the neck from the gallows."

"Lord Rathbone believes that the scandal, the stain on her name, is the reason she downed two bottles of laudanum."

Perhaps some people might clap their hands in joy or relief upon hearing the news. But how could she be happy knowing someone's life meant less to them than their reputation?

"I doubt the coroner will rule suicide," she said, "not for someone of Lady Rathbone's standing." The same rules that applied to Jack Jewell did not apply to the aristocracy.

"The coroner concluded the matter rather quickly. As expected, he cited an unstable mind. The most important thing for the Crown is that a peer receives his inheritance."

Oh, the hypocrisy of society left a bitter taste in her mouth.

"Lord Rathbone assures me he knew nothing of the plot against you. Since the death of Lord Steele, he has tried to persuade his grandmother that his marriage to you would prevent you from revealing the truth."

A shiver ran the length of Scarlett's spine as it occurred to her that Lady Rathbone was her grandmother, too. Still, after everything she had learnt, doubt flared.

"Are you certain this isn't all a terrible mistake?" She would rather have the father who never visited than the one who gave her away.

Wycliff's mouth twisted into a grim line. "Lord Rathbone travelled to Paris and bore witness to the confession. He explained how they used the information to find you." Wycliff exhaled a weary sigh. "It would serve Rathbone better if it were a lie, which is why I believe it's the truth."

A pulsing pain in her temple saw her press her fingers there and massage the tender spot. Wycliff shifted, and she feared he would insist on leaving the room to let her rest.

"So how did Lady Rathbone find me?" she said, hoping conversation would keep him at her bedside.

Wycliff pushed his hand through his mop of dark hair. "Lord Rathbone said his grandmother visited Jack Jewell and demanded to know the truth. He refused to reveal the information and so she hired an enquiry agent to investigate."

"When was this?"

"Almost four years ago. A month before your father's death."

A chilling thought settled in her mind. "The coroner recorded my father's death as suicide. Perhaps someone else pulled the trigger."

"Or perhaps your father believed you were safer if he was dead. He knew Mr Flannery would take care of you. The Irishman knows enough criminals in the rookeries to ensure no one would dare hurt you." Wycliff shrugged. "Either way, you will never know for sure."

Scarlett didn't want to think that someone had murdered her father so callously. She would rather think that he made the ultimate sacrifice to protect his daughter. Tears sprang to her eyes.

She had sat at the window week after week and cursed him for not loving her.

"The enquiry agent kept a watch on your father's premises," Wycliff continued. "At some point after leaving the seminary you went home."

It had always been her intention to plead with her father, to drop to her knees and beg him to let her remain at The Jewell. "When I got there, the doors and windows were boarded. A neighbour told me what had happened and took me in for the night. I didn't know what else to do as my father had never mentioned Mr Flannery. His neighbour's daughter was an actress and found me work on the stage, a room to rent in Covent Garden."

"And you remained there until you married Steele." His tone turned frosty.

It was time she made him see her reasoning, the foolish thoughts that seemed so logical at the time, the error of her judgement.

"Marrying Steele seemed like the simple solution. I knew it was only a matter of time before some drunken buck followed me home and forced his advances." Wycliff didn't know what it was like to have men grope you when all you wanted was to earn an honest living. "Letters arrived, threatening letters—"

"You should have come to me."

"Yes, I should have, but you were not offering marriage, security, a way out from the pit of despair." He might have offered her another role, one equally precarious. "The night Steele saved me from the attack in the alley, I would have done anything for a moment's peace."

Silence descended.

It was as if those memories came alive. The air thrummed with the same tension.

"Things happened that way for a reason," Wycliff eventually said in a melancholic tone.

She liked to think that, too.

"In some twisted way, perhaps marrying Steele saved your life," he added.

"Saved me? How?"

"When you married Steele, the matron believed it was only a matter of time before you met your end, and so she called off her dog. Apparently, some older members of the *ton* were aware of Steele's predilection for violence. There were whispers concerning the death of his first wife."

How the previous Lady Steele had survived her marriage for fifteen years was anyone's guess. "Lady Rathbone rarely spoke to me during my marriage, yet extended the hand of friendship the moment I donned my widow's weeds."

"Lord Rathbone is happy to recognise you publicly as his kin. Equally, he understands if you would rather refrain from associating yourself with the family."

She didn't want to be a Rathbone.

She wanted to be Scarlett Jewell—Ruby as her mother often called her.

Scarlett forced a weak chuckle. "Then Lord Rathbone has given up all thoughts of marrying the Scarlet Widow?"

"I imagine his offer stands, though he wouldn't dare say so to me." He stared deeply into her eyes. "We have yet to determine the nature of our growing relationship."

The need to reveal everything in her heart burned brightly. But after a life filled with deception and betrayal, she had one final test. Besides, Wycliff needed to have an honest conversation with his father before his heart was free to commit. And his love and commitment were the only things she wanted now.

"Slip out of your coat and lie with me for a while."

Wycliff moistened his lips. "I thought we agreed that would not be a good idea."

"I didn't say strip naked. But I would like for you to hold me as you did that night in the lodging-house." She wanted nothing more than to make love to him, but the man was as stubborn as a mule, and she had to say something to get him to join her in bed.

After some reflection, he stood and removed his coat.

As he draped the garment on the chair, she said, "Perhaps you ought not crease your breeches. You know the marquis hates those in shabby attire."

Wycliff glanced back over his shoulder, his eyes alight with mischief. "He's rather particular about rumpled shirts and cravats, too."

"Indeed, you wouldn't want him to throw you out. Not when you're eager to ask the questions you've held back for so long."

He turned to face her and set about undressing. "No, I wouldn't want that. And I'm sure Dr Redman would support my reasoning."

"Dr Redman is a logical man."

Scarlett watched him in silence as he stripped down to nothing but his breeches. She imagined those hard, rippling muscles soaked in sweat, those pert buttocks clenched as he thrust long and deep. The pulsing between her legs replaced the pulsing in her temple.

Judging by the length of his arousal springing free as he slipped out of his breeches, he was just as excited to join her in bed. He prowled towards her with a sleek, predatory grace.

Scarlett drew her chemise over her head and dropped it on the floor before peeling back the sheets in welcome invitation.

His body was warm, his skin carrying the earthy masculine smell that made her want to lick every inch. They settled onto their sides, huddled together in the tender way that spoke to her soul.

"While I recall being hard for you that night, I do not recall being quite so solid." He brushed her hair off her forehead, brushed his erection against her abdomen.

"And while I recall placing my hands on your chest, I do not recall draping my thigh so brazenly over your hip."

He clutched her thigh, opening her legs wide as he breached her entrance and pushed deep inside.

"Damian!"

"Had we indulged our desires that night, I imagine it would have been a slow, sensual coupling."

"Nothing vigorous. You were recovering from an injury." Scarlett welcomed him into her body with a pleasurable sigh. "But it would have felt as divine as it does now."

He kept his gaze fixed on hers as they made love, his dark eyes flashing hot with each delicious slide. Every profoundly tender moment pleasured her heart and soul as well as her body. She could remain like this for a lifetime, a lifetime to soothe his pain, to bear his children, to create the happy home they were both denied.

As a sweet moan fell from her lips, she imagined him reading her letter, opening the gift which should convince him how much she cared. And as her body thrummed with rapturous ecstasy, one thought filled her head.

I love you, and I pray you love me, too.

CHAPTER TWENTY-ONE

"Forgive a man for being mildly curious," the marquis said with his usual aplomb, "but having refused every invitation to spend time in my company, I find you in my study for the third time this week."

"It is not entirely out of choice."

Having kept Damian waiting for twenty minutes, the marquis sauntered into the room and dropped into the sofa opposite. Damian need not have bothered appearing presentable. Today, the marquis greeted him wearing a burgundy silk robe thrown over an open shirt and beige breeches. He reeked of wine and perfume. Clearly, Damian was not the only one who had enjoyed making love to a woman this afternoon.

But there was a difference.

Damian loved Scarlett—with his heart and soul. The feeling had crept up on him like a thief in the night. There had been no warning, no sign to arouse his suspicions. With surprising clarity, he knew he could not live without her. The question was—after surviving one disastrous marriage—would she risk her heart for a reckless rogue?

"As it appears we're able to converse without resorting to

veiled swipes and verbal blows," Damian said, "I wanted to tell you I plan to marry."

Hell, the words were as much of a surprise to Damian as they were to the marquis. But he recognised the truth in them. Indeed, his heart swelled at the prospect.

The marquis narrowed his gaze. "I don't suppose you speak of Lord Bromley's daughter? No, of course not, you do not love her."

"No, I am in love with Lady Steele."

The marquis snorted. "And you think she will have you?"

"I can only hope."

"If you align yourself with the widow, you understand there is no hope of saving your reputation."

"I rather like my scandalous reputation and enjoy the power that comes with not giving a damn." No one told him who he could marry.

A faint smile touched the marquis' lips. "It must be quite liberating."

"What? Not giving a fig for other people's opinions?"

"That and having faith in requited love."

Damian glanced at the ceiling. "I expect the same cannot be said for the woman currently warming your bed."

"Why would I chase love when the pain of a broken heart lasts a lifetime?"

Damian understood his father's logic. If he lost Scarlett, his heart would wither and die. Bitterness would beat in his chest. And he knew that feeling all too well.

"I find it hard to believe you have experienced loss," Damian said. The man acted as if he were impervious to all emotions. "Particularly when your selfish actions have caused others immeasurable pain."

An uncharacteristic sigh escaped the marquis. "Your mother—"

"I am not speaking about Maria. Do you know what this is?"

He opened his arms wide and gestured to his impeccable clothing and devilish facade. "It's a wall. A wall to keep the marauders at bay. Protection from the vile comments, the vicious blows. Illegitimacy is frowned upon regardless of rank, but try living at boarding school with a host of privileged little lords. Try feeling like nothing you do is ever good enough."

The marquis swallowed deeply. "And yet you have found the one thing that eludes the best of us. You have found someone to love, someone to love you in return."

What the hell did the marquis know about love?

Thoughts of his mother filled Damian's head. Life had not been perfect. She had entertained a few men during his childhood but never married. "Maria would have loved you if only you had given her a chance."

A long, drawn-out silence filled the room.

"Have you nothing to say?" Damian prompted. Had the marquis ever cared for Maria? Had he ever held his son in his arms, ever felt the urge to fight against society's dictates?

"Your mother loved singing more than she loved me." The marquis stood abruptly, moved to the drinks tray and sloshed brandy into a glass. Without turning around, he downed the contents, panted a few times as the liquor burnt his throat. "We wanted different things. Despite our truce, we were too selfish to save you." He stared at the wall as if lost in another time, another place. "I could have snatched you from her arms, and she would have been powerless to prevent it. I could have raised you here. But I loved her, so I let her keep you like a trinket of our lost affection."

Frustration flowed like hot lava through Damian's veins. He wanted to call his father a liar, but the marquis never lied about anything. He wanted to challenge the story, but his father dealt only in painful truths. Not once had Damian questioned his mother's affection for the lord. Not once had she spoken his name with disdain, only love and respect.

And so his situation was like Scarlett's. The people who might confirm the truth had departed this world, and so all they could do was realise that the past had no place in the present.

"Why did you not tell me this before?" Damian knew the answer yet still asked the question.

The marquis turned to face him. For the first time, Damian saw water glistening in his eyes. Unshed tears of regret, perhaps. "I am not a man who carries his bleeding heart in his hands and begs others to take pity. I loved and lost. And I hope never to love again."

Then the marquis was doomed to live an empty existence.

"Wish me luck." Damian came to his feet. The heavy burden of his parents' failed relationship dissipated, leaving him feeling lighter. Free. "I am about to ask the woman I love to marry me. Pray she does not reject my proposal." Else he would rain the devil's wrath on everyone he met. "Pray that in years to come, I am not bedding every woman breathing in the hope of purging my pain."

"We all wear masks when it suits us." The marquis inclined his head. "You will find me here should you wish to peruse my story books again."

During the journey back to Bruton Street, Damian's mind was plagued with doubt. Surprisingly, his concern did not stem from his own feelings on marriage—he wanted Scarlett more than he'd wanted anything his whole damn life.

But did she want a rogue with a tarnished reputation?

Or was he destined to a similar fate as his father?

Once home, his anxious heart thumped in his chest as he mounted the stairs. He paused at the bedchamber door, recited a romantic declaration in his head and tapped lightly before entering.

Scarlett was not asleep in bed.

She was not in bed, not in the room.

He went to investigate the room next door, found it empty, her valise missing.

Returning to his chamber, he rang the servants' bell but then noticed the letter and leather pouch on the night table.

Dread's icy hand settled on his shoulder, leaving him frozen. Immobile. Nausea roiled in his stomach as he anticipated the worst. His heart pumped a painful beat in his throat. Hours earlier, he had thrust deep into her body, been so close to declaring his love. Was she thinking about writing her letter when she kissed him so passionately? Was she planning the best way to say goodbye?

But then another thought struck him—one far more terrifying.

He yanked the pull again.

A maid entered. One glance at the empty bed brought some confusion.

"Has Lady Steele taken ill, taken a turn for the worse?" Panic squeezed its fingers around his throat. Many people died days after receiving a blow to the head.

Through trembling lips, the maid said, "No, sir, she was tucked in bed the last time I checked."

Relief flooded his chest.

"Then do you happen to know if she has left the house?" Of course she had left the house. Why else would she scribble a note?

"I'll speak to Welton, sir, see if her ladyship mentioned an outing."

"No matter." Welton would have conveyed the message when he greeted Damian in the hallway. Equally, he would have broken the bad news to his master should the lady have perished during his brief absence. "You may go about your duties."

The maid curtsied and left.

Damian stared at the letter. Hell's teeth! He'd fought duels at dawn, survived a stab wound to the leg, a shot to the arm. So why was he scared of words scrawled on a slip of paper?

Marching over to the night table, he snatched the unsealed note, peeled back the folds and scanned the lines. One word —*love*—drew his gaze further down the page.

Uncertainty and insecurity have plagued me my whole life. I have learnt to hide behind a mask, a facade. Deep down I'm a coward, far from perfect. But I know one thing with absolute clarity—I'm in love with you, Wycliff, madly in love, and there is nothing to be done about it.

The next few words were smudged, as if her tears had dropped onto the paper.

I pray you feel the same. I pray you will come rescue me, that we will not waste another three years in abject misery. In the meantime, please accept this token as a symbol of my abiding affection. Know that I have never stopped thinking about the day I might return it to you.

Damian placed the note on the bed and picked up the leather pouch. It felt heavier than expected. Loosening the drawstring, he delved inside. The moment his fingers settled on the cold metal, he knew what it was.

His heart skipped a beat.

A rush of euphoria flooded his chest as he withdrew his mother's gold necklace and cross. "Maria," he whispered, pressing a kiss to the symbol representing the only other woman he had ever loved. "You sent me an angel that night."

He stood for a moment and let the light of love touch his soul. Then he untied his cravat and fastened the chain around his neck.

Capturing the letter from the bed, he pressed his lips to the words. "Scarlett. You gave me your trust, and I shall never give you cause to doubt me." After a brief pause, he continued with this newfound habit of talking to himself. "Then why in the devil's name are you still standing here, Wycliff?"

Within minutes he'd summoned Cutler to bring the carriage.

"Did Lady Steele instruct you to convey her home?" Damian said as his footman raced behind ready to open the carriage door.

Cutler shook his head. "No, sir."

Then she must have walked. Why in damnation would she walk whilst recovering from a head injury?

"Where is Alcock?" he barked.

His coachman's cheeks flushed. "In the mews, sir. Shall I send for her?"

"No!" He would not have Alcock fretting over her mistress. "Take me to Bedford Street. As quick as safety allows."

Cutler was as skilled at driving as he was sewing. He navigated the overturned cart on New Bond Street with ease, flew through the streets as if carried by the hands of the gods.

Once in Bedford Street, Damian burst into the hall, though the butler seemed surprised when he asked if the mistress was at home.

"No, sir. We were under the impression her ladyship wouldn't be home for another few days."

"I see." A prickle of frustration ran the breadth of his shoulders. "Thank you—?"

"Hanson, sir."

"Thank you, Hanson. Should your mistress return, please inform her that I came to call and ask that she send word to Bruton Street."

Perhaps she had questions about her parents and had gone to

visit Flannery. And so, The Silver Serpent was his next destination.

Perturbed by the thought of Scarlett's mysterious disappearance, Flannery's face turned deathly pale. "But you said the matron was to blame for what happened, so you did. Now you tell me Scarlett is missing."

"The matron was to blame. Rest assured, she is dead." Damian's patience was wearing thin. "Scarlett is not missing. She left me a note."

"Well, what did the note say?"

Damian was not in the habit of discussing intimate details of his private life. Still, he would have Flannery know his intentions were honourable, and this man was the closest thing Scarlett had to family.

"Scarlett loves me. I intend to ask for her hand in marriage—"

"Ah, then that saves me asking O'Donnell and the men to twist your arm." Flannery grinned. "And you've tried the house on Bedford Street, you say?"

Damian nodded. All this racing about roused memories of those months after she had disappeared from the lodging-house. Why did he feel like he was losing her all over again?

"Do you know of any other houses she owns in town?"

"Can't say that I do." Flannery frowned. "But if the lass loves you, what business has she running away?"

"She has not run away." Damian thrust his hand through his hair and sighed. "She wishes me to rescue her." To rescue her from the lies and deceit, to create a life together filled with honesty and truth. Most people presumed he ruined women, not saved them. "To do what I struggled to do three years ago."

He had not exactly struggled. Had she opened the door to the lodging-house when he delivered the food parcels, things might have been vastly different. He had lost count of the times he'd sat in his carriage in Drury Lane, staring at the—

"Bloody hell! I think I know where she is."

Without saying another word, Damian hurried from The Silver Serpent and had Cutler ferry him to Covent Garden. He alighted on Drury Lane, spent a few seconds staring at the small window of the lodging-house.

After crossing the crowded street, dodging carts and carriages and wild dogs, he entered the alley. Memories came flooding back. The vicious attack. Him slumped against the cold stone wall, his angel standing over him dressed in white and clutching her scarlet shawl.

With his heart thumping in his chest, he walked towards the blue paint-chipped door and let himself into the hallway, stood outside the entrance to the shabby room that held a treasured place in his heart.

Damian raised his hand to knock, paused when he imagined being met by a toothless hag with a babe at her breast. He shook the picture from his head and rapped on the door.

With the noise of the street echoing in the hallway, it was impossible to hear the pad of footsteps, to hear the sweet voice he hoped would bid him entry. But he stared at the doorknob, his pulse racing as he watched it turn.

Scarlett opened the door, a nervous smile playing on her lips. She wore a simple day dress in a dull, moss green. Her ebony hair hung over her shoulder in a single braid.

God, she was so beautiful.

"One must do one's best to blend in when walking the alleys in Covent Garden," she said, gesturing to her plain skirt. "Won't you come in, Damian?"

"If we're to reinvent the moment lost to us three years ago, should I not drape my arm around your shoulder and let you settle me into bed?" He had been incoherent that night. Now, for the first time in his life, his mind was sharp. Lucid.

Scarlett arched a coy brow, looked just as eager to play this game. "As long as you don't intend to spew brandy over my boots."

"Love, I have the funds to buy you a thousand pairs."

She took a step towards him. "Let me help you, sir. It is but a few feet to the bed."

Damian grinned. "Wait. There is something I must do first." He unbuttoned his waistcoat, pushed his fingers between the gap in his shirt and withdrew the gold cross. "Mother, if you are watching from your heavenly plane, send me an angel, someone to love."

"I don't remember it being worded quite like that."

"No, but a mother can hear the secrets in her child's heart." He glanced at the cross gripped between his fingers. "You kept it, even though you needed the money. Why?"

"Some things have a value beyond that of material possessions." Water filled her eyes. "It may not have bought me new boots, but it soothed my soul so many times during the last three years. As does coming here. I leased the room six months ago, and visit often."

A single tear hit her cheek, and he wiped it away with the pad of his thumb. He would make it his life's mission to ensure she never cried again. "How long do you intend to make an injured man wait at the door?" he said, hoping to lighten the mood.

"Your injuries are healed, sir, but I am willing to pretend if you are."

His mind raced forward to the moment she might cut his breeches and massage his bare thigh. "Just because I am not bleeding from my arm or leg doesn't mean I am not suffering."

Curiosity danced in her pretty blue eyes. "Then let me help you to the bed. Let me soothe your woes."

He made no protest when she captured his wrist and draped his arm around her neck. He limped as she helped him across the threshold, smiled when she kicked the door shut. When he fell onto the small bed, she almost came tumbling down on top of him.

"Now, tell me what ails you." Scarlett lifted his legs onto the bed and then sat down beside him and stroked a lock of hair from his brow.

"My heart is aching." He took her hand in his, massaged her palm with his thumb. "Every fibre of my being writhes in torment and agony. Only you can ease my pain."

Her eyes sparkled like crystal blue waters. "What can I do?"

"You can love me. Love me my whole life. You can marry me. Marry me and bear my children, our children." He tried not to choke on the sudden surge of emotion. "Marry me as soon as I can purchase a licence, and I believe my symptoms shall subside."

Her eyes misted, and she pursed her lips. "Are you certain you wish to settle? I've spent my life believing no one wants me and I couldn't bear—"

"I want you. I need you. God, Scarlett, I've never been in love. Now I know why. I've been saving every ounce of love for you."

A smile touched her lips. "You love me?"

Damian snorted—a sound between amusement and contempt for his own ignorance. "I believe I have loved you since the day you saved my life."

She caressed his thigh. "The stitching is remarkably good, even if I say so myself."

"I am not speaking of the wound. You saved me from a life of emptiness and misery. Thank the Lord—no—thank Maria. Had I not made that oath, I may never have seen you again."

They stared at each other for a heartbeat.

"I love you, Damian Wycliff. Promise me we will not waste another minute."

"Not a single second."

She bent her head and kissed him. It was a kiss that spoke of deep abiding love, one that soon turned wild and ravenous.

"Let us stay here tonight," she said as her nimble fingers set to work on his cravat. "Just this once."

He smiled as he covered her hand to prevent her from unfastening the knot. "I intend to indulge your every desire, every lascivious whim, but I'll not eat broth. Let me send Cutler back to Bruton Street so he may return with a picnic."

"Very well. I did promise never to serve you broth again."

Damian jumped to his feet, raced from the room to his carriage and instructed Cutler to fetch supplies—wine, food and candles, not firewood. On his return to the dingy room in the lodging-house, he locked the door and stared at the grate.

"What is it?" Scarlett crossed the room and closed the gap between them. "Is something wrong?"

"Yes, something is wrong." Damian cast her a wicked grin. "It's damn cold in here. What the devil shall we do to keep warm?"

CHAPTER TWENTY-TWO

Two weeks later

They married at St George's Hanover Square. Not because it was the church the nobility chose to forge their alliances, but because Damian had purchased a common licence and it happened to be the best church in the parish.

Mr Cavanagh and Mr Trent witnessed the discreet affair, the only other guests being Dermot Flannery and the Marquis of Blackbeck. Not that it mattered to Scarlett. Had a congregation of a hundred well-wishers watched them exchange vows, she only had eyes for Damian Wycliff—her dangerously handsome husband.

After the ceremony, they stood on the stone steps and smiled when the marquis offered his felicitations. From his expression, it was impossible to tell if he was pleased or indifferent. Mr Flannery shed a tear or two during his congratulatory speech and then invited Damian to partake in an arm wrestling bout once his wound had fully healed.

"Are you certain you don't want to invite our guests back to Bruton Street for a small breakfast?" Scarlett touched his arm, and her pulse raced. She didn't want to make idle chatter when she might spend the rest of the day making love to her husband.

"While I am done with hating the marquis, I'd rather not break bread with him around the table—not today. Flannery is intent on snapping my arm to prove a point. And I need the use of both hands tonight." His tone turned sultry, and his dark eyes scanned her face, her hair, and the midnight-blue gown she'd worn because she knew how much he liked the colour. "Have I told you how beautiful you look today?"

Scarlett couldn't help but grin. "Five times or more."

"Have I told you that I cannot wait to strip you out of that gown and devour every inch of your delectable body?"

Scarlett swallowed. "No, but I am keen to hear what you plan to do with me once we return to the privacy of our carriage."

"Then let us say goodbye to Trent and Cavanagh. There's somewhere I want to take you before we venture home."

Curiosity burned. "Is it to look at a house?"

With the need to put the past behind her, Scarlett had agreed to sign the house in Bedford Street over to Joshua Steele. The lord could sell the property and pay his debts, start a new life, free from guilt. Joshua had cried when she told him, had promised Damian he intended to wed the mother of his son. Having discovered that Jemima had been the one to spook Scarlett's horse and had paid the groom to let his hound loose in Green Park, Joshua had banished the girl to his country estate in Yorkshire.

"We are going to look at a house, but it is not for the reason you think." Damian stepped closer, so close she felt the warmth of his body. "As the man tasked with satisfying your every desire, I wouldn't dream of suggesting we remain in town. You once told me you want a house with countryside views that stretch for miles. A family who picnics in the park, children to love, a husband to adore."

"I have a husband." Her heart swelled with excitement, happiness and love. "But would very much like to have a child." She had feared it was too soon to broach the subject.

"And I am more than happy to fulfil my part in the task. Lots of practice is needed, I think, if one is to be certain of success. I'm sure Dr Redman would offer similar advice."

Scarlett chuckled. "Dr Redman is a logical man."

"Indeed." Those dark, hungry eyes dropped to her lips. A wicked grin formed though he said nothing. He gestured for Mr Trent and Mr Cavanagh to join them.

"You were right, Mrs Wycliff," Mr Cavanagh said with some amusement. It felt so good to lose the name Lady Steele. What did she care for a title? "And we were wrong. It seems that Wycliff is not doomed to roam the fiery pits of hell. Love has saved him from a stab to the leg, a lead ball to the arm and from a life of eternal damnation."

Mr Trent snorted. "If Wycliff can fall in love, there is hope for us all."

Once again, the brooding gentleman appeared preoccupied. While those vibrant green eyes were fixed upon them, his thoughts were clearly elsewhere.

"Did you happen to discover who left the flowers, Mr Trent?" She did not wish to reveal the full extent of their conversation lest the man preferred privacy.

Mr Trent shuffled uncomfortably. "No. But let's just say the person is persistent in their efforts to ensure my brother enters the gates of heaven."

Scarlett hadn't realised the grave belonged to his brother. Had she known, she might have given him an opportunity to discuss the matter further. Grief lurked behind many masks.

"Are we speaking of your mysterious graveyard visitor?" Damian asked.

Mr Trent's mouth formed a grim line, and he nodded.

"Well, we know the person is a woman," Scarlett said. Who else wrote poetic verse and tied it with a pink ribbon? "A young woman, I suspect." There was something of the whimsical, something romantic about the gesture that seemed too fanciful for a mature lady.

"We have no aunts or sisters. And our mothers are dead."

Mothers? They were half-brothers, then? It was a morbid conversation to have on one's wedding day, but Mr Trent looked as though he'd not slept in weeks, as though this problem plagued every waking hour.

"Have you asked the vicar?" Damian said.

"Of course I've asked the vicar. The villain comes and goes like a ghost in the night."

"She is hardly a villain if she is paying her respects," Scarlett countered.

"Then you must go there tonight." Damian patted his friend on the upper arm. "You must go every night. Wait in the darkness and discover the identity of this mysterious stranger. What I cannot understand is why you've not done so before now."

"Sometimes one fears what they might discover," Mr Cavanagh interjected.

Sadness lingered in Mr Trent's eyes. Anger simmered beneath the surface, too. She wasn't sure what had happened in his past but knew tackling the problem was the only way one might sleep soundly at night.

"Go tonight, Mr Trent," Scarlett said. The longer one spent worrying about problems, the worse they became. "Call on us in Bruton Street if you require our help."

Mr Trent inclined his head. Clearly aware that this was not a topic one wanted to discuss on their wedding day, he made his apologies and agreed to inform them of his discovery.

"Now mind neither of you suffers an injury," Mr Cavanagh joked before leaving them to join Mr Trent.

Damian and Scarlett took the carriage to Howland Street, where she was to learn of this mysterious surprise. During the fifteen-minute journey, her husband's ravenous mouth made her forget all about deceased brothers and graveyard meetings in the moonlight. Indeed, it took every effort to straighten her clothing and alight from the vehicle.

"Well, what do you think?" Damian draped his arm around her shoulder and stared at the three-storey townhouse in dire need of renovation.

"It would help if I knew why you're showing me this house when we intend to move to the country."

"I did what you suggested and collected my winnings from White's."

"As the only man who will ever grace my bed, you earned every penny." Had he not claimed his prize, the club would have returned the money to the pompous prigs who'd made the group wager. "But that still doesn't explain why you're interested in this house."

"I thought we could use the money to open a home for destitute women. A safe place where they might live comfortably while training for a profession." He turned to face her, pressed a soft kiss to her lips. "A place you might have come. A place that might have protected you from the likes of Lord Steele."

Shock rendered her momentarily speechless. "You wish to spend fifty thousand pounds helping downtrodden women?"

"Men do exaggerate. It was closer to thirty thousand. What better way to recognise the strength and courage of the Scarlet Widow?"

Scarlett stared at him, resisted the urge to claim his mouth in the wild, reckless way that heated her blood. Love for this man infused her body with a hot, vibrant glow. Every fibre of her being ached to join with him, join with him now.

"I think it's a wonderful idea." Thoughts of hiring staff and a matron to oversee the women's progress entered her mind, but she pushed them aside. "And you have my support no matter what you choose to do."

He kissed her then, a slow, sensual kiss—a prelude to what she might expect once back inside the carriage.

"Have I told you I love you?" he said in the tender voice of the man who no longer hid behind a facade. Not with her.

"Many times."

"Many times is not enough. I love you to the depths of my soul." A sinful smirk touched his lips. "But if I don't plunge deep into your body soon, I fear I might die."

Scarlett moistened her lips. "I love you more than you can ever know. But I need to feel full with you. Else my heart might simply give out."

Without uttering another word, he captured her hand and escorted her back to their conveyance.

"We'll take the long route home, Cutler," Damian said, opening the door.

The coachman nodded, but it was Alcock who spoke. "Down to the Strand and once around St James' Park?"

Scarlett glanced at Damian and bestowed a look of love, lust and a lifetime of longing. "Three times around the park."

THANK YOU!

Thank you for reading *And the Widow Wore Scarlet.*

What will Lawrence Trent do when he discovers a mysterious woman tending his brother's grave?

How will he react when he hears her incredible story?

Find out in *The Mark of a Rogue*
Scandalous Sons - Book 2

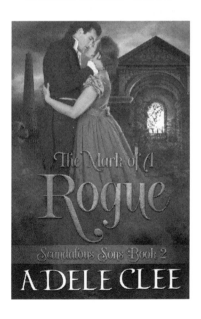